Reviews

Gripping and heart-wrenching doesn't even come close to the emotion that I found rising up in me over and over again as I read this book. *Out of the Mouths of Children* is the most horrific account of satanic ritualistic abuse that I have personally read.

It is difficult to fully comprehend how this sort of darkness and evil still exists today. It's especially heart-breaking when it comes to touching beautiful, innocent children!

Woven beautifully throughout the story, God, in His true fashion, shows up in one way or another with His unmatched love and comfort. He does prevail. His love for humanity, especially for His children, pours out. He is so good!

For anyone who has been sexually abused, there is hope! God longs to heal every shattered piece!

- Charleen Raschke, author of *The Season of Ashes*
(www.charleenraschke.ca)

The systematic sexual abuse of vulnerable young children is arguably the most incomprehensible and depraved of crimes against humanity. Holy God is our creative source of light and love. The Enemy, therefore, is dark, destructive hate.

In **_Out of the Mouths of Children,_** a fictional work based on true, historical facts, is an account of a Christian community's tragedy and ultimate triumph in this battle of good vs evil, God demonstrates His ever-present help during a family's darkest ordeal. The author clearly articulates, time after time, how only God understands the depths of confusion, pain, and despair and gives our only hope to truly overcome Evil.

Laura Fernandez

-Troxel Pickering, BA, MAT, 40-year career K-12 public school educator.

OUT OF THE MOUTHS OF CHILDREN

CHLOE WINSLOW

WESTBOW
P R E S S®
A DIVISION OF THOMAS NELSON
& ZONDERVAN

WestBow Press books may be ordered through booksellers or by contacting:

WestBow Press
A Division of Thomas Nelson & Zondervan
1663 Liberty Drive
Bloomington, IN 47403
www.westbowpress.com
1 (866) 928-1240

ISBN: 978-1-9736-5460-5 (sc)
ISBN: 978-1-9736-5459-9 (hc)
ISBN: 978-1-9736-5461-2 (e)

Library of Congress Control Number: 2019902546

Print information available on the last page.

WestBow Press rev. date: 03/15/2019

DEDICATION

To all adult children who have survived the ravages of sexual abuse.

inspired by true events

PROLOGUE

The light ocean breeze ruffled Paul's curly dark hair as he looked around the large cove. The waves were licking the shore, beckoning him to enter in. His soft brown eyes smiled at his wife Teri, who was clipping the life jackets on their three children. "Well, it looks OK to me! The waves are calm and the tide's going out. Let's give it a try!" He knew he was being extra cautious. The small green motorboat held the most precious people in his life.

"Ok!" She replied with enthusiasm. She was eager to see this adventure go ahead. They all needed a break from their busy lives. It seemed as if every day was packed full of activity.

Paul and Teri Nelson, with their three children, had arrived a year ago on the shore of the Echo Bay community. They were part of a mission organization that specialized in planting churches in remote areas. The five of them had happily settled in as missionaries to the local people. Although there was no church building, there were several Christian families who had been eagerly looking for a pastor. Paul had started services in the local hall shortly after their arrival.

Everyone carefully stepped into the boat. It wobbled as two- year- old Jacob crawled over the side. Wiggling with excitement, he grinned from ear to ear as Dad started the motor. Sitting beside his dad, seven- year- old Peter copied his dad's every move. Hannah, five- years- old, snuggled close to her mom as they headed over to the other side of the cove. Sea gulls laughed overhead at their slow progress. Teri couldn't help smiling. This was just what she had envisioned, a perfect day in the sun and surf.

Fifteen minutes later the little green boat slid smoothly onto the far beach. The three children scrambled out of the boat and raced down the shore. They started beachcombing among the rocks and driftwood. Soon,

Teri heard Peter shout, "I found a buoy!" They all gathered around him and looked at the beat up treasure. "That's a good one, son" Dad praised.

After an hour of hunting, each one had a bounty of shells, bottles and other washed up debris. All the while,Teri unpacked the picnic basket. The warm wind lifted the corners of the blanket as they ate. Sand mixed in with the food as they ate, but no one noticed.

Finally, it was time to head back. The kids helped Teri pack up and load the boat. She suddenly noticed Paul staring out over the water. He looked worried. Right away, she saw what he was looking at. The wind had come up and the tide had changed. Butterflies tickled her stomach as she looked at the rows of breakers crashing on their far landing beach. Hannah looked up at her mom anxiously. Teri lied "It'll be OK, sweetheart."

Paul tried to look calm, but his eyes squinted with anxiety. He looked up and called out, "Oh Lord, we are in danger. Please guide us through these rough waters!"

Hurriedly they finished packing the little boat and set off. The happy day went away and fear came crawling in. The landing shore disappeared behind the crashing waves." How are we ever going to beach this little boat?" Teri asked.

Paul didn't answer her as he concentrated on controlling the boat. Hannah and Peter pressed together on the middle seat, while Teri hugged Jacob tightly in her arms in the bow.

Drawing nearer to the shore, they became even more alarmed. The rows of breakers rose higher than the boat, which was tossed to and fro like a cork. Paul yelled, "Hang on!".

He gripped the throttle and surfed the tossing boat between the waves, which were racing them towards a collision with the rocky beach. Terrified, Teri wondered if their world was about to crash.

"Jesus, Help us!" Paul called out.

The boat was out of control. The rocks rushed past . Then, amazingly, a large wave picked up the boat and gently slid them on to the sand. They were safe!

All five looked around in bewilderment. What just happened? Paul proclaimed, "This was God helping us! Children, never forget this great answer to our cry for help."

Little did they know that their lives were about to be changed forever by the crashing waves of evil. Calm would become chaos and it would be only by God's mercy and grace that they survived. During that time Teri would often remember how Jesus saved them from the angry waves as they called upon His Name.

CHAPTER 1

Two years later

The south- east gale bent the trees and dropped branches onto Teri's path as she wrapped the ribbon around another tree. For the last hour, she had weaved through the many trails behind their house to lay this paper chase. The rain slapped Teri's face as she crossed the log. *Is it too slippery for the kids?* she wondered. *Well, they wanted it to be challenging.* Despite the rain, wind and danger, she smiled, thinking of the kids trying to find the soggy paper strips. After all, it was Peter's ninth birthday and this was his choice for a game.

As she came back to the house at last, wet and bedraggled, the faces of the eager group told her it was worth it. She thanked the Lord that Peter had made a few good friends in Echo Bay. This was not always easy when you were the only family to home school in the area. Teri counted seven heads, not including four- year old Jacob, who was too young for this birthday game. Thankfully, the gale force winds had eased along with the rain. *Much safer!* she thought as the excited children disappeared into the trees. "City kids would not do this" She smiled at Jacob. "They would more likely go to a movie". He smiled back, his baby teeth gleaming in the light.

After only forty-five minutes, Teri watched the group burst out of the trees and race to the tree house where treats awaited. Sighing to herself, she realized that it had taken her nearly two hours to lay the trail. Looking at their excited faces, it was impossible to tell that they held secrets that would not only overwhelm the family, but also the church and the entire community.

Paul and Teri both had a deep sense of satisfaction and joy as they served God in this remote area. Despite having no TV or computers and little income, their children were active and happy. They were a close family in every way. They couldn't imagine being anywhere else. The waters of their lives were calm.

While Paul was busy with visiting and getting to know the community, Teri had started to teach the two older children while trying to keep their two- year- old occupied. The couple had decided to make the hard decision to educate their children after discovering that the school lacked the ability to teach their over- achieving child, Peter. Because he was new and therefore different, he endured constant bullying from the students. He and a friend often spent their recesses hiding and running from these tormentors. Early on, Teri had a feeling that there was something wrong with this school. For instance, why did they call the sports teams the' Demons' and 'Demonettes'?

Teri found it difficult to balance ministry and schooling with mothering and keeping everyone happy and healthy. However, she often thought, *I wouldn't trade this for anything, despite the hard work!*

Two weeks after Peter's birthday, Teri and the kids waited at the airport, north of Echo Bay. They were watching with anticipation for her mother to arrive. Peter, Hannah and Jacob jumped up and down in excitement as the jet touched down. They had waited for weeks for their Nan to arrive. Teri had been delighted when her mother had phoned from down south to tell her that she was coming to Echo Bay.

As the plane taxied to a stop, Teri reminded herself that her mom would inevitably bring up her usual tirade of questioning why they had come to this isolated place. Her mom had never accepted the fact that Paul and she had converted to Christianity fifteen years ago. Nan was a loyal and devoted parent, but there were some things they couldn't talk about. Teri would avoid telling her that their purpose in coming to Echo Bay was to bring the gospel to the area, which included logging camps and native Indian reserves.

The kids rushed to hug her as she walked toward them. " Hi, Mother!" Teri said as she embraced her. "Are you tired? Here, let me help you!"

"Thank you dear. I am quite weary."

"Do you want to go straight home, or would you like an early tour?"

Nan replied with a tired smile, "I really would like a cup of tea and a rest before we do anything else."

Later that afternoon, they all piled into the van to show Nan the town. Of course, they started at the waste dump so they could show her the huge scavenging black bears. After taking pictures and appreciating Nan's awe-struck comments, they drove along the windswept shore that spread along the front of the community. "You don't have many stores," Nan said pointedly, as they passed through the most populated part of town.

Paul stopped at the grocery store."No, but they have most of the things we need. I just have to run in and get some milk."

As soon as he was out of sight, Nan started the age-old argument. "Why did he bring you all the way out here? This is no place to raise children. What is there to do, anyway? Don't think I didn't notice those gangs of teens. I'm sure there are plenty of drugs and drinking around. They even glared at us."

Teri wanted to defend her husband. *Keep quiet*! she concluded. *There is nothing you can say to change her mind.* Instead, she changed the subject. "How about later we drive to the place where our Bible camp-site is? It is one of the most beautiful beaches that I have ever seen. Some of those teens and younger children come to camp. They all seem to enjoy it."

In some ways, Teri wanted to tell her mom about some of the deplorable conditions the town's kids had to endure. She thought back to the night when a two-year-old boy from next door had shown up on the Nelson's doorstep. Crying, with his filthy diaper dragging around his feet, he obviously wanted help. Paul and Teri entered the run down little house with the little boy in Paul's arms. She was shocked to find that his older brother, who was babysitting while his parents were at the bar, had disappeared. His baby sister was wailing in her crib. The smell made her want to plug her nose. As she busily cleaned up the older child and changed the younger baby's dirty diaper, Teri was upset. "Why on earth would these babies be left like this! What is wrong with this family!"

Paul went to find their parents. Unsuccessful, he returned frustrated. Acting on a hunch, Teri went over to a nearby trailer blaring loud music and found the "babysitter." He defiantly refused to return home. Not wanting to interfere further and wanting to connect with the parents, Paul and Teri watched carefully from a distance. " Should we phone social services or talk with the family in the morning?" Teri had asked Paul. Finally, they decided on the latter.

The next morning they had sternly told the parents about what had happened the night before. Teri had frowned as she warned, " If we witness another incident like this again, we will be forced to report it." The parents looked at each other with a smirk and shrugged.

If she had told her mom this story, it would add to her already prejudiced opinion about why they lived here. Paul climbed back into the driver's seat with the milk. "Let's drive by some of our friends' houses, then go home for supper. How about that?" he asked.

They drove by Jackson and Tabitha's home. Teri could see the goats and chickens in their backyard hobby farm. "There are quite a number of our friends living in this area of town, Mother." She pointed to Joe and Katie's house across the street, the two lived right beside Selma and her two sons.

"I suppose they are all part of your religious group," Nan said sarcastically.

Neither Paul nor Teri responded to her comment. Again, Teri changed the subject. "Jackson and Tabitha have three children around our kids' ages. Susan is your best friend, isn't she, Hannah?"

"I think she is, Mom. I also like Leona a lot."

Leona lived in a remote logging camp that Paul boated to on Sundays. She was part of the Bible club he had started there. Her parents attended the church service that Paul lead and were the most mature Christians in the camp. Sometimes he brought Leona back to play with Hannah.

Nan's visit ended four days later. Teri appreciated that her mother had come all this way to visit, but felt relieved too. Mostly they had a good time. She loved her mother, but becoming a Christian had put a rift between them. Every day Teri prayed that her mother would come to salvation through Jesus. Teri longed to be able share this, but her mom continued to put up walls.

CHAPTER 2

Several days after her mom had left, Teri sat in the living room looking out at the ocean. Home school was over for the day. Paul was out visiting. Now, she had a rare moment to just sit and think. The sun poured over her through the window and she allowed her eyes to close. Sighing wearily, she leaned back against the couch. *This homeschooling is a lot of hard work, but so rewarding. I'm so pleased with how well Peter and Hannah are progressing. All three seem very happy with this arrangement. Why do so many people think that homeschooled kids lack socialization? That's not true in our case! That's for sure! The kids all love the field trips we go on with the other home school families who have joined us.*

Just that morning, Teri remembered watching Peter's handsome young face as he leaned over his books in deep concentration. *What a reliable and obedient guy!. Hannah is a pleasure to work with, too. She is such a good student. Loves every part of her school work!* With her curly hair and pretty features, it was no wonder people told her that she looked like a little blond Shirley Temple. She loved Jesus and enjoyed memorizing Bible passages with her mom. Four- year- old Jacob was an energetic, loving little boy who played happily as the rest of them worked. Blond and slight, he was nearly always smiling.

Teri sat up as she heard Paul drive in. When she looked out the kitchen window, she saw her husband slowly backing the van up to the garage towing a new boat. Friends in the area had pooled their money to buy this safer and faster means of travelling to remote communities by water. Teri smiled at their act of love. These wonderful people had encouraged Paul to use the boat for pleasure as well as ministry. Cruising the shore line looking for beachcombing opportunties, was a pastime that they especially enjoyed. She quickly donned her coat to go out and see Paul's new treasure.

After exploring the new boat, she walked down to the sandy beach in front of their house. *How amazing! I'm all by myself for a change.* Two seals popped up right in front of her. As they cavorted in the waves, she remembered the amazing day when a group of gray humpback whales fed off the seaweeds only feet off shore.

What a beautiful place! I am so grateful to the Lord for leading us here!

A short time later, Teri returned to check on the children playing in the basement. "Mom!" Hannah yelled, "Come and see the town we made with the blocks!"

"Wow! That is an amazing little city. Good work! This might be a good time for you all to get some fresh air. I'm going out to work in the backyard."

Teri wandered over to the chicken coop. *The hens are laying enough eggs to supply our needs these days. I think I'll let them out to forage for awhile.*

She bent over and picked some clover to feed to the bunnies in their hutches. Their noses wrinkled in delight as she fed them. Her hands slid over their velvet coats."The kids will let you out later into our fenced yard," she told them.

Teri strolled into the garden she had painstakingly planted. It had taken months to pick up all the rocks and put a mix of seaweed and horse manure into the sandy soil. *At least the peas and chard are growing well!* She began pulling the weeds which always threatened to over grow her vegetables.

Peter, Hannah, Jacob and Cricket, their faithful little dachshund, came over. "Can we go exploring in the woods?" Peter asked, "We'll be back in an hour."

"Sure," replied Teri, "Supper will be at 5:30, so why don't you come back at 5:00".

She knew her reliable son would return right at 5:00. The forest crouched at one side of the backyard with an elevated fort peeking through the trees. This had become a favorite hangout for their children, as well as for some of their neighborhood friends. Along a trail from there, Peter would lead his brigade on excursions to the ponds and swamps half a mile away.

The next morning, Teri had to put aside school as she prepared the house for her Thursday morning Bible study. Teri looked out her window to see the first arrival. Two women in a rusty red pickup drove into their driveway. She felt a surge of excitement race through her gut. This was her favorite day of the week.

During these past few two-years of living in Echo Bay, about ten adults had turned to Christ as their Savior. They were eager to learn what the Bible had to teach them. Paul's Bible study for men was on Tuesday night. He always had a good turnout. He delighted in seeing these new Christian men growing in their understanding of Scripture. Teri's group of women was increasing in number every month. Some of them were interested in just seeing what had caused their friends to become Christians. Others were new in the faith and enthusiastic learners. Another few were professing Christians who attended church, but were weak in their knowledge of the Bible.

Paul babysat the children downstairs while the moms studied. He made it fun enough for them to race down the stairs to the waiting collection of toys. The kids loved Paul's easy manner and the fun routines he created. His voice drifted up the stairs, "Now, everyone stand in a straight line. That's good! Let's recite the play rules together!"

Others arrived and gathered around the kitchen table. Silence did not exist. Teri enjoyed hearing their happy chatter, but her mind drifted elsewhere. *Good! Selma and Cathy have not shown up.* Relief washed over her. She couldn't explain why she felt so uneasy around those two. Usually she was quite good at reading people, but whenever she talked with either of them, she always felt sick and tense.

She especially felt this way towards Selma. Her son, Brandon, often babysat the kids during church meetings. Teri remembered the time she had tearfully asked their ministry director, Drew, to pray for her regarding this woman. She wanted to love all the women in the community. Cathy, a domineering, imposing personality with penetrating dark eyes, affected her the same way. It seemed to Teri that both would try to intimidate Paul and her with their attitudes. Selma would often complain about others, while Cathy seemed manic. *What a pair! They are so difficult to relate to.*

Enough of this! She turned with a smile to the group, "Let's open in prayer."

✦━━━━━━━━━━━━━━✦

Darkness fell quickly. A misty fog enclosed the house where they met. She kept looking out the windows to see who was arriving. Nobody yet,

but she knew they would arrive soon. Didn't she tell them that it felt like something special was going to happen tonight!.

Her faded green eyes gleamed below her thin black hair. She thought with delight about her well kept secret. She remembered how successful she had been at enticing those teenagers. She knew they were bored, so she planned parties with the promise of unlimited drugs of their choice and the heavy rock music they loved so much. That had been at the start. Now, they were ready for the children.

She shook with the thrill of remembering the time when those so very naive Christian missionaries and their three young children had come to her territory. She was especially stimulated by all the new families who had joined Paul and Teri's congregation in the past two years. She calculated that there were at least 20 children among them. "We love little kids!" She laughed out loud .

Her plans were nearly complete. Tonight she would tell the participants how their mighty god, Darkness himself, would help them have fun and to use these little victims anyway they wanted. Their prince had put these little innocents right into their hands.

She heard scuffling at her back door. They were arriving!

CHAPTER 3

It was Friday morning, and Teri was busy correcting Peter's school work. *We need to work on his untidy writing.* She mused. However, she found most of his math questions were correct. She smiled at his doodling down the side of the page. The phone startled her, but she answered cheerfully, "Hello!"

"Hi! This is Ursula calling. Are we meeting tonight at the same time?"

Ursula and her husband, Don, had two young children, Jasper and Cynthia. They were both eager to learn more about Christianity and attended every meeting. Both were always concerned about their children.

Teri responded, "Hi, Ursula, I was about to phone everyone. Tonight is a spiritual emphasis time, so bring your Bibles. We are meeting at Jackson and Tabitha's house. Brandon is babysitting here in the basement."

She knew that Ursula would be happy that Brandon was taking care of her little ones. Brandon was highly recommended. After all, he had won ' The Citizen ' award at school two years in a row. " I phoned Selma last night to see if he was available. Glad he is!"

Ursula relaxed, "I like to make sure that the children will be OK while we meet. Brandon does a good job. Don's coming tonight, too, but he wanted me to find out who was looking after Jasper and Cynthia first."

"Sure, that's fine, Ursula. We'll see you tonight." After they had hung up, Teri went to search out Peter to discuss his corrections.

Just before the seven o'clock meeting, Teri went downstairs to set up the toys for the kids. She asked Brandon to help, but he had no interest in doing this. It was a bit strange that he watched all the children come in without greeting them. She guessed he was waiting for the parents to leave before playing with them. The teenager was polite and pleasant, but the children showed no interest in his presence. They quietly started playing with the toys scattered about. "Teri, are you coming?" Paul's voice sounded impatient. Teri knew that he wanted to be early. She hurried upstairs.

Tonight, Straps, an older man of great faith, greeted them at the Morrison's front door. His short, square frame blocked a clear view of Tabitha standing behind him. She was nearly dancing on her toes at the joy of having the meeting at their home. Smells of freshly cooked treats wafted from the kitchen!

Straps started off the get- together by booming, " God saved me from the pit! I was so lost! So unhappy that I became an old drunk. I praise Jesus for loving me so much even as I was. Now I am a new creation, praise God! Let's sing to our great Lord and Savior, Jesus Christ!"

As they joined in singing a favorite hymn, Teri looked around to see who had come. She counted fifteen. *What a great turn-out!* She noticed Katie singing with obvious reluctance. Her husband, Joe, stoically standing beside her, was not singing at all. He was trying to understand this Christian life from the outside. He tossed back his long brown hair, with confusion and uncertainty clouding his face. He looked like he would rather be at the bar, where he and Katie usually went on Friday nights. Earlier, Katie had shared with her, "It is so hard to stay away from the bar. I have such great friends there. Maybe this Christian life is too hard." Teri silently prayed for them to put God first in their lives.

Jackson and Tabitha sat opposite Teri, sharing a hymn book. They had changed so much since they had received Christ last year. Jackson had been short tempered, but was now much more mellow. His loud voice, often heard by most of the community when he called his kids, had softened. Tabitha's personality, calm and thoughtful, radiated joy when she talked about her faith. They had become close friends with the Nelsons.

Next to them, Diana and Sam, professing Christians, sang together with obvious enjoyment. The Haywoods had moved to the house next to the Nelson family a few months after they had arrived in Echo Bay. Their three children, Caleb, Mary and Ali, enjoyed playing with Peter, Hannah and Jacob.

Teri heard Wes laugh at something his wife Sharon had said. She turned to smile at them sitting next to Paul. Although Wes had worked as a social worker for years, he now worked for the Echo Bay logging company as a faller. He was also a changed man after he accepted Christ into his life. His wife Sharon was still skeptical.

Yes, Ursula and Don had come! They must have dropped their two off at our house to be babysat by Brandon.

As the hymn finished, Teri watched as Michael and Katherine briskly entered the house. Michael took off his coat and turned to the others, "So sorry to be this late! A phone call came in just as we were leaving with the kids. We just dropped them off at babysitting." They had two children and had lived in town for many years. The couple loved the Lord. Michael was active in helping Paul any way he could. Tall and lean with sandy brown hair, his eyes often twinkled when he spoke to others. Katherine was fast becoming a good friend to Teri. Tabitha found a few more chairs to fit them with the others in the group. Paul smiled, "We don't mind if you are late. We just want you to be here."

Paul asked Straps, "Could you read the first chapter of Acts for us?"

"It would be my joy to read this great chapter," Straps answered with glee.

Teri smiled to herself. *I just love these people! I don't want to be anywhere else than here in Echo Bay with this group of friends. This is what Christian fellowship is all about.*

It turned out that most of these friends agreed with her. They shared much later that these fellowships had been the best and closest Christian meetings that they had ever experienced. Teri hadn't realized that these special times had been part of God's plan in preparing them all for the overwhelming events that were about to hurtle into their lives.

After closing with Communion, the couples started to disperse. Teri happened to glance out the window. She was surprised to see Selma pull into her driveway next door. *Wonder where she been? There's not much going on at this hour. Oh well, it's none of my business!*

Paul and Teri arrived home, tired but happy. Most of the kids had already been picked up. Teri herded the older two upstairs. Jacob was asleep on the couch. Teri came back and gently picked him up and carried him upstairs. Hannah never said a word and climbed sleepily into bed. Peter went straight to his room too. Teri whispered, "Paul, isn't it weird that the kids are always sleepy like this when we get back?"

Paul answered quietly, "They're OK. We are a bit late tonight. That's all!

Just wait, they will be ready to go in the morning. Wait and see them hurry out after breakfast to play with the Haywood kids! I'm happy that they are so relaxed when we leave them with Brandon."

Shortly after the evening fellowship, Selma phoned Teri, "You must do something about your son, Peter!" Her sharp tone was intimidating as she continued. "If you don't do something about his disobedience, I will not let Brandon babysit him. He certainly needs to apologize to us and do what he is told!" Dismayed by this report, she mumbled something about being sorry and promised that she would deal with this. After Selma hung up, Teri thought unhappily, *Peter doesn't behave like this. Something is wrong with this picture.*

"Peter!" She called outside the door When he came breathlessly into the kitchen, Teri asked him to sit at the table with her. " I just had a phone call from Brandon's mother. She told me that you were not obeying Brandon at babysitting. You know that when Mom and Dad are away, you need to listen to those who look after you for us."

Peter folded his arms and looked away. He muttered, "He is mean!"

Oh, how she wished later that she had probed further, but instead she replied, "Peter, he may have to be strict at times, but it is important that you respect him and do what he asks. This is not like you. I don't understand why you are behaving like this. Now Selma wants us to go over and have you apologize to her for not obeying her son."

With some misgivings, she drove him over to Selma's house the next morning. After they went inside, Selma commanded that Peter work in her garden for an hour to show he was sorry. Teri was shocked! Again she felt helpless in this woman's presence and Peter went tearfully out to pull weeds.

Later, Teri would feel guilt and shame that she had not interceded for him. She had reacted in fear of this imposing woman. She continued to be concerned that Peter had acted this way towards Brandon. She later realized that she had not stopped to hear what Peter had to say.

That should silence Peter, she thought with glee later that day! She did not like the way Peter tried to defend the others. The other day he went after Brandon with a metal broom. Her son had told her that the broom was dented by the force of Peter's strikes.

She sat on her porch in the sun with her two little dogs. She was thinking how well it was going with her group. The teens were certainly enjoying themselves on their special nights. The Christians were all such fools! So easily deceived! It was easy to find out their meeting times as they always invited her. She realized that she would have to go to one of the get-togethers soon. It's so much fun to mock them at these times. Her hoarse laugh filled the air.

Drugging the children with 'Angel Dust' in their apple juice and candy seemed to work. She very much doubted that the kids would remember much. No one would believe them anyway! Threats were good silencers too! Just the other day she told the Nelson brats that she would kill their dog, Cricket, or burn their house down, if they ever said one word about the secret times.

She moved her ponderous body towards her swimming pool. She chuckled as she leaned forward to pet the dogs, then lowered her bulk into the water.

CHAPTER 4

In the months to follow, the smooth water of their happy life began to show ripples. Lately, a number of moms from their group had begun to drop in to visit Teri, all with growing concerns about some of their children.

One day, Diana had come over from next door. She had confided in Teri. "I am having lots of problems with Ali. She has become almost unmanageable. I really need some help here. She has stopped doing what we ask. Her favorite word is 'No!' She screams when we send her to her room but won't stay there. Yesterday, after we had tried everything, Sam locked the bedroom door from the outside. I thought that she was going to kick a hole through it. She's only three years old! I'm wondering why this is happening? Ali was pretty easy going until a month ago. What should I do to help her listen to us?"

Katie had recently phoned up to talk to Teri. "Our Kim is becoming disrespectful and rude to me. How can a five year old change so much! I thought we had a good relationship."

Josh, Wes and Sharon's young son, was being severely bullied both at school and in the neighbourhood. Susan, Tabitha's daughter who was best friends with Hannah, had become moody and unhappy. Teri was wondering about Peter, who recently started to avoid adults and stayed alone in his room for hours. He stopped smiling as often as before and didn't like groups. Little Jacob had walked into her brother's house on a visit and punched his cousin. *Why is all this happening?* Teri was worried. She couldn't think of a single reason why these children were suddenly behaving like this. Their lives were so healthy and secure. Nearly everything the children did was supervised and guided.

That wasn't all. Hannah lately had complained of irritated and painful private parts. Teri would help her and encourage her to wipe herself more gently. "I'll try and be careful, Mom. That must be the reason it hurts so much."

Teri had asked, "Are you sure there aren't any other reasons for this? Maybe I'll buy softer toilet paper."

Also, Jacob started needing help to use the bathroom and was reluctant to have a bath unless she was there.

Much later, she would be asked by friends, "Why didn't you connect all these things and figure out that something was wrong with this picture?"

Teri would always reply, " We had no reason to suspect anything. It's easy to look back and put it all together, but none of it made sense at the time."

Meanwhile the church was growing in number and spiritual growth. It was an exciting time. Easter was coming and nine adults wanted to be baptized. Paul prepared this group with special Bible studies. The only hesitant one was Katie. "I'm just not sure yet," she confessed, "I need more time to think about it." Her oval, light brown face looked thoughtful as she considered all the ramifications of this big step. "If I get baptized, I want to be sure in my heart."

Katie's Dad, Bill, a member of an Indian tribe in another area, had earlier professed Christ as his Savior. He was the first in his family to make this decision. Both of his daughters lived in Echo Bay with their families. There was no doubt that Katie had become a brand new Christian, but still had one foot on the fence. She just wasn't sure that she wanted her friends to know about her new found faith.

Finally the big day arrived. Everyone gathered at the south beach for the Easter sunrise service. Straps got there at the break of dawn to start a fire. As their family approached the beach, Teri looked with dismay at the strong gale blowing the waves into crashing breakers on the shore. " This could be a challenging day to baptize nine people!" Paul said with glee. Nothing could dampen his enthusiasm!

Groups of the Echo Bay Christians arrived and gathered around the fire. 'Up From the Grave He Arose' they sang with gusto. What a joyful sound it made with the rolling waves thundering nearby! Some of the children were wrapped in blankets and looked sleepy as they huddled near the fire. Paul stood and opened the Bible. With a loud voice he read chapter twenty of the Gospel of John, which describes the resurrection of Christ. After he sat down, some of the group shared about what this fact had meant to them. There was a hush as they worshipped their great God and Savior.

Straps prayed, "Our great Father, we gather here to give our praise and adoration to You. How thankful we are to be your children! We ask in Your great name to calm the storm for the sake of those being baptized. In Jesus Name, amen."

The crowd gathered up their children and drove over to a more sheltered beach. Paul exclaimed, "Wow! Will you look at that! It's actually calm and where's the wind? What a wonderful answer to prayer!"

By the time they arrived, the waves had flattened. Amazement showed on faces all around. The winds in this area usually built during the day. Wes spoke for all of them, "I'm in awe this morning. This is clearly the work of God. He is blessing us on this special day!"

Paul had managed to fit into a wet suit, which was too small. The participants had blankets and towels draped over them as they waited. Paul waddled towards the ocean, looking like a robot. Teri tried not to laugh. At the edge of the sea, he spoke, " Could each person being baptized, share their story of what this means to you?" Teri looked around for Katie. *Where is she? I so hoped she would come."*

Jackson spoke up first. "You all know that I am anything but perfect." He shot a quick look at Tabitha. "God saved me anyway! I want to live for Him the rest of my life. I will not turn back." He marched through the water to Paul, who was now up to his waist in the water. Paul took a strong hold of Jackson's back and lowered him beneath the surface."I baptize you in the Name of the Father, the Son and Holy Spirit."

As Jackson popped up, someone started to sing, "I Have Decided to Follow Jesus." Everyone on the beach joined in with praise.

As the song concluded, Tabitha walked to the water's edge. Smiling at Jackson she said, "I'll go next. Might as well join my husband!" The wind ruffled the papers she clutched in her hands. Standing tall, looking confident, she turned and read with emotion. "Before accepting Christ into my heart, although I didn't realize it, I was failing as an individual, wife and mother. Years searching for that indefinable something had left me beset with fears and a very clouded mind. I started going to church because my husband and children did and I wanted us to look, at least, like a united family. The things

I yearned to be, a strong competent individual, wife and mother, were the goals of my heart, and after many attempts, I felt defeated.

I started attending a women's Bible study at Teri's. I felt very open minded, although at that point didn't know what I believed. Eventually I came to understand what salvation through Christ really meant, and asked Him into my life to forgive my sins. Then, I only wanted to hear about the goodness of being a Christian. I still felt unsettled by sermons regarding evil, Satan and persecution. This was alright for others but not for me.

Finally, I couldn't deny that there was evil all around us, even here in Echo Bay. That's when the full reality of a living God and His love for me hit. I realized my tremendous need for Him. Now I understand why I had an indefinable yearning for God, although at that time I didn't know it. That emptiness has been filled today. Now I know that Christ did enter my life when I asked Him. "Ask and it will be given to you; seek and you will find; knock and the door will be opened for you."(Mathew 7:7). I thank God for His infinite wisdom and patience that fills my heart's desire to be who I was meant to be."

Little did Tabitha know that in the near future the evil she already felt would surround her and her family. The strong faith in her heart would help see her family through unspeakable circumstances. Right now, she was filled with joy as she stepped into the water to be baptized.

Suddenly, Teri saw movement out of the corner of her eyes. There was Katie at last. Teri's heart beat rapidly as she thrilled to see this beautiful woman head straight to the water. Her face was set like a flint. With determination in every step, she walked out to Paul standing just off shore. She turned. "I acknowledge Jesus Christ as my Savior and Lord. Nothing in my life is as important as this!" As she came up out of the cold water, an eagle flew right overhead. It seemed to be a symbol of Katie's heart set free.

Later in the week, Katie asked to come over. Teri was delighted, as she wanted to ask her friend about her baptism experience. They sat down in the kitchen. Teri poured them both coffee in her most special mugs. Katie spoke first. "I want to talk to you about Kim's behavior." She paused and looked directly into Teri's eyes. "First, though, I want to tell you about Sunday."

"Yes, I really want to hear what it was like for you!"

"What a morning I had! I think it was a spiritual battle. I did not want to go. In fact, I wanted to give up on the whole idea. I've never, ever felt this way before. It was very dark, like I was fighting an enemy. It was so hard, Teri. Finally, almost at the last minute, I prayed to God. I thought of what all you and Paul have taught me. I pleaded with Jesus to help me. Right away, I had a strong impression to get down to the beach as fast as I could. As soon as I got there, I felt a freedom like I've never experienced. I almost ran into the water to Paul.

Jesus loves me! Now I understand! I desperately wanted Him to be my Lord and Savior after all. Oh, Teri! I'm so glad I did! Like the Bible says, I am a new creation. The joy and peace I felt as I came out of the water! I can't even express it. Did you see that eagle? From my native culture, it is especially significant. It was a symbol to me of the choice I had just made to follow the Creator." Her dark brown eyes twinkled. " Now I can honestly say that I am a Christian."

Teri felt chills run down her back. The hairs on her arms stood up. "Oh, Katie! Nothing can make me happier than what you just told me!" She came around the table and wrapped her arms around her friend. Do you understand that God the Holy Spirit came into your heart?"

Fetching her Bible from the counter, she turned to Ephesians 1: 13 -14. "Here Katie, let me show you something. 'In Him you also trusted, after you heard the word of truth, the gospel of your salvation; in whom also, having believed, you were sealed with the Holy Spirit of promise.'"

Katie's face lit with understanding. After Teri gave her some more passages to study, she got up to leave. "Got to get back to my kids! I'll talk to you later about Kim. Thanks for helping me so much. I'm really getting what this Christian life is all about."

Dear Father, this is one of the happiest days of my life, Teri prayed later. *Can anything be any better than this?* She thanked the Lord for the believers who had found Christ as a result of Him leading their family here.

"I don't think we can ever leave here," she said to Paul later that night. " Living here seems so right for us!"

Paul smiled as he replied, " I sure don't miss the TV, or any of the other things we could have if we lived elsewhere. I hope next Easter we will have another baptism with just as many people." Unknown to them, that was not going to happen.

CHAPTER 5

The next day Teri sat down to read the government test results for Peter and Hannah. She felt a rush of pleasure that they had gained two grade levels since she had begun teaching them. Teri had never felt so fulfilled and happy with her life.

Hannah called up from the basement, "Mom, come quickly!"

Teri rushed downstairs, wondering why her girl sounded so excited. Cuddled in her hands was the goose egg that Tabitha had given her several weeks ago. It was hatching. They watched as the tiny gosling freed itself. Teri knew that from now on the baby would think Hannah was its mother. School was certainly finished for the day! Peter was ready to quit too cause he had big plans to go exploring with his friend, Len.

After settling the gosling back under the heating lamp, Hannah and Jacob ran to the beach to play on the nearby swing. Len arrived and disappeared into the woods with Peter and the ever present Cricket. Teri snuggled into the living room couch and read a booklet in the living room. It was a tool to prepare young children about the touchy subject of how to avoid sexual abuse. It was a typical teaching book that helped young children be aware of strangers and what to do if approached by a potential molester. She didn't even want to bring up the subject to her naive kids, but it was a requirement for school. *I really don't think this is necessary!* She thought, as she scanned each page. *The children are so well protected. Every activity they do is supervised. Hope this doesn't shock them too much! If I didn't have to do this for school, I would skip it.*

That night she started to teach the kids what the book said. *They are being awfully quiet.* She pondered. *Wonder why? Guess it is as uncomfortable for them as it is to me.* As Teri tucked them in that night, she knew that she had done her job. *No one will ever touch these kids! Besides, we are too close a family for anything like this to happen anyway. They would always tell me about anything like this.*

As the year came to a close, the church congregation started to shrink in number. Some had moved away and others were planning to. Jobs were the main reason for this.

Among those moving were Jackson and Tabitha. Although they wouldn't live very far away, their close presence would be greatly missed. Hannah was despondent about not having Susan nearby to play with.

Teri drove Hannah over there the day before the Morrisons left for their new home. As they pulled into the drive way, Hannah sadly told her mom, "I love my goose, but he attacks Peter and Jacob and anyone else who comes into our yard. Do you think the Morrisons will take him back? I know I can't keep a goose that hurts people."

"All we can do is ask, but I'm sure they will. Here comes Tabitha now."

Kindly, Tabitha calmed Hannah's fears. She gave her a hug, "We will take good care of him for you. There will be a pen at our new house for the other geese and chickens. I think he would be a good husband," she chuckled.

To Teri's complete surprise, Tabitha had decided to start home schooling her three. She explained, "There are just too many weird things that have happened at the school. The bullying and nastiness have reached a new high. All my kids were coming home depressed every day. I question some of the teaching methods, too. Teri, can you help me get started? I've also heard the school where we are moving to is just as bad. I think it would be a good solution to teach them at home."

Later, after some difficult adjustments, Tabitha and the kids relaxed into the fun curriculum that Teri had given them. Both families delighted in getting together at the monthly home school outings.

CHAPTER 6

After a busy summer Bible Camp season, normal life had returned. Even though the church fellowship was smaller, nothing dampened the special closeness they all shared.

Two couples had decided to get married, after living together for a number of years. At each ceremony, the many children were babysat at different houses with faithful Brandon. At one of the receptions, the kids were allowed to join in. Tabitha and Teri went to pick them up and pay Brandon.

Teri's good friend, Katherine, came over to stand beside Teri, "Oh my! The kids are so hyper tonight! Do you think Brandon is giving them too much sugar?"

Teri watched a group of younger kids on the dance floor. They were acting like idiots, pushing and wrestling. "Ya! Your right! There's Jacob in the middle of it! They look very worked up. Kinda weird, eh?"

An hour later, some families started to leave. Many were chasing their children all around the room, trying to herd them to their cars. Teri whispered to Paul, "It looks like I need to take the kids home. Jacob is wild and is not listening to me. Can you get a ride?"

He nodded and replied, "Sure! I'll see you at home. I don't mind walking, either."

Teri tried to settle the restless children into bed. By the time their lights were off, she was exhausted. She had no idea why they got so over- stimulated and displayed unusually bad behavior.

The next morning, Hannah sat in her room playing with Sparkles, her new guinea pig. Picking him up, she cuddled him and whispered, "You don't have anything to worry about. I will never let them touch you. I will stab them with my knife if they come into our room." Sometimes she felt overwhelmed by the dark feelings that crowded her. Thoughts continually flitted across her mind of the people hurting her and being mean. Everything seemed foggy and blurry, as she tried to put her thoughts together.

"I wish I could tell Mommy." She worried. One thing she couldn't forget. Cricket would die if she told. She was horrified at what she saw them doing to that stray dog. Hannah quickly pushed it to the back of her mind. Instead she thought of the Bible verses Mom was memorizing with her. Isaiah 26:3-4, was one, "You will keep him in perfect peace whose mind is fixed on You, because he trusts in You. Trust in the Lord forever." she quoted.

She especially liked the verses in Philippians 4:6 -7. "Let me quote something to you, Sparkles."

Her quiet voice lisped as she shared, "Be anxious for nothing, but in everything by prayer and supplication, with thanksgiving, let your requests be made known to God; and the peace of God which surpasses all understanding will guard your heart and mind through Christ Jesus." She laid on her bed with Sparkles on her tummy.

"God, I don't understand what is going on, but I know it is bad. I'm scared to tell Mom and Dad, cause the people said something very terrible would happen to me if I said a word about what they are doing. Please help me not to be scared! Cause I know You are looking after me, even when they hit me."

She had felt so weird when Mom had read her the book about bad touches by strangers. It didn't say anything about friends of her family. Did her parents know about this? "Please let them figure it out, Jesus. You know that I can't tell them." Hannah felt sorry for Peter. "I wonder if they are doing bad things to him, too?" she wondered."I'm scared about what they are doing to Jacob."

She suddenly wanted to be near her Mom. She dropped Sparkles into her cage. Running to the kitchen, Hannah saw her cooking supper. "Can I do something?" she asked, hugging Teri's arm.

"Hi sweetie, do you want to set the table?" Mom was listening to her tape recorder. It was playing the song Hannah loved, called "You Are My Hiding Place".

Hannah hid her tears as she busily put the knives and forks in their right place."I like that song, Mommy. Will you play it again?"

Teri stopped her stirring and rewound the tape. "I like it too, Hannah. The words are sure good, aren't they? How's Sparkles today?".

Hannah replied, "He seems a little sad today. Can I get some lettuce for him?".

"Go ahead," Mom answered, "I wonder why he seems sad. Did you play with him?".

"He really seems to like me, Mom; he loves snuggling."

Teri smiled as she remembered how excited Hannah was on her birthday when her dad had brought the cage with the guinea pig in it up from the basement. Paul was glad to get rid of that noisy little critter. He had hid it in his office for a few days. Sure was a good idea to get that for his only girl!

Soon the family came to the table. Teri had made clam chowder, one of their favorite suppers. Dad prayed, thanking the Lord for their cozy little house and especially for the clams. Mom and Hannah had dug them out of the windblown sand near their property. Peter eat silently, looking a bit moody, while Jacob wiggled around trying not to spill his supper. "Did you finish that book?" Paul asked Peter.

Without looking at his dad, he answered, "Yes, I have started the last book in the series.".

"That's really good, son. Do you like all the encyclopaedias I brought you? I see you reading them a lot these days."

Peter smiled happily, " I'm already on the third one." He then rattled on about what he had learned that afternoon. Teri marvelled at his amazing memory. He could remember every detail of those books. She was relieved to see the tension he had developed lately disappear as he talked about the Caspian Sea.

I wonder why he has become so shy. He doesn't talk to anyone any more. Where has my happy, outgoing boy gone? There's definitely something wrong, although he says there isn't.

Peter had not being sleeping well either. Teri went into his bedroom that night before she went to bed. He was wide awake with his mind racing. "Would you like to invite Sean over tomorrow" she asked softly. She wanted him to get out and play with a friend, instead of reading so much.

"I guess so. We could work on our fort."

"OK, I'll phone his Mom after school. He sure enjoys coming over here to play, doesn't he?"

After, she crawled into bed beside Paul, Teri talked to him about Peter. He had also noticed a change in him. "I'm sure it's just a stage. He's growing up so fast. It's hard to realize that he will be ten in a few months," Paul assured Teri.

"It sure is strange that he won't look at other people like he used to, though." she commented.

She could feel Paul smiling at her through the dark. "It's OK to be shy. Just watch, he will get over this in time." Teri was not comforted. She finally slipped into a restless sleep.

She woke with a start as she heard Hannah crying in her bed. Teri hurried in and found her shaking and sweaty. "Mommy!" she sobbed, "I had a really bad dream about a bear. He was trying to get into the house. He can't, can he, Mommy?"

Her Mom answered calmly, "No, you are safe from bears. Remember, Dad would protect you. We haven't seen any bears near our house, ever. It is just a bad dream. Do you want me to lie here with you for awhile?". Sighing with relief Hannah gave a nod and tucked herself close to Mommy.

CHAPTER 7

The phone rang right after lunch the next day. Katie's voice greeted Teri. Right away, Teri noticed that her usually cheerful voice had a much more serious tone. "You remember that I wanted to talk to you about Kim's behavior the other day? Well, this morning she was so angry about going to school! Boy! Talk about moody! She slammed the door as she went. I hate it when she acts like this. What am I doing wrong?"

Teri scrambled to think of an answer to satisfy Katie. Nothing of substance came to her mind. "Do you have some sort of consequence when she acts like this? Have you talked to her about why she is angry? Maybe something is going on at school that she hasn't told you."

"Yes, Joe and I do correct her for this attitude. But, we need to do this multiple times a day and we don't think that is good either. When I ask her if anything is wrong, she won't even answer."

Teri didn't know how to respond to this. She ended the conversation by saying lamely, "Well, you could try to spend more quality time with her. I know how busy you are with the new baby. Maybe Joe could take her fishing and see if she opens up to him. Let me know how she's doing in a week. Paul and I will certainly be praying for you all."

After she hung up, she remembered uneasily of Diana's recent visit from next door. Her neighbour had also run out of ways to control her little daughter, Ali. If she put her in her room she would come out. No matter what she did to help her three year old to obey, it always ended up in a rage. Everything that Teri had suggested earlier had not worked out.

I'll phone that Christian foster mom I know. Teri thought. *Shirley has raised so many kids successfully, she may be able to help.*

Later, she did just that. Shirley gave her some firm instructions to pass on. In her heart, Teri knew that, although good advice, it had already been tried to no avail.

Around the same time, a young Christian man who had befriended Brandon had stopped over after work to talk with Paul. Davy explained, "For some time now, I've been aware that Brandon is having trouble at home. Yes, he's finished high school, but, as you already know, his learning disabilities have kept him from graduating. His mom has become bitterly angry, even hostile towards him. How can we get him out of there? "

Paul thought for a minute." Brandon has just finished helping us at Bible Camp, as you know. We certainly didn't realize he was having such a bad time with his mom, though. Hey, do you have any idea why Selma would park her trailer down the beach while Brandon was working with us? She never set foot into the camp! It was almost like she was keeping an eye on her son. Really, something is very odd about their relationship, don't you think?"

"Oh, there definitely is!" Davy answered. "I have to admit that I really don't like her at all. Poor Brandon gets nothing but verbal abuse from her. He needs to get out of there. I've been considering letting him room with me, just until he finds something else. Do you have any other ideas?"

Paul promised that he would think about alternatives and ask around.

Davy picked Brandon up later that week and moved him into his house.

Eight days went by. Then an agitated Davy phoned Paul, "This isn't working! Brandon is so bored with my being away most days." Exasperated, Davy continued, "He just sits around and watches TV. He never helps with anything. I think he needs help learning how to take care of himself. Do you have any ideas of what I should do? I hate to kick him out, but it can't go on like this"

"I think I do have an idea we can explore. " Paul answered. " Jackson and Tabitha, who you know have recently moved, have told me that they are thinking about having Brandon move in with them. They have an extra bedroom where he could stay. They would help him find a job and do chores. Give them a call to see if they have made up their minds yet! How does that sound?"

Davy gave a sigh of relief. "That is great news. Just a warning for them! By the looks of his behavior while living with me, he will need a lot of work. Knowing Tabitha and Jackson, I think they will be a big help to this guy. They will need to be firm. He seems very unmotivated, even lazy. Have to admit, I'm not sorry if he goes! To me, he seems kind of weird. I just haven't felt comfortable having him live with me. I really can't pinpoint why. Maybe it's just me!"

A few days later, Brandon moved over to his new home at Morrisons and settled in their basement suite. This seemed like a good solution. Teri felt relieved at this arrangement, although what Davy had shared lingered in her mind.

CHAPTER 8

It wasn't long after this that their world started to cave in. One quiet afternoon, the phone rang shrilly in the kitchen. When Teri casually raised the receiver to her ear, she heard an agitated, angry male voice on the other end. "Who is this" she asked anxiously.

"You should know my voice by now." the caller snapped. Teri instantly recognized Jackson.

"What's the matter, Jackson? You don't sound very happy!".

"You won't be either after you hear this," he yelled. Teri pulled the phone further from her ear. Jackson often spoke loudly. but not like this.

His words tumbled after each other as he tried to express himself. With an effort of his will, Jackson tried to calm down. Bluntly he told her why he was calling. "Tabitha went into Robbie and Jamie's bedroom this morning with some laundry. Brandon was standing with his pants down! Robbie had no clothes on!" Jackson's voice broke.

"What? I don't understand, Jackson." Teri's heart fell to the floor.

"He had just finished abusing the boys, That's what!" Jackson was nearly in tears.

Teri broke into a sweat. "Oh Jackson, this is just awful!"

Jackson continued, getting right to the point, "Don't think that your children are OK! Brandon, when we confronted him, confessed to sexually abusing Jamie and Robbie. Tabitha and I both heard him say this. Brandon has moved back to Davy's. Let me talk to Paul."

Paul picked up the phone, "Jackson, what has happened?" Alarm filled his voice. Teri's heart immediately went out to the Morrisons. *How absolutely awful! I can't believe this is happening. What!! After all that they have done for Brandon!* Her mind collapsed into chaos. *Can this really be true?* She moved close to her husband as she saw his face grow pale. He looked very disturbed as he listened to Jackson's frantic voice.

"Can I speak to Tabitha?" she mouthed to Paul. He shook his head, looking upset.

After a few minutes, he slowly hung up and looked at Teri. "Jackson told me that he thinks our children could have also been abused by Brandon. He thinks that this is not an isolated event. However, I'm pretty sure that Jackson is over wrought and a bit panicky. I can't imagine Brandon abusing our kids. Besides, they haven't given us any reason to think this. Our kids are fine! You know how worked up Jackson can get, especially with something this urgent."

Teri hesitantly added, "Also, our kids would tell us if Brandon had touched them. Just last month I read them that little sexual abuse book. Hannah especially tells me everything. Oh Paul, this is beyond shocking! I never thought that Brandon would act like that! This is so very serious!"

"Well, I want to tell our friends here about this, but think we should wait until Jackson says it's OK. Let's hope that this is an isolated event! Jackson told me that the children are not saying a word about what just happened. Oh, and also, Tabitha said she would phone you tomorrow."

Teri looked tearfully at Paul, "That poor family! I was the one who asked them to take Brandon in the first place."

"It's not your fault. How could you know?"

This would become common refrain throughout the next couple of years.

Teri didn't sleep well that night. Troubling dreams about children in crying out for help invaded her rest. She woke up with a start. She heard a terrified wail from Jacob's room. As she hurried into his bedroom, she saw him curled up with no blankets. What shook her most was his position. He was curled into a fetal position and crying, "Go away! I don't like you. Go away!"

She tried to wake him up, but he seemed to be far away. " It's OK Jacob! Wake up!"

Slowly his eyes opened, but they looked vacant, unseeing. Teri picked him up and cuddled him gently. "It's Mommy, sweetie. Everything is OK! You were having a bad dream." Finally, after a half an hour, she put him back under the covers. He had not awakened.

Back in bed, Teri lay with her eyes wide open. Why were Hannah and Jacob so disturbed these nights? She entertained the thought that maybe Brandon had done something to them. He had babysat often enough. But, why was there no evidence and why hadn't Hannah told her if he had done something terrible? Finally, Teri must have dozed, because the next thing she knew was Paul asking, "Are you going to get up, or should I feed the children?"

Later that morning the phone rang. She hoped it was Tabitha. As she rushed to pick it up, butterflies flew around her stomach. It was Tabitha, but she sounded so different than the last time they had called. With a deep, husky voice, she said a quiet, "Hi, this is Tabitha. What did Jackson tell you yesterday?"

Teri carefully related all that he had told Paul and herself. "Tabitha, I am so upset for you! Praying lots! How you doing?"

"I have been better," she understated, "We are trying to sort this all out. The kids are so quiet and seem scared. They are not saying anything about Brandon. Robbie is very hard to control right now. He is angry and lashes out at everyone. We have reported what Brandon did to the RCMP and a social worker. The police are planning to lay charges and already Wanda, a case worker, is encouraging us to go to Hudson for counseling as soon as we can."

"Are you going then?"

"We are planning to go down in a month. Jackson will need to take a week off from work."

Teri voice was a whisper," We sure didn't have any idea that Brandon would sexually abuse kids. I wonder how many children have been devastated by him. He sure has babysat a lot! Also, he worked at camp this summer. On the other hand, maybe it was only your children that he abused. After all, you have been neighbors of that family for years. How unspeakable for you to find out in your own home! You have been so kind to Brandon. Maybe he has been doing these things for years! I really don't think that he has hurt our own three, though." She hesitated before she added, "I'm sure Hannah especially would have talked to me about anything that had happened to her."

Tabitha's voice raised a notch, "Teri, don't think that your own children have not been abused by Brandon! I think that an unknown number of children could have been involved. This could include yours."

Chastised, Teri's stomach cramped again and she felt sweat on her forehead. "Oh, Tabitha, sad as I am that your family is going through this terrible time, I can't even imagine that other children could be involved too. I wonder, though, if I should let the other parents know about this."

Tabitha sounded tense. "No, please, not yet! We just need a bit more time to talk to our own children. I'll be in touch."

As they finished the call, Teri's mind whirled. *I'm so glad that we haven't passed this news on yet. I can certainly understand where Tabitha is coming from. I can't even imagine what they are going through. It just can't have happened to our kids, too!*

That afternoon, she asked Paul, "Do you think we should ask our kids if Brandon has touched them? Tabitha seems to think that he may have abused them, too". She felt nauseated. Her guts twisted with waves of anxiety as she nervously waited for his response.

Paul reached over to hold her clenched fist. "Don't worry too much at this point, Teri! Let's wait until the Morrison kids are able to give some details to their parents about what Brandon has done to them. I'm sure we will learn more soon."

———————◆◆◆———————

She turned to her younger son, Barry, fury written all over her. "Brandon is even more stupid than I thought he was. Didn't know that he would be THAT careless! Now we are all in danger! What an idiot! He didn't keep his big mouth shut! I sure wonder how much he has 'confessed' to." Her voice dripped sarcasm.

"Don't you even THINK of telling anyone, Barry! You know what I'll do to you if you ever did. There is no way that I can get to Brandon. He is being carefully watched. " She kicked the garbage can as hard as she could. "Now, I have to contact every single person in the group. It could take hours!"

———————◆◆◆———————

CHAPTER 9

Jackson finally had enough! He was tired of watching the three kids moping around looking like they'd been beaten. They were so scared. Now was the time to show them that they had nothing to fear! He went to the basement and grabbed his shotgun. He loaded it with one round of ammo, then walked with determined speed up to the living room. He had asked Tabitha to gather all three children there.

"I know that you are all petrified and don't want to tell us what happened." He walked to the front door and locked it. Turning around, he held up his shotgun." If anyone tries to harm us, I will use this. You can say anything you want to."

Jamie, nearly eight, glanced fearfully at Robbie and Susan. "I'm going to tell them something. Brandon can't hurt us anymore." His lips started to tremble." Brandon did bad things to us." He looked up at his Dad, "But he also hurt Ali, Caleb and Mary."

While her brother talked, ten year old Susan turned ashen white and ran to the bathroom. As they heard the bathroom door slam, Robbie suddenly stood up and blurted out what Brandon had done to him. Tears blinding her eyes, Tabitha hurried to the bathroom to help Susan. Jackson looked almost green and nearly used language he no longer spoke, although he knew that it was important to be as calm as possible for the kids' sake.

"Thank you, boys! You have done the right thing. Don't worry! I will never let him do anything to you ever again. You all realize that I have to tell the police what you have told us."

Tabitha, with her arm around Susan, returned to the living room. "Susan, do you want to say anything? Has Brandon done bad things to you too?"

Her young daughter hid her face, shook her long hair and didn't say a word. Her mom assured her, "That's OK, dear! Why don't you all go to the kitchen and have a cookie! Your Dad and I need to talk."

The parents kept their voices low as they discussed what they had just heard. Neither of them were prone to tears, but they were close. Tabitha whispered, "One thing we must keep in mind is to try and keep calm at all times."

Jackson gave a weak smile. "Easier said than done! You're right, though. Guess I'll have to try harder!"

Tabitha almost smiled at this, knowing that this would be next to impossible for her husband. Instead, she quickly added, "They need all our love right now. We must trust the Lord for the future. I'm struggling with that right now, but I know He is Sovereign.

"Brandon is such a monster!" Tabitha could not hide her anger. "The poor kids! I think the RCMP should send Brandon far away for his own protection."

"We failed the kids. " Jackson mourned. "Why didn't we know sooner?"

Tabitha reached over to hug him, "It's not our fault, Jackson! We just didn't know."

"Well, we are not going to fail them now! I will keep the gun by the door. I sure agree with Brandon moving away. We'll phone Davy and fill him in."

"Don't you think we should phone the police first with this new information?" Tabitha, the ever practical one, was thinking ahead. "Then, we had better phone Diana and Sam and let them know about what Jamie told us."

Diana was washing lunch dishes when her phone rang. She casually picked it up. Tabitha was on the other end. "Diana, I have some bad news to tell you. Is Sam working?"

Diana quickly looked out the window to make sure her three children were in view. "What could be wrong, Tabitha? You sound awful!"

Gently, Tabitha explained to her friend what she had discovered about Brandon. "Jamie just told us something about your children, Diana. Maybe you should sit down".

In stark contrast to her black hair, Diana's face looked white as snow. She trembled as she waited for the terrible news. Tabitha carefully told her friend what had happened that morning, "I'm so sorry to tell you this, but I have no choice. My son just disclosed to us that Brandon has not only sexually abused him and Robbie, but also your children, too."

"Oh, he must be mistaken! Our kids are fine. When did this supposedly happen?" Diana had the gut feeling that her world had just crashed.

Tabitha spoke softly about finding Brandon in the bedroom with Jamie and Robbie. "Jamie told us that Brandon has, quote, 'done bad things to Caleb, Mary and Ali too.'"

Diana felt sick as her mind spun out of control. "What else do you know, Tabitha? Is this why Ali is so unmanageable? When could this have happened? What are you going to do?"

Tabitha told her, "The kids are very reluctant to give us more information right now. The boys are scheduled to talk to the police tomorrow, but, of course, I have no way of predicting whether they will say anything more. They are very scared right now. Why? We don't really know, but I think there is a lot they are not saying. Susan is miserable! I'll update you with any news that affects your family. I promise!"

Diana hung up, feeling completely overwhelmed. She staggered over to her worn out couch and sat with her head in her hands. One thing ran through her brain. *Our lives will never be the same if this is true!*

She cautioned herself. *I need to talk to the kids when I am calm. Also, I need to think and pray before I call them to come inside.* Her petite face contorted as tears rolled down onto her lap. "Oh, Lord Jesus, please pour your mercy and grace on our family. Why have you allowed this unspeakable thing to happen? Help me talk to the kids. If this has happened, let them open up to me and talk."

An hour later, she called to her three who were outside playing. Caleb urged his sisters to come as he ran for the door. As soon as he entered and saw his mom, he knew that something major had happened. "What, Mom?"

Diana sat them down. She wondered if she had the courage to even ask them.

Next door, Teri couldn't keep her mind on school work. She kept thinking of the Morrison family. *Wish I would hear from Tabitha again! It's been nearly two days.* Finally, in the afternoon, she couldn't wait any longer. Her tummy tensed as she dialed her friend's number. After some small talk, Teri dove right in. "I've been thinking about you all morning. Have you any updates?"

"Yes, I do! It's getting worse, Teri. I just phoned Diana to inform her that Jamie told us last night that Brandon also abused her children. You should have seen him! He looked almost panicky as he blurted out about the Haywood children. I thought that he was going to be sick. Oh Teri, I think this is just the tip of the iceberg! Something much bigger than we can imagine is going on. Tomorrow the two boys are talking with the RCMP. Who knows what they will or will not say! Jamie would not tell us anymore last night but ran to his room in tears. It took hours before he calmed down enough to sleep. Poor kids! I think our lives are about to be changed forever! Who knows how many other children have been involved with this abusive man! Diana will talk to her three and maybe we will find out more information."

"I have no words, Tabitha. How awful for you and now Diana! How are you holding up?"

"I haven't spent much time for myself lately. Jackson and I are praying a lot. Jackson is angry and wants to do something. He tries not to let the children know how he is feeling. It's hard for him to keep his feelings in check. You know him!"

Teri invited them all to come for a visit on Saturday to go for a walk on the beach. "Bring some sandwiches and I'll supply the rest."

Teri hung up in despair. What was happening to them all! She got up and looked out the window and watched as Diana called her children inside. "Oh Lord! Please give Diana great wisdom as she talks to her children. Help her to be calm and reassuring."

CHAPTER 10

Saturday arrived. Teri was busy in the kitchen preparing for the picnic. She hadn't heard back from Diana. She guessed that she would come over when she felt ready. As far as she knew, her neighbors were planning to join them on the beach.

No sooner had the Morrisons arrived, then the boys, including Caleb, all went into the woods to play. The girls rushed downstairs to play with some toy ponies that Susan had received from her grandmother. While Jackson and Paul visited in his office downstairs, Tabitha and Teri worked in the kitchen.

An hour later, everyone gathered at the beach . Tabitha and Teri went next door to help Diana. They found her tired and teary. "My three still have not said anything to me about Brandon. I so want them to tell me nothing has happened, but I know that they are hiding something. Every time I even touch on the subject, they just look terrified and won't say a word. Sam has set up an appointment with a counselor in Cassidy for them. I'm sure hoping that they will open up to her, cause they are feeling awful right now. I don't know what else to do."

Sam, Jackson and Paul were throwing stones into the water with the kids. Some sort of competition was going on. The three women were snacking on potato chips and watching. Teri picked up her Bible. "I've been looking for assurance in the Bible and I found a wonderful passage in Psalm 91: 14-15. Is this a good time to share it with you?"

The other two said in unison, 'Yes!"

She read out loud "' Because he has set his love upon Me, therefore I will deliver him; I will set him on high, because he has known My name. He shall call upon Me and I will answer him; I will be with him in trouble;

I will deliver him and honour him. ' I love the first two verses too. 'He who dwells in the secret place of the Most High shall abide under the Shadow of the Almighty. I will say of the Lord, He is my refuge and my fortress; My God, in Him I trust.'

As I thought about these verses, I was reminded that God is not only in control, but is also our refuge and fortress. He is Sovereign God and will always be with us in trouble. We certainly are in trouble here. We need to ask God to be our strength and wisdom, cause we sure can't cope with this huge situation without Him."

The three bowed their heads and asked their Heavenly Father to help and to pour His peace and safety upon them all.

"I'm feeling better now" Diana sighed. "I think I will memorize that passage. Right now, I am just confused and helpless. It isn't possible for me go on without walking close to God."

Teri felt a surge of peace as she watched Tabitha and the kids leave. Tabitha's parting words had been, "We must keep in touch often. Diana, please let us know how the counseling goes next week. OK?"

CHAPTER 11

A week after the beach picnic, little Jacob watched out the window as the police visited next door. "Why are the police there, Mommy?"

"They are going to talk to Caleb and Mary about some bad things Brandon did" Teri replied, watching him carefully for any reaction.

Jacob turned and stared wide- eyed at his Mom. "Oh!"

Hearing Hannah calling him, he ran down the stairs without another word.

"Hmm!" Teri thoughtfully considered what she had just witnessed. That wasn't quite the normal response she expected from him. This inquisitive little four- year- old usually asked lots of questions. She prayed quickly for her friends, asking God to help the family as the police questioned the kids. *Please help Diana with Your mercy, O Lord! Encourage Caleb and Mary to have the courage to talk to Constable Jay!*

She knew that Jay was the right cop for them to talk to. She had met Constable Jay several times and enjoyed his gentleness and good humour. It looked like he was going to be the one to take care of this case. If her three were involved in any way, he would be the one she would most want to help them.

She finished cleaning up the kitchen and waited for Diana's inevitable phone call.

After supper, all the kids hurried down to the beach to watch some whales feeding off shore. Teri looked out the window and saw Caleb run over to join them. Now is my chance, thought Teri. She jogged over to see Diana. Sam answered the door looking grim. Things did not seem happy in this household! "Are you guys OK?"

"No! " Diana answered. "Sam and I were having a discussion." She paused with a sarcastic look at her husband. "Sam thinks we should forget this is happening and carry on with our lives. Caleb and Mary never told Jay anything, so Sam thinks nothing happened. You should have seen their faces, Teri. They were terrified and wouldn't even look at Jay and the police woman who was with him." Her voice raised with frustration, "I want to take the kids to Cassidy to see the counsellors. Sam thinks it's a waste of time, because they are not disclosing anything. Jamie and Robbie both told the cops that our kids were involved. Has Tabitha told you what her boys said about what happened?"

"Some, but I heard they said quite a bit."

Diana continued, "Well, some of the details they described involve more than just touching. Believe me! I can't even speak about it."

Teri was deeply shocked. "Imagine what it must be like to hear such things coming out of your own children's mouths!"

"If you put two and two together, it seems the same things probably happened to ours."

Sam winced at his wife's words and argued, "We don't know this for sure, Diana. We just don't know!" He spoke as if he didn't believe his own words.

Teri couldn't think of anything to say. Sadly, she said goodbye and went home. *This family is facing impossible circumstances . No wonder they feel this way! Lord, help them!*

Later that evening she found out exactly how her friends were feeling. She had called the children up from the basement to read their night time story. They enthusiastically joined her on the couch. Jacob snuggled next to her. "Wha- wha what is the st-story about t- t tonight?" He stuttered.

Teri was confused, *What! This is something new! He's never stuttered before. Usually he speaks very clearly. What has started this?* Jacob squirmed restlessly as he continued trying to express himself. Peter and Hannah stared at him in astonishment. Suddenly, Teri remembered. A short while ago, he had watched the police show up next door. Was there some relationship here? She knew it was important to not draw attention to him at this moment. She felt nauseated, but said gently," It's OK, sweetie. Let's all find out what the story is about tonight. I think you'll really like it."

Tonight was Jacob's bath night. Teri had to fit it in before bed time, because he always insisted on her being in the room when he bathed. He was quite quiet until she helped dry him off with his favorite towel.

He stepped back from her and looked into her face. "Mommy, Brandon did bad things to me. He hurt me and he hurt Peter, too! He did it to you, too, Mommy." Teri's heart fell to the floor. The bathroom walls started to spin. *"Help me Lord!"* she prayed silently.

Teri knelt down beside her precious, innocent little boy and calmly replied, " Brandon did not tell you the truth. He has never done bad things to me. I am so sad he hurt you, my little sweetheart".

Jacob continued, " He did bad things with sticks too".

No! This can't be happening! Teri wanted to plug her ears as he described things she couldn't bear. He struggled trying to speak, but he was finding it more and more difficult to get the words out. Tears of frustration slid down his ashen face. She tried to snuggle with him and hold him close, but he pushed her away.

She believed everything he said and it crushed her. There was no way that he had made it up. Numbly, she helped him get ready for bed. Teri tucked him in and prayed that God would comfort him. She asked the Father to let her son know how much Mommy and Daddy loved him. As she prepared to leave the bedroom, he pleaded with her to stay. "Mommy, pl- please don't leave me alone!"

She was heart-broken that every time she tried to snuggle him, he rolled away. She sat on the bed waiting for him to fall asleep. She desperately wanted to talk to Paul, but here she was, stuck. She heard him putting the other two to bed. An hour later she felt Jacob relax. Finally, he was asleep! She carefully got up and slipped out of the room.

Her mind swirled with emotion. Paul was in the living room reading the book she had just read to the kids. She threw herself down beside him and started to moan quietly, rocking back and forth.

"What is it dear? What happened?" He whispered in alarm.

Teri poured out the words that their little son had revealed to her. She pressed her face into his chest and sobbed quietly. Paul held her but was too stunned to speak. Finally, he got up to pace in the darkness. "I guess we will have to let Jay know right away. Did Jacob mention any other children being abused by this wretch of a human being?"

Teri swept the sweat and tears off her face, " Yes, he told me that Brandon had done things to Peter. Oh, I haven't told you that he also mentioned Caleb, Mary and Ali ."

"This is unbelievable!" Paul anger spilled over. "Too bad he's been charged already by the police and sent to Hudson for psychiatric evaluation! I sure would like to talk to him face to face!"

Teri sighed, "Well, I'm just glad the court accepted the charges. It's probably good that Brandon's not living near us right now. I wonder if they will find a screw loose in his brain. Selma will be furious."

"Do you know what this means?" Paul continued as he bowed his face into his hands. "It means that all these kids have been sexually abused together. I wouldn't be surprised if there are others involved."

As it turned out that would prove to be an understatement .

The house was dark as she rustled through her files. Selma muttered away angrily as she pulled out some magazines. "I wonder if our fun is over. Stupid Brandon! Confessing to the cops! What is wrong with him. Has he completely lost his mind? How soon will the cops come sniffing around here? I must get rid of anything they can tie to me. These magazines would sure give us away!"

She slammed down the one with a front page picture of Brandon in the act with Mary. "I must let everyone know, so they can get rid of their stuff too. If not, we are all in big trouble. Those little brats better not talk. They know what will happen to their families if they do!"

Storm clouds had enclosed three families now. Life had completely changed for Paul and Teri. Instead of their usual ministry, they were immersed in trying to cope with this horrible turn of events. Teri had phoned the Morrison's counselor who, among other things, had advised her to not rush Peter and Hannah into talking about Brandon. Instead, she encouraged Teri to rely on her own intuition.

As a result of this conversation, she started to ease up on school. Instead, she and Paul took them for frequent biking and hiking trips. They also frequently took the kids on long cruises through nearby islands. Sometimes Peter and Hannah were let off to explore the shores by themselves. As well as trying to relax the three children, the couple tried to think and do anything to take their own minds off the unspeakable.

However, they couldn't stop the wheels of justice from turning. Brandon's preliminary hearing was held in Fort Smith. A few days after, Tabitha took the kids to visit the Nelsons.

Teri thought Tabitha looked exhausted. Her clear blue eyes had dark smudges under them. Her voice was subdued as she explained what the last week was like. "We all went to Fort Smith last Wednesday. Our lawyer met with Jackson and me that night, while the kids played with toys in the next room. " She sighed. " They've been so scared lately, so we were glad that they had enough courage to go and play without us. Anyway, Ken, our lawyer, told us to not worry about Jamie needing to testify. He said that they had enough police witnesses that heard Brandon's confession. Besides, I was the one who walked in on Brandon! The court day went just as he said it would. After Crown presented our case, the Court accepted the evidence and Jamie never even had to go in. Jackson looked after them in our motel room. Ken, our lawyer, told us that the case would go to the District Court this fall. That gives us seven months to prepare. Teri, this is so absolutely awful! Never would have thought anything like this would ever happen to us! Why, Teri, did God allow this?"

Teri and Paul had already discussed this at length. Teri looked intently at Tabitha, "There is no way we can understand the ways of the Lord. He has promised to be with us in all our troubles. He will walk with us through this, even if we don't feel His Presence. It's sometimes even hard to pray, isn't it! I keep looking at His Word for answers. One thing I find are an array of amazing promises for us right now. There are so many! He has allowed this awful thing to happen for His purposes. Why? We probably will never know on this earth! I also want to make sure that you both know what good parents you are. You were deceived as much as the children were deceived. Let me tell you what Jacob told me the other night."

After Teri finished, Tabitha looked even worse." That must have been beyond sickening!"

"It was! I thought I would throw up. Do you see what lies he told the kids! He deceived the parents as much as the children. Imagine telling Jacob that he did the same thing to me! We had no idea what was going on. How could we?"

"Yes, but for several years, all three of mine have acted as if something was wrong. Robbie especially was so hard to handle. I never could pinpoint why. I knew it wasn't all genetic." She laughed for the first time since the discovery. "I just thought he was taking after his father. Sometimes, though, his behavior was over the top. Disobedient, angry and very easily frustrated! Honestly, I think we should have known there was something more going on."

Teri had already thought this through. Even though many families had seemingly difficult child issues, it was impossible to put all the pieces of the puzzle together. They hadn't had any reason to suspect child abuse of this nature and magnitude. She said as much to Tabitha and encouraged her not to lay guilt on top of their many other emotional stresses.

CHAPTER 12

"There he is." Peter whispered to Hannah. They watched Jacob play with Lego blocks in the living room. "It'd weird that he won't even go downstairs or play outside anymore. Silly guy!"

"I'll talk first," Hannah whispered back.

"Hey, Jacob, we want to talk to you." Hannah spoke in a soft voice. "You should not have told Mommy about Brandon. Don't you remember what they said about telling anyone? Don't you care about Cricket? They told us that she would disappear if we told." Tears filled her eyes. "Now they know! We are mad at you! And don't you even dare tell Mom or Dad about what happened to us! Do you understand?"

Jacob started to cry, "Bu- Bu- Bu- But he d- d did do those th- th things!"

Peter burst in, "You still didn't have to tell anyone. Now they think we are all involved and we don't want to talk about it. Now stop crying before Mom comes upstairs! Oh, Oh! Here she comes, you whiny little brat!"

The older two crept quickly into Peter's room. They listened carefully as Mom asked Jacob what was wrong. They were relieved when Jacob told her that he couldn't find a Lego piece.

Despite their conversation with Jacob, they overheard Mom talking with some of her friends about Brandon. Both of them felt ill at ease, wondering if they would have to eventually tell.

Caleb reached up and turned the light off and shut the door of his bedroom. His mom had just come in to say goodnight. Instead of climbing into bed, he sat beside her and turned his face away. "I need to tell you something, Mommy."

His mom sat in shock, knowing that her oldest child was about to tell her something awful. She had mixed feelings as she stared at his shaking body.

He blurted out " Brandon did do bad things to me, Mom. There were some of us on the beach by the swing . Brandon made us take our clothes off. He hurt us with sticks behind the logs. He did bad things at our house with Hannah and Mary. Once it happened at the Morrison's house. It was really scary, Mommy."

Diana fought for composure as she listened to her oldest child go on to describe some terrible things. *What in the world would cause Brandon to abuse these kids? What is wrong with him? He sounds demented. This is unbelievable!*

Close to tears, she tried to comfort him, "I am just so sad that he did these things to you, Caleb. I didn't know this was happening. Do you know that the police took him away? He will never hurt you again." She pulled him over to her lap and laid her hand against his trembling back.

The next day, Diana took her three to the north beach to play in the sand. She watched Mary shake the sand off her sweater and slowly walk towards her. She sat down quietly beside her mom, while the other two built a sand castle. "Mommy, can I tell you something?"

"Of course you can. You can always talk to me anytime you want to."

Mary went on, " Caleb told me that he talked with you last night. He didn't tell me what it was about. But I know! Cause one time we were next door and Brandon made me bleed. Jacob and Hannah were there, too."

Hiding her horror, Diana gave her a long hug, "I love you, Mary. I hate what Brandon did to you! I wish I had known, cause I would have thrown him out of the house!"

Mary gave a sad smile, "Would you, Mommy? I sure wish you had been there. How come you didn't know?"

Diana couldn't stop the tears sliding down her cheeks. "Cause he fooled all us parents! He pretended that he was a nice babysitter. If we had known about these bad things he did, we would have called the police. Let's go home and I'll give you all ice cream and cookies."

Mary hesitated, "Do you have to tell the police now? I'm scared about that!"

Diana hugged her, "Yes, my sweet princess, I do have to. They will need to know so they can put him in jail."

Immediately after she spoke, a tremble rumbled through her gut. She knew it wasn't going to be that simple, but kept her thoughts to herself. Mary was too young to understand.

After they got home, she gave each child a bowl of ice-cream and sent them into the living room to watch cartoons. She quickly phoned Constable Jay to tell him what her kids had told her. He promised to come over to get statements from them as soon as possible. She dialed again. "Hi Teri, this is Diana. Well, it has happened! Caleb and Mary have both told me what Brandon did to them. I was so hoping that they weren't involved. Teri, these kids are all telling the truth. I'm sorry to have to tell you this, but I must! Both Caleb and Mary mentioned that Jacob and Hannah were there during the abuse and that Brandon hurt them, too. What terrible times we are in! Has Hannah given you any clue about this? It is just disgusting! I have already phoned up Constable Jay. You may want to talk to your kids about this."

Teri had known this was coming. She knew she couldn't put this off any longer. " Oh, this is so horrible! I feel just sick about it! How are you doing? Does Sam know?"

"He doesn't know about Mary yet. I can't phone him, so I'll have to wait until he comes home. Right now, I'm just trying to keep the kids busy. I sure hope that they will open up to Jay this time. I'd better go. Ali is needing me."

"OK, Diana, I'll try to find a way to encourage the older two to open up. Talk to you later!'"

This horrendous news added to her already bad day. It didn't help that she had just experienced an awful time with Jacob. He had changed, almost overnight. He could barely speak a sentence and took out his frustrations on Peter and Hannah. He had even kicked Teri in the shins this morning. The other two would retaliate, causing the once peaceful household to change dramatically into one of tension and chaos.

Teri found Paul outside washing the van. She updated him right away about what Diana had told her. They held hands and prayed desperately for all the children who had revealed this awful secret and for those who hadn't yet.

Afterwards, they called Hannah and Peter into the living room. Teri knew she would have to find a creative way to help Peter and Hannah talk to them. Now she had a plan. First Paul explained to the two that Mom and Dad had heard new information about Brandon doing hurtful things to other kids. Then he encouraged them to tell them, anytime they wanted, if Brandon did anything bad to them too.

Teri handed out papers to the children. "Here are some questions that I want you to write the answers to! We won't tell anyone what you write down." She handed them pencils.

Hannah looked with dismay at the paper. Two questions were written there. The first one read, "If Brandon did something to you, who would you want to tell?" The second, " Where would you like to go to talk privately?" She glanced at her parents, *What will happen to us if we tell? I have to answer these. I have no other choice!* Without thinking any further, she wrote, *"I would like to tell Mommy in the back of the van at North Beach."* After she wrote the words, she felt sick knowing that she had given her parents a clue. She tried to hide her anxiety. *Now she would have to tell her secret! Would these bad people hurt little Cricket? Would someone set her house on fire?*

Peter was just as worried. *Will Mom and Dad blame me for not protecting my brother and sister? Would showing them the broom handle that was bent from me hitting Brandon show them that I had tried?* He thought long and hard before he picked up the pencil. He didn't want them to know that Brandon had embarrassed and shamed him before other kids. *If I do talk, I will only tell about what happened to the other kids, but not what had happened to me.* Slowly he wrote," *I would talk to Mom in the van away from town."*

As Teri read their answers, she felt an odd sense of relief. Although she was pleased that they had moved a step forward in being able to tell her what happened, she felt sick about what she might hear. She passed the answers over to Paul, who nodded sadly.

The next day Hannah was ready to talk to her Mom. They drove to the beach she had chosen and parked. Teri had a notebook. She had decided to write down everything the kids said about Brandon. Her guts were twisted with anxiety as she waited. Hannah moved to the very back of the vehicle and looked out the window. She then proceeded to tell the awful truth about what Brandon had done to her.

It was beyond sickening for Teri to hear this, but she made a huge effort to keep her composure. In explicit detail Hannah described two episodes. Teri was shocked when she described an appalling scene at the beach near their favorite spot by a swing. An overwhelming urge to vomit gripped Teri. It was a struggle to keep calm. She wanted to pull her little girl onto her lap and never let go, but Hannah was still talking. She had lowered her voice as she breathed out some more scenes. Asking for a piece of paper and pencil, which Teri quickly supplied, Hannah drew a shaky diagram of the beach swing and where the kids and Brandon had stood. In this picture, she drew children with tears running down their faces and Brandon looking very angry. Teri's mind swirled as Hannah remembered several other events at the Haywood's house. Tears ran down her face as she continued to describe a time when Brandon had taken some of the children down to Mary's bedroom.

Teri's tried to keep up with what she was hearing. *This is far worse than I could ever have imagined! It is impossible for Hannah to make this up. It is so unthinkable!*

As if to confirm her thinking, Hannah asked, "Mom, do you believe me?"

"Oh yes, my wonderful girl! I'm so devastated these awful things that happened. How are you feeling?"

Hannah's curly hair fell forward as the tears continued to flow, "I just don't know, Mommy. I feel scared and sad. I didn't want to tell you cause I felt so bad."

"I am very glad you told me, Hannah. Now we can help you feel better. You know how much Mom and Dad love you, don't you. You can always tell us anything."

"I know." she sniffled. "But you won't tell Peter about me telling, will you?"

"Not as long as you don't want me to, but I will have to tell Jay, the nice policeman, about what you told me. Brandon did terrible things to you and the police need to hear you so they can put him in jail." This is what they all fervently wanted, but she didn't want her little girl knowing that it was up to the court. "Is it OK for me to explain to Dad what happened to you?"

"That's OK, Mom. I just felt better talking to you. Do you think Dad will be hurt that I only told you?"

"No, he won't be, honey. He will be glad that you told me. Do you want to drive around for awhile and listen to some of your favorite songs?"

Hannah responded, " No, I just want to go my room and play with my guinea pig. Could you play my songs in the kitchen?"

Back home, Teri gave her a big squeeze and again told her how much she loved her. Hannah slipped out of her arms and slowly walked to her bedroom.

After she put on her girl's favorite music, Teri hurried downstairs to Paul. "Was it awful?" he asked as he saw the anguish on his wife's face. His own face reflected the dismay she felt. She tried not to weep as the words came rushing out. "Oh, Paul, it is way worse than either of us can imagine! I took notes. Would you like to read them first?"

Wordlessly, he picked the papers from her hand. Teri watched as her husband broke down crying . He bowed his head, "God, we need your strength and wisdom. Please help us!"

He got up slowly and put his arms around his wife. They stood like that for a long time. "At least we have our children," Paul finally said. It wouldn't be the last time he voiced that.

Teri wasn't ready to go along with just that. She thought that there weren't many things worse than what she had just heard from the mouth of their precious daughter. She wasn't angry at God, even though she understood that for some unexplainable reason, He had allowed this. She needed more time to grapple with what she had just heard.

The next day, Peter was particularly quiet. After breakfast, he informed Teri he wanted to tell her something in the van beside the sea down the road. As she drove over to the look out, anguish filled her at what her beloved first- born would tell her.

He sat directly behind her and looked out at the waves. "What do you remember about Brandon hurting kids?", Teri gently asked.

He muttered sadly "I remember lots, Mom."

She was amazed at how detailed he was as he spoke. He described the same events that Hannah had shared. Not once did he relate anything that had happened to him. Instead he focussed on what he saw. During the next fifteen minutes he talked about abuse happening at the Haywood's, Bible camp, on the beach and even in their own home.

Brandon had been busy abusing kids right under their noses and they never had a clue. Teri turned to look at her son. "Peter, I just feel terrible that all these things happened to you all. We never had a clue to what's been going on. I can't imagine how hard this must be for you! Do you think you'll be able to tell Constable Jay about this?"

He looked beyond stressed as he considered this; then answered bravely that he would talk to their local policeman. He seemed to withdraw into himself as they arrived back home. Teri could not seem to comfort him. After communicating with Paul, she dialed the police station with trembling fingers and asked for Jay. He answered right away and sympathetically said that he would be over that afternoon.

All three children left their lunch untouched as they waited for the police car to drive in. She saw the older two wince as, finally, the car drove up to their door. Constable Jay had brought along a police woman to help with the interviews. Teri and Paul were allowed to be in the room while they questioned each child individually. As they set up, Jay turned to them. "Please don't interrupt or comment as we listen to the kids! I can't imagine how difficult this all is for you, but it is very important for you to not give any leading questions during these interviews. Eventually they will be used in court as evidence. Do you understand this?"

Both of them readily agreed.

First, Peter came in to face his worst fears. As Jay chatted with Peter, his gentle and relational attitude helped their son relax. Peter kept his head down and wouldn't look at anyone. Nevertheless, he was able to share pretty much what he had told his mom.

Hannah was next. She entered the room smiling in embarrassment. She continued to smile, even as she spoke of the horrors she had experienced. Jay could hardly contain his anger at all this terrible information. Admiringly, he kept a kind expression, but his eyes revealed how he really felt. Although each child was questioned separately, their stories blended into one from their different perspectives.

Jacob found it hard to be still. He wiggled constantly as he haltingly told Jay some of the things that Brandon had done to him. Paul looked ill as he listened, for the first time, at what was coming out of his dear children's lips. He struggled, as Teri had done, to keep his face calm.

Finally they were done and Jay asked to speak with the parents privately. He looked at them for awhile before he could speak. He was visibly shaken. Finally, he cleared his throat and brushed his large hand over his short black hair. In a husky voice, he told them that he was utterly dismayed at what he had just heard. "The older two are very credible and I'm amazed at how courageous they are. From the sounds of it, they have also experienced some serious threats from this offender." He looked at his partner and asked, "I believed every word that they said. How about you?"

Sharon was no stranger to testimonies of abuse. "I have never heard of anything close to what these children have told us." She turned to Paul and Teri. "Your children are so well spoken. There is no doubt that this happened to them. Peter and Hannah's descriptions are so detailed and believable. I can tell that you are excellent parents."

Tears glistened in Paul's eyes as he thanked them for their help. "What happens now?"

Jay explained the process of compiling evidence and follow up. "We have to follow the routine of submitting disclosures like this very carefully. You can expect calls from social services, as well as some child counsellors that I will contact. This case looks like it involves a number of children, so eventually you will also hear from a prosecuting attorney. We have a lot to do first in putting this all together."

CHAPTER 13

After supper, Teri felt ready to explode. She needed her own space for awhile, to try and sort out her feelings. She called Cricket and went for a walk in the woods. She turned on her music and put the earphones in. The tall trees enclosed her as she walked towards the lake. Birds sang all around her, but she never heard them. The gentle worship songs she listened to soothed her heart

After she had travelled a way, she sat down on a log at the end of a swamp and wept. Satan was attacking not only her family but also some of the new Christian families. Anger was not part of her agony today. Grief overwhelmed her! She tried to pray, but couldn't find the words. Teri knew that the Lord saw her pain. The comfort only the Holy Spirit could provide seemed to enclose her. She remembered the many times she and Paul had prayed for spiritual protection. She imagined God opening His Hands to allow this horror for purposes she did not understand.

Swiping her sleeve across her wet face, she finally looked up. She sighed as she watched ducks bobbing in the water, with the ever present wind ruffling their feathers. Overhead, a pair of eagles glided by. The ducks disappeared into the shallow water. All was still; life went on. But Teri only saw chaos and pain in their future. In her heart she knew that things were going to get worse. There were police reports, court decisions and the very necessary counseling that all these children needed. As the news circulated to the others in their close circle about this overwhelming abuse, these friends would undoubtedly look to Paul and herself for assurance and direction. At this point she felt too weak to help anyone.

She picked herself up and strolled slowly home. It was nearly dark when she opened the door and entered the living room. Paul met her, looking distressed. "Hannah is asking for you and Jacob can't go to sleep. You were a long time!"

Not waiting to respond to his complaint, she hurried into Jacob's room. He was busy kicking all his blankets off and fussing with his pillow. Teri sat down beside him and talked quietly to him until he started to settle down. "Please fix your bed the way you want it and I will be right back."

She went into Paul's and her bedroom and lay down beside Hannah. Her sad little girl wrapped her arms around her mom and snuggled. " You are having a rough time, aren't you sweetie. Do you want to listen to music?"

"No!" she answered quietly, " I just want you to hold me. I am having bad thoughts."

Teri would hear this often in the days to come. "I can cuddle you for a little while, but Jacob needs me, too. He can't get to sleep, either."

For ten minutes she held Hannah close and together they recited the twenty-third Psalm. After Hannah finally fell asleep, she found Paul and asked him to carry their daughter to her own bedroom. Entering the boys' room, she found that Peter, on the top bunk, was still awake. Teri looked at her watch which read nearly eleven o'clock. "Will we have to go to court, Mom?" he whispered.

"Let's not think about that now, honey. We just have to take it day by day. At this point, Dad and I just want to help you and the others in any way we can as we try to sort this all out. Try to think about something nice, my sweet boy. How about the last boat trip when you and Hannah went exploring? Think about what it was like to walk from one side of the island to the other. That may help you go to sleep. OK?"

He sighed unhappily and rolled over to face the wall. Bending down to Jacob, she saw that he was nearly asleep. Carefully she held his little hand and tried to get herself comfortable. In fifteen minutes he was sound asleep. Quietly, she slipped out of their room.

Paul had carried Hannah to her own bed and was ready to lie down. He smiled softly at Teri as he climbed into bed. She quickly got ready and curled under the quilt beside him. Paul sighed, "I feel completely exhausted!"

Teri agreed, "Me too! I guess bed times will be like this for quite awhile. All three are so unsettled and upset. It seems that the terrible stress of telling is taking a toll on them. Especially at bedtime! I guess they are all being flooded with bad memories. At least they won't have to see Brandon around here! He sure is a very troubled guy! I have trouble feeling sorry for him, though. Wonder what they will find out during the psychiatric examination Jay told us about?"

Paul was too sleepy to answer her and soon went to sleep. Teri was restless. Her mind keep spinning to the awful things that were shattering their peace. Jacob was turning into a different child. One moment he needed her to be close, then a moment later would bang his head against her legs. The night before, Hannah had slept in the living room on the roll- out couch with her mom. Grief had poured out of her as she gripped Teri's hand and wept quietly. Soothing music played softly beside them. This helped, but could not reach into the intense emotional pain of her little girl. It had been in the early hours that Hannah finally drifted off to an uneasy sleep.

Teri listened to Paul snoring away. That was not what kept her awake. The night light in their room cast a friendly, warm glow. It didn't help Teri, who was unable to shake feelings of intense despair. She thought of Peter, who remained closed and never smiled any more. He didn't want to talk about his feelings. Paul and Teri tried to support him, but he brushed them away with an "I'm OK." It was obvious he wasn't. He was angry and moody, often lashing out at Jacob who made a point of purposely aggravating him. Both parents were heartbroken at these changes. Their once quiet home was in chaos.

Teri dropped into a light sleep. It didn't last long. Jacob climbed in beside her. "I c-c-can't go back to sleep, Mommy. C-c-can I sleep here? I'm s-s-scared."

"That's OK. Let me move over a bit." She crowded next to Paul who rolled onto his side. Little did she know that this would be a pattern for many years to come.

CHAPTER 14

Disclosures of Brandon's abuse kept rolling in. Susan started to open up to her mom. Jamie had given the police even more information. Other children from the church families were mentioned as victims. Paul decided that it was important to inform the rest of the families with small children who had been babysat by Brandon. Teri spent hours on the phone to the concerned mothers, carefully telling them that it was possible that the abuse had also happened to their little ones. Consequently, Paul and Teri spent time with each of these families to give what comfort they could.

Drew and Katherine started to question their children. Others were swept away by panic and didn't know what to do.

The next week Paul received a phone call from Officer Jay, who asked him to contact the families of interest about a meeting he was planning soon. It would also involve social services, a doctor from Hudson, who was an expert on child abuse, and two counsellors from the Family Counseling Service. "Tell the parents that they are all welcome to come and find out what is being planned to help you all."

Their fellowship meetings turned into times of sharing and prayer. Some were angry at God and confused by what He had allowed to happen. One father thought sexual abuse would be the worst thing that could ever happen to his children. Paul answered by repeating what he had said earlier. "We must all keep calm. Remember that we still have our children. The Lord spared them from physical harm. He is providing help so we can cope better. The best thing we can do now is pray. Allow our Father's comfort to fill your hearts and ask Him to give you wisdom and peace! What we do, and how we do it now, are essential to our children's healing. They have had some terrifying experiences and probably haven't told us everything."

Teri knew that her husband was thinking of Hannah's recent description of Brandon holding Jacob upside down over a well near their house. Brandon had menacingly warned the other children that if any one talked about what he was doing to them he would drop them down the well. This and other threats had obviously terrified these little ones into silence.

Teri agree."There are so many things we don't understand. I'm sure the counselors will fill us in when they come. Right now, my youngest is impossible to manage!"

Diana lamented, "Our family seems to be in ruins these days."

Katie's voice rose in anguish "What can we do? I'm getting very little sleep. I have to admit that I'm wondering how long we have to deal with all this behavior."

Teri knew that she certainly didn't have any answers for them. "Guys, it's only four days until this important meeting with the experts. Let's try to hang on until then. OK?"

Paul closed the discussion, "Let's have a time of prayer."

The group bowed their heads and one by one asked God for His wisdom and help in the dark days to come.

Finally, the day of the special meeting arrived. The Nelsons, along with the other families who had children babysat by Brandon, gathered in the conference room. The mood was somber as the RCMP, social services, the doctor and child counsellors took their seats. Jay started the meeting by introducing each professional to the parents.

He said gently, "I know you are all full of questions and concerns. First, though, let's listen to what these people have to say. I'm sure they will explain the procedures and give you options to consider. Remember, they are all on your side and concerned about your children. Feel free to ask questions afterward?"

Teri saw Sharon sit back in relief.

Dr. Scott was the first to speak. He rolled his chair closer to the group. His eyes matched his steel gray hair. His sincere manner and quiet voice reassured them all. "I'm glad to see you all. I am here to help you. One thing that I need to do is physically examine each child thought to be victims of this sexual abuse. I realize this is a difficult process and the children will undoubtedly be upset. However, this will help you know if any damage has been done; as well, it is necessary for court. I will be very gentle and your local nurse will be with me at all times. You will need to prepare your children for this. Your counselors will also help them ahead of time."

Teri felt her stomach flip and tense with anxiety. She knew right away that Peter would refuse this. He had become noticeably more private since his first disclosure. If anyone so much as touched his door when he was dressing, he would shout in anger at the suspected intruder.

The doctor went on to comfort them by explaining his credentials and experience. " I have been a referral doctor for fifteen years for abused children and adults. I want to make sure that you explain to your children the importance this examination has on this case. We want to make sure that the children are OK physically as I'm sure you do, too."

Wanda, one of the counselors, was busy scribbling notes as Dr. Scott spoke. Linda, the social service's representative was next. She looked around the room, oozing confidence. " We are here to make sure your children are safe. Although we know that Brandon is unlikely to come back to this community, we want see if the children feel protected in their homes by their parents. They may have feelings of being vulnerable in the presence of those around them. We will visit each family to insure that the children are feeling secure. For instance, all of you must be careful not to get angry in your children's presence, or use physical correction for negative behavior."

Several hands shot up. Jay shook his head and explained that questions could be asked after the presentations. Tabitha and Teri exchanged an irritated look. Distrust of this woman was obvious.

Then it was Wanda's turn. "We are working hard to arrange regular visits from our Family Counseling Center in Hudson. Doug McIntosh, our most experienced worker with child sexual abuse, will be the one you will see first. He is very gentle and loves to work together with parents and their children. Some of his techniques involve using fun toys, drawings and games to help these victims be able to talk about what has happened to them. He will also prepare those who may need to appear in court."

Katie turned to Teri and gave a small nod. The mood in the room relaxed.

Jay announced, "Now you can ask questions. We can answer some of them here, but please remember that you may want to wait until you have the opportunity to ask questions privately. First, I want to ask Wanda when you can expect to see Doug."

"We are hoping to have everything arranged in three weeks. We want Doug up here as soon as possible. At that time, Doug will meet you all at a collective meeting, before he arranges private times for each child."

Sharon was the first to raise her hand, "What I want to know is how can we cope with our children's behavior? We need help now!"

Linda, from social services, answered, "I'm hoping to visit you all in the next several weeks. I have some helpful guidelines to help with this."

With a worried expression, Katie spoke up next. "I think I speak for everyone here. Are you suggesting that we are at risk of you taking our children away from us! What if you judge that we are not providing a safe environment?"

Linda clasped her hands together and raised her thick brown eyebrows, "I think you have misunderstood. It hasn't entered my mind that children would be removed from your homes! Instead, we want to work with you to see that your child is feeling safe here and that you are cooperating with the guidelines I will be sharing with you. I think you will see this at our visits."

Teri explained boldly, "We are Christian parents here. We need to feel freedom to parent our children in a godly way. The Bible teaches a lot about how to do this. I guess I'm asking that you respect this. We just may not be able to agree with everything in your guidelines."

Frustrated, Linda looked to Jay to answer this remark. Wanda replied instead. "Our purpose here is just that. We will work with your beliefs in mind. You have the last word on everything that we suggest. We are not here to cause you stress."

Jay spoke up," Are there any more questions? No? Alright then, I will finish this meeting by asking that you all try to remain calm. I know that this is a lot to ask at this stage. Concentrate on just being there for your children."

Katherine went over to talk to Wanda. Teri knew she was concerned that her children had not reported any abuse. She knew that several other children had mentioned their presence at the abuse locations. Sharon hissed at Teri, "I don't like any of this! Maybe nothing has happened to mine! I especially don't like that Linda. Guess I'll wait until Doug comes up! Maybe he will think they are fine."

Teri paused before she answered, "I hope you're right, Sharon. However, you have told me of your difficulties with their behavior. You remember that they have also been mentioned at being there when Brandon hurt others. I think, at this point, you need to keep an open mind. Like you said, we need to wait for Doug to come."

Sharon shrugged her shoulders and went over to talk with Katie.

CHAPTER 15

The emotional trauma that the children were suffering persuaded Paul and Teri to leave the community for two weeks. They all needed a break from the relentless stress.

Paul's sister gave them a gift of a cabin to stay in by a lake near where she lived. After a long day's drive, they arrived at the small cabin snuggled into the trees. A dock jutted out into the large lake. Peter, Hannah and Jacob all leaped from the car and raced down the dock. Hannah came running back. "Mom, do we have some bread to feed the ducks?"

A gentle breeze kissed Teri's face as she joined them with some old bread crusts. "Isn't this a beautiful lake! Look at those loons out there. You will enjoy their mournful calls this evening."

Paul packed their luggage into the two story cabin. A quaint little living room met him. Large windows looked out on the lake on one side. A brick fireplace sat at the far end. Sofas in multiple designs sprawled around the room. *Hmm?* He wondered. *Where's the kitchen*? To his right some steep winding stairs reached up to the second floor. *It won't be up there.* Finally he gave up and looked out the window. As he watched Teri and the kids playing on the dock, he noticed a cooking stove with a grill on the grass in front of the cabin. *Well! There's our kitchen. Outside! I wonder if Teri will mind that. I guess if it rains, we will need to use the wood stove in here. Oh well! We wanted it to be rustic.* He walked through the living room to a bedroom off to the left and dumped some suitcases on one of the bunk beds.

Teri joined him there. "Hey, Paul, this is perfect. Did you look upstairs? There's a tiny bedroom with a large double wide bed. It's all made up. We will be right over the kid's bedroom. They should feel quite safe here and we can finally enjoy some privacy ourselves."

Her husband's eyes gleamed with anticipation. He moved over to her side and gave her a warm hug. "I agree. This is the first time in months that we can all relax. Although, I'm not sure that you will like cooking outside."

"I don't mind that. I love cooking over a fire pit. I noticed it when I came in. You know I like roughing it! There's a small fridge in the living room. I'm glad we have some place to put our milk and eggs. Otherwise, we'll just keep our food in the boxes."

The sound of a loud argument from outside slipped through the cracks in the logs to interrupt the peace. Teri sighed, "I guess this camping trip won't be entirely tranquil!"

As the sky started to darken, Teri bent over the fire pit to cook supper. The breeze blew wisps of hair into her deep blue eyes while she concentrated. Paul had taken the kids fishing in the little white rowboat that had been tied at the end of the dock. It was quiet all around her, but her mind was disturbed. Her memory reluctantly reached back to what had happened yesterday.

The drive had become tiring in the relentless heat. Little fights in the back seat were increasing in frequency. "Hey guys! Do you want a fun break? I have a surprise for you in a half an hour."

"What is it, Dad?" "Can you tell us now." "Please, Dad! Tell us."

Paul laughed. "Don't you think it would be more fun if I kept it a secret?"

Teri smiled knowingly. "Let's have a guessing game! What do you think it might be?"

The half hour flew by. Paul turned into a parking lot filled with cars. Peter was the first to exclaim. "It's a Zoo!"

"You got it, son. This is quite a famous place. There are many different animals here that you have never seen in your life."

As they walked through the wide gate to the booth, they saw a huge elephant looking over a high fence. Peter blurted, "Oh, look at the real elephant! Do you think they have rides, Dad?"

"I'll ask the lady in that ticket booth."

Suddenly, Jacob turned and ran back to the car. Teri quickly followed him. Reaching for his hand, she pulled him to herself."What's wrong Jacob?"

He had turned and looked up with fearful eyes. "I-I-I'm s-s-scared!"

Peter and Hannah glared at him, but their brother refused to move. Jacob glanced at the crowd of people all around him and shrunk against his mom. Paul had asked with concern, "What are you afraid of son? Mom will hold your hand the whole time. Just think of seeing all those animals! I promise that you will really like this."

Jacob had kept shaking his blond hair, "N-n-no! There's too many people. M-m-maybe they will grab me!"

Hannah had stared at him in disbelief. "What do you think you're doing! You are just trying to hold us all up. Don't be so stupid!"

"Come on sweetheart! Dad and I won't let any one touch you." Teri soothed.

Reluctantly, Jacob had gripped his mom's hand harder and let her drag him toward the entrance. Teri thought, *Man! If he squishes my hand like this the whole way, I'll lose all circulation to my fingers!*

The slim young woman at the booth had smiled at them. "Do you want to include elephant rides? If you come back in an hour, the rides will start up."

Peter had jumped in glee, "Yes! Please Dad!"

Teri remembered that although Jacob had watched in amazement as a pride of lions circulated around the pen, his tense hand did not relax. He had seemed distracted by all the people crowding around them. If anyone looked at him, he hid his face in her clothes. A couple of overweight women had been laughing next to them as they took pictures of each other. Shockingly, Jacob released His hand from Teri's. His face had turned red with rage. As hard as he could, he had savagely kicked the woman closest to them. Teri was beyond embarrassed. The woman had clutched her shin and yelled in disbelief. All Teri could do was to grab her distraught son and profusely apologize for his behavior. "I'm so very sorry! My son has never acted this way before."

The ruffled lady turned to Paul, "You need to do something about this spoiled little boy. Obviously you don't discipline him!"

The Nelsons had quickly left the area and moved towards the monkey house. Paul had crouched down in front of Jacob. "I'm not going to ask you why you did that, but I'm telling you to control yourself. That woman hadn't done anything to you. I know that you are not used to crowds, but you must never do anything like that ever again. Do you understand!"

Tears rolled unchecked down his face as he nodded. "I hate them! Th-th-they are scary."

The rest of the zoo visit had gone well. Peter and Hannah rode an elephant together, while Paul bought them all some snacks.

Teri's scalp prickled at the memory. Besides being very ashamed by their son's behavior, Paul and she had wondered why he was angry at these women. She had taken him aside during the elephant ride to ask him why he was acting this way. He had stubbornly refused to answer her.

As she flipped the hamburgers on the grill, frustration engulfed her. *This couldn't be the result of the abuse! Something else is going on! How are we going to break through to the heart of Jacob's anger and aggression? Were they raising a permanently disturbed child? Why was he so upset by the crowd and especially by the woman he had kicked?* She hoped the up-coming meeting between parents and Doug would answer some of her questions.

CHAPTER 16

All too soon they were back in Echo Bay. While they had been away, Susan, and now Katherine's and Drew's seven year old, Christina, had both described more details of Brandon's sexual abuse. Again the Nelsons wondered how many other children were involved. Teri was amazed at the close similarity of the disclosures of these children. A grim picture continued to emerge. Groups of innocent children had been tormented by this rampant abuser! Only a few days to go and hopefully the experts could tell them what help was available.

Cathy and a few teenagers slipped through Selma's back door. Sitting on her couch dressed in black, Selma gave them a terse welcome. "I've been waiting for nearly an hour. Why are you so late?"

"I was trying to get off the phone with that Teri. Imagine, she was inviting me to a get together with her group!" Cathy vented."I was held up by this stupid phone call! Then, we had to wait for your neighbors to go inside before we came over. You're the one who told us to be extra careful. You don't need to rant at me!"

"OK,OK! I got that invitation too. I just might go. Maybe I can have an opportunity to mock them without them catching on." Selma smirked. "They are so easy to fool. They even pretend to like me. Ha! If they only knew"

Cathy said sarcastically, "I wouldn't laugh too soon. You do realize that more of the 'poor little victims' are telling their parents and the police about what Brandon did. At least they are too scared to mention our names yet."

One of the teen boys peered around nervously at others with his dark eyes, "I sure hope they don't mention me! Do you realize how much trouble I will get in?"

"You worry too much! After all the threats and demonstrations of what would happen to them if they talked, should keep their little mouths shut." Selma snapped.

"Come on! We need to meet with our supreme ruler to find out his pleasure." Cathy interrupted.

Selma snarled, "Well, let's go upstairs. I've got everything ready to call him into our presence."

The Friday after the Nelsons returned home, the monthly social event met at Joe and Katie's house. The children were all there in the play room downstairs. Paul and Teri were pleased to see a good turnout. Katie had made some cookies for the kids and raisin tarts for the adults. They were all surprised when Selma marched in. Paul didn't miss a beat and opened their fun time with prayer.

"Let's all start by singing some favorites hymns and choruses," Paul encouraged, "Call out your favorites and we'll try and sing them." He was referring to the lack of song leaders in their midst.

Before they even got started, Selma, who seemed in a particularly good mood, asked for the children's song, " Spring Up O' Well". The song called for silly actions to go along with the words. Selma started doing the motions, laughing loudly. Teri had never seen her like this. She was usually reserved and non-participating. The thought crossed her mind that perhaps she was drunk. *She almost seems like she is mocking both the song and us,* Teri discerned. Diana picked up on the mood and asked for, "I Have Joy, Joy, Joy, Joy Down in my Heart". They all heartily joined in. Teri noticed that Selma had stopped singing and sat watching them all with amusement. *That is not a smile! It's a smirk. Weird! Teri thought.*

After the singing, Drew gave a short devotional about how to care for your neighbors with God's love. Selma spent the time staring stone- faced at him as he spoke. All her laughing had disappeared, replaced by a look of disdain. The thought entered Teri's brain that perhaps Selma knew more than she let on about her son's activities. She quickly put it out of her head.

CHAPTER 17

Paul and Teri soon found out that they had become the information centre for all aspects of the 'case', as it was now called. The phone rang too many times to count. Teri tried to keep the children out of voice range, but at times it was useless, as Jacob needed her close at all times. New disclosures from an increasing number of child victims were popping up nearly every day. Teri ended up hearing about all these details. She started to keep a log of everything she heard. She often thought, *Oh, so many children! They are all saying the same things. How could Brandon have hurt so many!* Teri did her best to encourage and help, although she knew so little about sexual abuse.

It was still a week before their first appointment with Doug, the counsellor. Teri was learning fast about how children react to being sexually abused. Her own three were good examples. All of them were especially fearful at bedtime. Jacob had moved permanently into Paul's and her bedroom. Hannah tried to stay in her own bed at night, but so often nightmares drove her to a special little foamy on the floor that Paul had laid beside their bed. Peter stayed awake for hours.

Breaks away from the house became essential to Teri. At least twice a week, she walked and jogged alone on a path by the ocean. As she ran, the waves blended into the music of her music player. She always felt a release from some of the stress as she worshiped and wept before God. She felt His love surround her. She often had the sensation of being lifted by the comfort of the Holy Spirit. She cried out to the Savior to give her wisdom and strength for each day. At these times, she tried not to think of the future but concentrated on the present. Sometimes, though, disturbing questions would creep in. *How did Brandon become such a vile offender? Was his mother in the equation? Where did Brandon's behavior come from? How could he intimidate and abuse so many children he was babysitting all by himself? Selma ruled her son with an iron fist and organized his every activity. Hmmm!* She always tried to push these thoughts aside by telling herself to "press on" and trust her loving Father.

One day, Paul decided it would be a nice distraction for the whole family to boat to the logging camp where he visited each weekend. His new friends there were eager to visit with the rest of his family. He realized that some of the folks there were lonely and felt cut off from the Christians in Echo Bay. Leona, Hannah's good friend, always asked Paul if Hannah could come for a visit. Her mom, Jean, also yearned to have Teri visit, as well.

As he discussed these plans with Teri, he reminded her, "At least these families are safe and uninvolved with Brandon. Don't you think it would be a good time for the kids to have a break by visiting their friends there?"

"Yes! It's great that all three have friends living there." Teri agreed. " They can all go off and play without fear."

Teri was relieved so see happy expressions on the children's faces when Paul told them of the trip. She felt a rush of happiness flow through her. *This is just what we all need right now!*

CHAPTER 18

The very next weekend the boat bounced over the waves on their way to the logging camp. Even Peter smiled with anticipation as he sat with Hannah and Jacob on the bow watching for fish to jump. Teri lay back against the seat and watched some sea gulls squawking along the shore. The wind blew her unruly hair away from her face. Freedom! *So glad that Paul suggested this! It will be great to get away from the phone's constant ringing.* She felt the stress wash away with the spray.

As the dock approached, they could see a small group eagerly waiting for them. Rob, Leona's dad, tied up the boat and helped Teri and the kids step off. Rob's wife, Jean, gave Teri a hug as the children all ran off to find Benji, Peter's good friend. Jean comforted Teri, "Paul told us of some the terrible things going on in Echo Bay. How awful for you all!"

"I'm so glad that your children have been spared from all this. It's refreshing to be here," Teri happily replied. " We have all been under tremendous pressure these days."

Jean was quick to invite them all to her house for tea and refreshments. Rob and Paul declined and went off on their own to talk about trucks and logging machinery. Teri was glad to have some time to confide in Jean. She was always encouraged by her friend's calm, friendly manner. "I'm so glad to have you for a friend, Jean." Teri felt affection for this woman whom she knew had times of loneliness in this isolated spot.

Just as they sat down at the kitchen table, the phone rang, making both of them jump. "Wonder who that could be?" Jean said as she hurried to the living room.

She returned quickly with a worried expression on her face as she passed the phone to Teri. "It's for you."

Who could be phoning me here? Only a few know where I am. Her stomach tightened with anxiety as she picked up the phone.

"Hi, Teri. It's Sam." He sounded tense and close to tears. "Well, we wondered if things could get any worse! This information will change everything."

Teri couldn't think of anything that could make their situation any worse. "Oh Sam, what has happened?"

He replied in a whisper, "Selma is very involved with this abuse, Teri. Caleb told us something this morning that defies the imagination. He woke up very disturbed and wouldn't eat breakfast. He suddenly burst out, 'I heard you talking about Selma last night. You think she's strange. Well, I'm terrified of her!'

Then he tore off to his room. When we followed him, we found him crying his heart out on his bed. Then, the world fell apart! He told us that many times Selma had entered some of our homes shortly after Brandon started to babysit. I won't describe some of the things he proceeded to tell us. Apparently, she had started 'hurting' kids and taking their pictures. Those were his words.

Teri, when Caleb described what happened with Selma, he was so scared. He shook so badly that we quieted him after a while, so he could rest. He mentioned Peter and Hannah as being there. I hate wrecking your visit with Jean and Rob, but we thought you should know as soon as possible. What on earth are we going to do now?"

Teri didn't know what to say. Her voice was gone.

"Teri?"

She was finally able to croak, "Sam, sorry! I can hardly think right now. You did the right thing to phone us. I'll phone you back after I talk to Paul. Is that OK?"

Nothing was OK and she knew it. After she hung up, Jean looked at her intently, "I think you should sit down, Teri. You look very pale."

Dizziness swept over her as she grabbed the chair. Jean had made a cup of tea and put it in front of her friend. "Can you tell me what that was all about?"

Teri spent the next hour unloading her pain and grief. She ended with, "I don't understand why our children haven't told us anything about Selma? Maybe it's because they are petrified of her! What do you think, Jean?'

"I know nothing about this sort of thing. This sounds like it's too much for us to understand. May the Lord help you! He's the only One who can."

For the next thirty minutes they cried and prayed together.

Hannah burst enthusiastically through the front door. "We are all over at Bejii's house. Just wanted to let you know! Jacob and Melanie are coming over here soon to play with her toys."

She disappeared back out the door. "You would never know anything was wrong with that girl looking at her." Jean commented. "You are doing so well helping your kids."

"We are doing our best. Sometimes I feel that our efforts are futile, but I'm glad that Hannah is holding her own."

Teri knew that she needed to tell Paul, but when he came in, she found no words. He looked relaxed and happy. She didn't want to burst his bubble.

After supper, she asked him to go for a short walk to check on the boat. He looked confused until he looked into her eyes. Once again, Teri poured out Sam's news. Paul's reaction was no surprise. His face flushed to the roots of his hair. "That miserable, wretched woman! All this time cozying up to us, while she was using her son to be part of her madness! I'm starting to think that we are only getting a glimpse of everything that happened to these poor little children. Did Sam phone Jay?"

The rising wind rocked the boat against the dock. Teri felt like cutting it loose, so they wouldn't have to return to the turmoil tomorrow. "I don't know, Paul. Right now, I feel like running away somewhere. I can't even imagine what is going to happen next!"

The visit ended way too quickly. The next morning, as the Nelsons stepped aboard their boat, Jean hugged Teri and whispered, "I'm so sorry that this wasn't the visit we hoped for. We are all coming to Echo Bay next week for groceries and stuff. Until then, know that we will be praying hard for you. OK?"

"Thanks so much for everything, Jean! You are a special friend. It really encourages me that you will be praying for us."

Soon they were at full throttle heading home. It was like turning their faces towards a horror story. If Teri had known the future, she would have asked Paul to return to the dock.

Hannah and Jacob sat up front enjoying the waves splashing up over the bow. Peter and Teri sat at the back . Paul was at the helm. Half way there,

Peter turned and looked at his mom for a few minutes. He thought long and hard. *They think I didn't hear them when they talked about Selma last night. Maybe this is a good time to tell Mom cause no one can hear us over the engine noise! Maybe Dad and Mom won't be mad that I didn't tell before! I know Dad will be able protect us better if I tell them.*

"Mom!" He asked in a tremulous voice, "I have something very important to tell you. You are not going to like it."

Teri straightened up in high alert. "Please go ahead, Peter!"

"Brandon was not the only one that hurt children. There were others."

Her heart froze with horror. "Peter, please tell me what you remember. There is nothing you can say that would surprise me."

Peter put his hand to his face to shield his mouth as he tested what to say first. "Well, first, Selma was also there."

Teri felt the blood rushing from her head.

Peter continued, "She was with Brandon when he showed us pictures from a magazine. We were in some of those pictures, Mom. They were disgusting, because they showed Brandon hurting Hannah, Jacob and other kids. Also, I remembered that every time, before Brandon started to hurt us, he got phone calls. They sounded like they were from his mother." He paused and looked down in embarrassment. *What will she think about Selma? I know she's a friend of hers.*

Teri could tell how difficult it was for her son to tell her this. *How much more is he going to tell me? I guess he heard us talking. I thought he was asleep.*

"Oh, Peter, how awful! It must be so hard to talk about this. I can't begin to tell you how sad I am that this happened to you and the others. We will not let these evil people hurt you ever again!"

She didn't want to ask him any leading questions, so she pulled him close and waited. However, she could tell from his guarded expression that this was all he could manage just now.

Teri continued to hug Peter and for once he didn't resist. It was reassuring to her that Peter was finally able to let himself be comforted. "I love you so much! You are such a brave boy! I know it is huge for you to tell me this."

Several hours later they arrived home. The children ran to sort out their laundry, so Teri could do the washing. Teri hurried to tell Paul about this news. His fist slammed down on his desk, "How can this get any worse! Did he say for sure that Selma was behind all this abuse?"

"No! But he implied it!" She added, "Do you think we should report this to the other families and the police, or wait until we get some more information?"

Paul rested his head on his folded arms and thought for awhile. Finally he raised his eyes and looked with anguish at Teri. "Let's wait on the Selma information. How many others are we going to find out about? Is this just the tip of the iceberg?"

It wasn't long before the telephone started to ring. The first call was from Katherine. The next from Ursula. After they had asked their kids if Selma had ever scared them, these moms also heard the awful news about Selma's involvement in the abuse.

Teri slowly hung up. She felt every cell in her body cry out, NO! The laundry forgotten, Teri went into Hannah's room. She was too stirred up to wait. Snuggling close to her little girl, she asked gently. "Sweetie, do you remember others that did bad things along with Brandon?"

Hannah, immediately, tensed and moved restlessly in Teri's embrace. "Yes, I do remember others, but I can't tell you." Her face flushed as she looked away.

Teri wanted to ask "Why not!" Instead, she held her tongue and waited.

"There were others." Hannah finally blurted, "But I'm scared! They told us they would hurt you, if we talked about it. They also showed us what they would do with Cricket, or Jacob. It was terrible, Mom! What if they found out?"

"Hannah, I will never let them near you again. Your dad and I will keep you safe now that we know." Teri said firmly.

"Are you scared of Selma?" Teri couldn't help but ask.

Her daughter started to cry. "Yes!" she whispered. "She's mean."

After cuddling and again reassuring her, Teri decided not to press her for details. "Would you like to help me with supper? We can listen to music together."

Hannah nodded sadly and followed her mom into the kitchen.

Jacob seemed to pick up on the tension in the house. Teri had triggered his anger earlier by asking him to clear the table of his toys. He responded by knocking his Lego truck on to the floor. His face contorted in fury as he yelled incoherently at no one in particular. Teri reached down to pick him up. He pulled away and landed a kick on her shin. Wincing in pain, Teri carried him into the living room and sat him firmly on the couch beside her.

"Jacob, control yourself! There was no reason to get mad at me for asking you to help. You sit here until you calm down; then we will talk about it." To her surprise, Jacob buried his head in a cushion and obeyed her.

Later that night, Teri phoned Tabitha and Katie. She did not mention Selma, but did tell them that there were other people involved with the abuse of their children. Uniformly, they reacted with shock and anger. Both asked, "What do we do now!" Teri encouraged them to continue an atmosphere of calmness and openness and see if any of their children talked about other individuals who hurt them. "This meeting with Doug can't happen too soon. We only have a few days to go now."

As Teri completed her calls, she heard Jacob crying from her bedroom. *Here we go again!* She was so tired. She trudged into the room and lay down beside him. "Let's give you a bath, then I'll read to you some of that book you like so much."

"N-n-no ba-ba-bath!"

She didn't have the energy to battle him to get him to have a much needed bath, so she just helped him get ready for bed.

CHAPTER 19

By now, all the parents realized that the abuse case was blowing up to be much more complicated and more overwhelming than ever. Officer Jay and his assistant again made rounds to the victim children to gather this new information. He had confided to Teri that he was shocked beyond words. He also cautioned her to be very careful to keep any new information confidential. "If word gets out to the community, it will not only affect the coming court appearances, but could prove dangerous."

Teri reassured him that she would do all she could to keep it within the victim families. However, she had a feeling that this close knit town would soon become suspicious of the frequent visits by the police to so many Christian homes.

Sunday came. Paul boated down to the logging camp and would return in the morning. That night, Teri found out that Jay's concerns had been warranted. The word was out! How? She had no idea. She had just finished helping Hannah and Jacob go to sleep and had decided to relax in the living room and read her Bible. She opened to Psalm 34 and started to practise her memorization.

Into her peaceful world, a loud noise of shouting voices startled her and made her lose her place. It sounded like a group of young adults yelling out on the street in front of their house. She got up and said to herself," What on earth is going on!"

She desperately hoped that the sleeping children would not be awakened. The curtains were open, but she didn't let the shouters see her. Instead, she went into the dark kitchen and carefully looked out the window. What she saw caused the hair on her arms to spike as a chill ran down her back! At least eight or more of the town's roughest teenagers crowded around each other on the street. While she knew that they couldn't see her, she felt very vulnerable. They seemed angry and their obscene language shook her to the core. "Get out of town! You'll all be sorry if you don't!! Your whole family are scum!! You better be careful and shut up or we will show you!!" The other words blended together in a unison of hatred.

Teri wondered if she should phone Constable Jay, but realized it would just make matters worse. She snuck back to the couch, picked up her Bible again and turned back to her spot in the Psalms. Reading in a steady voice, she quoted verses fifteen to seventeen. " The eyes of the Lord are on the righteous, and His ears are attentive to their cry. The Face of the Lord is against those who do evil, to destroy the remembrance of them from the earth. The righteous cry out and the Lord hears them, and delivers them out of all their troubles."

She was amazed at how calm and peaceful this made her feel. Anger and hatred filled the air outside, but her heart was still. She kept pausing to hear if they were gone. No, they hadn't stopped! Her eyes jumped back to verse seven. "The angel of the Lord encamps all around those who fear Him, and delivers them." She bowed her head and repeated the verse as a prayer.

Suddenly, every voice outside was silenced and she heard the sound of running feet. She clutched her Bible to her chest. Were they running into her front yard? She held her breath; then released it with relief as a car drove by. She felt like singing, "Victory in Jesus". Her mind started racing. *Why are they doing this? Was it because some had seen Jay's police car here? But why would these punks be shouting at her? Did Selma persuade them to harass their family? Would they come back later?* Teri got up and quickly checked each door and window to make sure they were locked. Then she checked on each child. Mercifully, they were still asleep! Back in the living room, she checked her watch. 11:30 pm! She turned the lights off and got ready for bed. This was a test. Would she trust her Heavenly Father or stay awake all night worrying?

As she lay, face up, she sang Hannah's favorite comfort hymn, "He Hideth My Soul" written by Fanny Crosby. Tears trickled down her cheeks as she sang, "A wonderful Savior is Jesus my Lord, a wonderful Savior to me. He hideth my soul in the cleft of the rock, where rivers of pleasure I see. He hideth my soul in the cleft of the rock that shadows a dry, thirsty land. He hideth my life in the depths of His love, and covers me there with His Hand."

The next thing she knew, it was morning. Immediately, she thanked

God for keeping them safe. Paul would be home in a few hours. As she lay in bed her troubled thoughts returned to the events of last night. *Why are these teens so angry at us? What will Paul do when he hears of this? Who should I tell? I must be very careful to keep the children more protected. This is getting so bizarre! I can't keep this incident to myself.* After much analyzing, Teri decided she must speak to her husband about this. *I wonder what his reaction will be? Would he drive around tracking these teens down?* She shivered at the thought. It would make everything worse if he did.

Sure enough, Paul was incensed! He marched down to his office and reached for his hidden shotgun behind his desk. Teri's heart was racing as he ran back up. In no uncertain terms, he demanded that she keep the gun in their bedroom closet. "You absolutely must keep this handy when I'm away. You know how to use it."

The gun made her uneasy, but she knew that he was right. They both decided that there was no point in telling the professionals about this just yet.

CHAPTER 20

Finally, the day arrived when Doug, from Hudson, came to town. Although he was only in his thirties, he had years of experience helping children who had suffered severe sexual abuse. Over the weeks and months ahead, as Teri got to know him, she enjoyed his fun way and his gentle spirit. He was of medium height, with dark brown hair and lively blue eyes. Almost immediately, he was able to connect with all the traumatized kids. Paul and Teri felt great relief at his presence. At last, someone was training them to find ways to help their troubled, frightened children.

Teri gathered her precious ones together on the morning of Doug's first visit. "Today you are going to meet a special man! His name is Doug and his job is to help kids like you. He is much different than the police because he wants to help you feel better. I'm sure you will like him! Try to look at this as a new fun experience, not a scary thing."

Peter looked sceptical. "Do I have to go? I'm doing fine."

His dad answered," Yes, son, you do! It may be hard this first time, but I know you can trust Doug. Your mom and I know how difficult this has been for you. You need someone besides your parents to talk to."

Later, Peter got reluctantly into the van with Jacob and Hannah. Paul drove them all to the local hotel, where Doug had set up a room for the counseling sessions. An adjoining room was for waiting parents and children. It had a TV and toys.

While the rest waited their turn, Teri took Jacob in to see Doug. Their little son looked fearfully at Teri as he saw his mom get ready to leave. Teri mouthed, "It's OK!" She had hoped that Peter would go in first, so he wouldn't have to wait. She had bought their favorite books to read. Hannah was reading a horse book, while their oldest looked at the new 'Guinness

Book of Records'. Although he was usually riveted by this type of book, Teri could tell he was not concentrating at all. He nervously tapped his foot and kept looking around. Thirty minutes later, Jacob reappeared looking happy enough. "OK, Peter, your turn." Doug called cheerfully. Their son got up grudgingly and followed the counselor.

Hannah leaned close to her Dad. "Is he going to ask us a bunch of questions? What if I don't feel like answering them? Will he get mad?"

Her dad answered gently, "No, Hannah! I don't think anything you do or say will make Doug mad. He just wants to hear how you are feeling about what happened to you. You can trust this man, Hannah."

When her turn came, she marched confidently into the counseling room.

After he had spent time with Hannah, Doug came out smiling. "Is it OK, for me to have a turn with your Mom and Dad," he asked the three." I will leave the door open a crack so you can see them."

The children looked at each other, then nodded their heads in agreement. Paul and Teri went in and sat down at the small table. Doug sat down opposite them and spoke quietly. " I know you two are the go-to people in this case. This is a very difficult responsibility, I know! Could you please tell me how you are managing?"

Teri let Paul go first. " We are doing well enough. You already know that we are Christians. We are experiencing the comfort and peace that only God can give. We are spending a lot of time trying to help the other families who have been deeply affected by the abuse of their children. It is draining, as we also spend a lot of energy caring for our own three. We are all so grateful that you are coming this far to help us all."

Teri continued, " We have been waiting a long time for you to come. None of us understand all the emotional difficulties that our children are having. We seem to be raising three completely different individuals these last six months! Jacob is unmanageable! Are we raising a permanently damaged and troubled child? I'm also feeling the stress of being the one that the other parents are turning to. All the authorities are contacting me for organizational meetings and information. Keeping a log of all this helps me to keep track. Also, I have found relief by jogging twice a week while listening to music.

Can you please tell us what observations you discovered as you spent time with our children?"

Doug flipped through his notes. He looked both serious and compassionate. This made Teri tense with fear at what Paul and she were about to hear. He started with Jacob. She gripped the edge of the table as he related deep concerns for Jacob. "I brought a variety of dolls and toys, as you can see. The first thing Jacob did, was pick up a female doll and punch it's stomach as hard as he could. I brought that punching clown over there. Jacob enjoyed hitting it so hard that it nearly popped. At the end of his session I asked him to draw a picture of something that made him angry. " Doug paused and looked directly at the couple, " He drew an ugly picture of a fat woman, with stick arms, reaching for a figure of himself. Tears poured out of the big eyes of the child who stood opposite the fat woman. Here's what it looks like."

He pushed the picture towards them. "When I asked him who he was most mad at, he told me that it was someone called Selma. He was moving around restlessly with his fists in a ball. I can tell from his play and behavior that he has been severely abused sexually, and perhaps physically. His speech got worse and worse the more he tried to tell me about incidences that terrified him. We finished up by playing a fun kid's board game to help him relax."

Teri, with tears choking her voice, whispered, " Yes, some of the children are starting to talk about Selma being involved in the abuse. She is Brandon's mother, in case you didn't know. As you saw, Jacob, like most of others, act scared of her. Will Jacob ever get better? He was such a happy, easy- going little guy before all this."

"I know you both have many questions. They will be answered eventually. First, I need to ask you if this woman has been reported to the police. Any new information the children disclose needs to be given to them. As well, I need to report my findings to them and the prosecution. Second, have you heard from your lawyer?"

Paul answered in frustration, "We have notified the police. They are still making rounds to gather information. We are still in the dark regarding any court appearances by our children. Your guess is as good as mine when this will happen."

"OK! We'll wait on that. I did hear that they were looking for a special prosecutor to handle this case. I'll let you know what I find out.

Now, I want to tell of some ways you can help Jacob, before I tell you my observations of Peter and Hannah. I think that Jacob will improve the more he is able to express his feelings better. I would like you to buy him his own punching bag. If you can't get one here, I'll bring one up next time I'm up here. When his behavior gets out of hand, encourage him to release his anger and frustrations on this inanimate object. Play with him as much as you have time for, especially with building toys and the Legos he seems to enjoy. He was very young when all this happened. We have found that the younger a child is, when they are victims of this kind of sexual and physical abuse, the more likely they are to suffer dramatic emotional disturbances. Please don't think this is a permanent state! With lots of help, love and support, most of these younger victims can often end up living fairly normal lives. Eventually, he will lose his memory of what happened to him. Believe it or not! The brain is so amazing! It seems that these very young victims, eventually, compartmentalize these awful memories and box them away in the deep recesses of their minds. Right now, you both have your work cut out for you!

Sadly, of course, you both will never forget. That is why parents need to be helped as well. Try to think of us as a team all working together to bring this child back to normalcy. He will need many more appointments with me. At this point he is not able to testify in court."

Paul asked about Peter, "Were you able to get Peter to communicate?"

Reluctantly, he responded, " As you probably were expecting, he was uptight and closed with me at first. He told me that he was fine and did not need counseling. I didn't ask him any questions about what he has told you and the police. He didn't play with any of the toys I brought. Just sat there, pale and quiet. Yes, to answer your question, I was eventually able to connect with him by asking what interested him. That young man is very smart! He told me in great detail about ships, planes and some of the books he's read. Anything except what has happened to him and about his own feelings. My impression is that he has a great deal of things on his mind. He had trouble looking at me. He seems to have feelings of guilt and shame about what he has seen and experienced.This is quite typical of older children who have been abused by adults. Dad, take him with you as much as possible. Your role in his life is very important at this stage. Spend time with him! I would suggest that you give him chores that require physical effort. I would like to see him apart from Hannah and Jacob. I'm sorry to tell you that he will probably need to testify at court. So, I'm hoping that he will trust me and be more relaxed as we go along."

Paul assured him that he was already doing projects with Peter. "I will try to think of more ways that he could work alongside me."

At this point, Teri wanted to leave the room and cry her heart out. She didn't want to hear any more. With a titanic effort, she pulled herself together, realizing that the alternative was a coward's way out. She needed to get all the information she could from this wise man.

Doug smiled as he approached the subject of Hannah. " This young lady expresses herself extremely well; very articulate for a nine year old! She liked playing with the dolls and talking to me at the same time. I noticed that when difficult subjects came up, she smiled with embarrassment. This is also common with some children who try to cover up their pain this way. She was able to talk about Brandon hurting her, but didn't give any details to me. She will do well in counseling."

"Look!" He continued, as he watched the grief in Paul's and Teri's eyes, "This is one of the most difficult and stressful things that could ever happen to parents. Please remember that you are victims, too! You will need to take care of yourselves, as you help your children and the others in your congregation. You've been deceived by the very people you thought were friends, or at least acquaintances! Your children were seriously abused by those that they thought were friends of yours. A bit too much for them to handle! I realize you have your faith, but you also need someone to like me to talk to.

I would very much like to talk to all the parents tomorrow evening at one of your homes. Bring the children as well! Perhaps they can play in a toy area in another room with one of the parents supervising. You can all take turns watching them. Can this be arranged?"

After agreeing with Doug's request, they returned home to organize this meeting. The kids, thankfully, ran off to play in the woods, which gave their parents time to talk privately. After thinking it all through, Teri phoned Katie to see if the meeting could be held at her house. They talked for a long time, as Teri shared what they had learned from Doug. Katie was taking their oldest, Kim, to see him in the morning.

Paul and Teri sat down over coffee and brainstormed about what they could do to keep their children occupied and distracted from thinking too much about what had happened to them. However, as they discovered, this would be anything but easy.

The next evening, all the parents and children gathered at Katie's house. Doug was already there. Teri could feel the apprehension as soon as she entered the room. No one was smiling! Jacob did not want to go downstairs, and hugged Teri's arm. He had always liked Katie, and she was finally able to entice him to go down and play with Caleb. She left them playing with mechanical building blocks.

"I don't know how long he will last," Katie smiled at Teri," But for now he is happy."

Doug started the meeting by telling them how much he enjoyed Echo Bay. He asked where the best places for walking were. As the atmosphere became more relaxed, he began asking them questions. "I'm interested in knowing how your children acted after our sessions?"

At first the answers were slow in coming until Tabitha jumped in and said, " All of my three seemed OK with the time spent with you. I know I speak for the group in thanking you for coming all this way to help us. I heard that you plan on coming here every two weeks. Is this true?"

"Yes, the government will pay for my visits until I decide that the need for counseling is finished. I anticipate that this will continue until after the legal system completes this case. We don't have a court date for Brandon yet, do we?"

The group looked at one another. Teri spoke for them, "No, we don't! In light of new disclosures from the children and lack of preparation for those who may testify, I think it will be awhile before Crown sets a date. Is this correct, Tabitha?"

"Yes, you're right! We haven't heard much from the lawyers of when or even where Court will take place."

"OK!" Doug cut in, "That gives us some time to prepare. Now, what causes your children to remember the different individuals who abused them? Are you being careful to not put thoughts into their heads by asking leading questions?"

Katie thought carefully before she spoke, "I think we are approaching the information they give us carefully. For example, when I saw my daughter,

Kim, reacting with agitation at seeing Selma's van drive by, I asked her if Selma scared her. It was then that she told me that Selma had done bad things. When I asked her where this had happened, she told me that Selma had come over, often, to homes where they were being babysat by Brandon."

Teri continued, "For us, it's usually when something triggers their memories. Hannah, for example, asks me to go into the woods to a pretty spot she likes when she remembers something that happened. It seems to us, now that the kids know they are protected, they feel more able to talk about what happened. Why do children remember different circumstances at intervals, instead of all at once?"

All the parents nodded in agreement that this was something they didn't understand either. Doug answered by teaching them how young children's minds worked in these situations.

"One thing kids do is block out terrible memories because they don't want to think about them. Sometimes, they are too scared to tell their parents, even if they have a close relationship with them. Many times there are threats from the offenders that may seem unrealistic to us, but to the children, they are very real. They feel mixed- up and torn between telling you and keeping it hidden."

"That's right!" Diana continued, "Like Caleb trying to tell us about Selma. He was so terrified that he started to shake. I wonder what she did to frighten him so much? Sometimes, I'm too scared to hear what he has to say."

"That is understandable," Doug sympathized, " It is awful to hear these things! Remember to not react in anger or reveal your horror and grief. They don't want to hurt you. Keep calm, as hard as that might be, and give them as much time as they need. If any of you have to testify in court, the defense lawyers may try and prove that you put these thoughts into your children's minds or coerced them in some way."

Long conversations continued about the various ways that the children were acting out. After a pause, Sam asked, "Please tell us about ways to comfort our children, while putting limits on their behavior?"

Doug patiently gave them some ideas about how to handle abused children. Finally, the meeting came to a close. Jacob and Ali came upstairs and shyly ran to their moms. Doug concluded by telling them that these meetings would continue each time he came up.

CHAPTER 21

It wasn't long after the meeting that Hannah asked Teri to go to her place in the woods to talk. Teri dropped everything and grabbed her notebook. "Let's go, sweetheart!"

The sunshine and light breeze blowing through the trees on either side of them did little to calm Teri's nerves as they walked to Hannah's spot. She prayed that she would be able to hold herself together as little Hannah told her things that she did not want to hear. They soon reached the tiny lake. Hannah climbed a short way up a small tree by the water's edge and looked away.

"This is so hard, Mom, because I'm scared! Are you sure they won't hurt Cricket or burn our house down?"

Teri took a deep breath, "They will not try anything like that now, Hannah, because it will make them look more guilty than ever. Remember, Dad put a gun by our bedroom window to protect you all, including Cricket!"

Hannah spoke in a monotone, "Selma did terrible things, Mom. She really hurt lots of kids. She was always so angry and told us what she would do if we told anybody. She used sticks and things to hurt us. Once she hit me under my chin and said, 'This is for being the pastor's kid'."

She went on to describe, in detail, some of the sexual acts Selma did with each of the children there."One time I saw her coming into the Haywoods's house. She wore a long dress that was mostly red and a hat nearly covering her face. She wore sunglasses and gloves. I couldn't see her van anywhere. I was very scared and wanted to hide, but Brandon made us stay in the room."

These memories caused the seven year old to shake as she wept. Teri pulled her close.

Although, for some time now, Teri had a nasty feeling that something like this was coming, but to hear the details made her furious and close to throwing up. Her little innocent girl had experienced things that were overwhelmingly horrible. Teri, still, had absolutely no idea of what terrors her precious child had gone through. How strange that while the parents were enjoying their close fellowship meetings, their own children were experiencing this unspeakable nightmare right under their noses! Now, she fully realized that this demonic activity was an attack by Satan himself. He truly was the 'roaring lion' that the Bible described. How could it be any worse than this! Soon she would find out.

Again, the authorities were all notified. Constable Jay started yet another round of interviews. At last, it was the Nelson's turn. Paul and Teri were once again allowed to support the two oldest in the interview room. Jay started with Peter. This time their son seemed a bit more relaxed. He sat opposite Constable Jay. He was still unable to meet anyone's eyes. He stared at a plant on the windowsill.

"Did you see any others with Brandon when he babysat?" he asked.

Looking embarrassed, Peter replied, " There were more people than Brandon doing these things. Once I saw Selma coming to the Haywood's house. She joined in right away."

'Do you remember what she was wearing?" Jay continued.

"She wore different clothes each time, but this time she wore a colourful dress, a hat and sunglasses. She was also wearing rubber gloves. When Hannah and I tried to get out, Brandon blocked our way."

Teri's scalp prickled as she thought of this same description that Hannah had given her. She exchanged a quick glance with Jay. He seemed pleased that Peter had responded so quickly. Jay and Peter spent another fifteen minutes together. Although Peter seemed almost eager to answer all of the RCMP's questions, he continued to deny his own involvement.

Next, Jay called in Hannah. She had her usual smile to hide her discomfort. Teri had prepared her by emphasising how important it was to tell Jay as much as she could remember.

So when Jay started to ask questions, she was ready. She tried hard to remember details as accurately as she could. She repeated most of what she had told her mom. She described a particularly bad episode at the Haywood's Then he asked. "Could you describe what Selma was wearing when she entered the Haywood's place that day?"

Hannah repeated the exact description that Peter gave earlier. She then asked if she could draw a picture of Selma and Brandon at the Haywood's. Bending over the paper Jay gave her, she penciled a detailed drawing of the interior of Sam and Diana's house during this particular episode. The picture showed kids in separate rooms with Brandon and Selma. " They put the boys in one room and girls in another," she explained, without looking up.

"Have you ever talked to Peter about this?" Jay asked carefully.

Her face shot up a look of shock. Indignant, she replied, " Do you think we want to talk to anyone about this! We don't want to remember. I'm only telling you cause I have to. It feels awful talking about it. The only one I want to tell is Mom. She told me that it was very important to tell you what happened."

Jay looked relieved, " You are right, Hannah. We are trying to get all the information on Brandon and Selma that we can, so that we can help all of you. That is good that you don't talk to other kids. It's best to communicate about these things with just your parents and counselor. Thank you for being so brave!"

Later, Jay went with Teri next door to talk with Diana. He put Hannah's picture of the interior of her house in front of her. As soon as she saw it she exclaimed, " Why, this is exactly like I arranged the trailer two years ago! I've totally changed the design since then."

Jay looked up at Teri. " What an accurate memory your daughter has! This is extremely helpful."

As soon as Teri returned home, Paul met her in the kitchen. " Fill me in! What did you find out at Diana's?"

Teri repeated everything she had learned. " Isn't it amazing how everything the kids tell us fits together? All the disclosures match into the puzzle of these unspeakable events."

Paul looked thoughtful. "I think it's time that we write to our family and friends who support us. We certainly need lots of prayer!"

"Let's wait until Crown charges Selma. I'm sure this will happen soon." Teri responded.

CHAPTER 22

School had come to a standstill. The two older kids had finished most of the goals for the year. Also, Teri was too distracted by meetings with counselors, police, lawyers and the other parents.

To Paul's and her relief, Crown had selected one of the top lawyers in the country to represent the families. Robin Wyatt had prosecuted many child sexual abuse cases and, therefore, was an expert in these matters. Doug had explained that she was waiting for an opportunity to test the newly passed Government Bill-15 in court. This Bill allowed children to speak in court on closed circuit TV to protect them from having to face their abusers.

Two weeks later, Robin arrived in Echo Bay. She met with each family separately. They all found her to be surprisingly friendly, open and even fun. Right away, the children trusted her, even though it was difficult for them to talk to her with cameras rolling. Robin's secretary, Deborah, was recording everything they said.

After Robin had interviewed Peter and Hannah, she assured Teri and Paul that the two had done very well and that, most likely, they would be good witnesses in court. "We need to spend more time gathering all the evidence, but at this stage, I would say that we have quite a solid case against both Selma and Brandon."

Like new explosions, more information flowed out of these little victims' mouths every week. The numbers of known abused children grew. Some of kids, who had never spoken about what they had experienced, started to open up to their parents or Doug.

Both Peter and Hannah remembered more details as time went by. Each time, Teri thought she had heard the worst. Every piece of new information that her own innocent children told her, shattered her. Some days, she felt close to despair. She was so grateful that Doug came so frequently. Without his help and counsel, she felt that their world would completely collapse. Paul started to look older than his forty -two years. Some parents had waves of panic as they continued trying to comprehend what had happened. They often turned to the Nelsons for advice. Paul became more and more a shepherd to his flock. He visited parents frequently to try to calm and assure them. He often referred them to comforting passages of Scripture. Bible studies continued, as they tried to build these new Christians into strong believers. Despite the overwhelming stress and pain, amazingly, most were hungry to know and understand their Heavenly Father, the God of comfort.

One day, Teri was outside de-worming the kid's rabbits. Jacob watched as she forced the pills down their throats. Obviously, they fought against this procedure. After a while he stuttered, "M-m-mom, w-w-hy did Selma give us the funny apple juice? W-w-we didn't want to, but they forced us to drink it. It made me feel fu-fu-funny. They gave us c-c-candy too."

Teri stopped in her tracks and stared at her youngest. "Oh Jacob, that was terrible!! How scary that must have been!"

She put the rabbit back in its hutch and pulled him onto her lap. "How did the juice and candy make you feel?"

As he sobbed into her sweater, he tried to explain. "It un-un-minded me. I couldn't do anything. It made my eyes g-go blurry, Mommy."

This was brand new information. Teri tried to work through all this. *No wonder these children found it hard to remember! They were drugged! Was there any way to prove this! I'm sure by now they would have destroyed any evidence.* She very much hoped that some of the older kids would collaborate this new information.

"Oh, Jacob, that was awful! I'm so sorry these bad things happened to you." Teri put her medicine down and pulled him closer. He cried softly against her chest. Fighting tears, she held him until he stopped sobbing.

"Let's go into the kitchen and we'll eat some of those cookies I just made," she smiled.

That evening, Teri went down to the basement to check on Jacob. To her delight, Paul was bending over the work bench, with Jacob staring intently at something they were working on. She backed up a step so as not to distract them. A small pile of wood pieces and elastic bands lay strewn across the table. Jacob was riveted as he helped his dad by hammering a nail into a piece of board. Peter was lying on the basement couch reading a thick book. Relief flooded her! Now she could spend some time with Hannah.

She found her daughter cleaning out her guinea pig. "Good job, Hannah! Are you nearly finished? Do you want to go for a walk on the beach? The guys are all occupied so it's a good time to have a girl chat."

Ten minutes later, they were strolling down in the darkening light to their favorite spot. It was good timing as seagulls were busy fighting over a dead salmon. "What a racket!" Hannah observed.

"Yes, they sure are making a fuss! Look at how the littlest one has to work extra hard to get a bite!"

They laughed at the wily young gull as he grabbed a morsel behind the others. After this entertainment got a little old, Teri took a quiet breath and turned to look at Hannah. She found the courage to ask the question burning in her mind. "I'm wondering if this is a good time to ask you something about the case." After seeing her faint nod, Teri carried on. "Did Selma or Brandon give you snacks when they were doing bad things?"

Hannah hesitated, wondering how much to tell her mom." Yes!" She paused and looked up at her. " They always gave us juice before they took us down to the bedrooms. It always tasted kind of funny and made me feel a bit sick. I felt weird all over. It seemed to make me sleepy. Everything became kind of fuzzy, every time they forced us drink it! I tried to refuse it, but Mom, they made us do it. What was in it, Mommy?"

"I don't know, dear, but we will ask Officer Jay what he thinks. Can you tell him what you just said?"

Hannah hesitated, her blond curls danced in the breeze " I think so. Will he be mad that I didn't tell him before?"

"Absolutely not!" Teri answered quickly." He will just want to know about it."

The next day she phoned Jay at the police station. She was put through to him right away. Teri was grateful that he was in his office for once. "Jay, I think you will have to come over here again. Hannah and Jacob have given me some information that is really scary."

She repeated what her two youngest had told her. She heard him give a sad sounding sigh. "This is important, Teri. I'll try and come to your house this afternoon. Please tell them that I am coming, so they won't be worried when I arrive! I'll actually talk to all three about this. OK?"

Teri agreed, thinking to herself that she wouldn't ask Peter anything so that he could tell Jay directly. Before he was due to arrive, Teri phoned Tabitha and repeated what Jacob and Hannah had told her. "Did any of your kids mention these drinks before?"

Tabitha paused, "Hmm? The older two did mention something vague about strange apple juice and candy awhile ago. We've just been focussing on other things."

Teri asked them if it was OK if Jay came over to talk to them about this within the next few days. Tabitha sighed, and said that she would phone Jay sometime that day.

History repeated itself once Jay arrived at their house. Paul asked Peter if he would play downstairs with Jacob while Hannah visited with Jay. Then he joined them in the kitchen. As Hannah related events at various locations involving the candy and apple juice, Jays' assistant, Sharon, took notes. Their little daughter gave more details than they had ever heard before.

"Once, Selma gave us gum- like candy, " Hannah whispered. " After we ate them, Selma talked to Brandon, but I couldn't hear them. I felt really weird. The other kids looked the way I felt. We just sat around looking at each other. Another teenager, who Brandon called Morris, was there, too. He was mean, like Brandon. He told me to shut up when I started to cry. The room started to spin around. I don't remember what happened after that."

The faces of both RCMP officers turned grey with this disclosure, while Teri fought tears. She felt like screaming and never stopping. Paul held her hand under the table and gave it a squeeze. Rain started to splatter against the window, as Hannah continued to pour out some of the terrible things that had happened to her. Teri felt like the storm outside was raging in her heart. Just when she thought she could not take any more, Jay thanked Hannah and sent her to change places with Peter. Teri wanted to follow her out, but stopped herself with a strong act of her will. She must be there for Peter and Jacob.

She pleaded silently to God to give her strength and self-control, as Peter started to answer Jay's questions. To her surprise, their son seemed open, even though Teri could sense his tension and fear.

"Peter, have you talked to Hannah about what you remember?" Jay abruptly asked.

Their oldest jerked with dismay and angrily responded, "No! I never want to talk to her about it. I want to forget this has ever happened. I'm only talking to you because I have to. I hope Selma and Brandon go to jail forever!"

Despite Peter's emotional response, Jay expression seemed to be relieved. "That's good Peter, because that makes everything you tell me more helpful. Now, I want to ask you more about Selma and Brandon. Did you ever see them give the children snacks before the abuse started to happen? If you did, could you describe how these children acted after getting these. What kind of treats did Selma give them?"

Peter looked down at the floor as he replied, "Whenever Selma arrived, she would go to the kitchen and prepare the goodies. I noticed that she did not ask any of the kids if they wanted them. She made them take the apple juice and some candies. When I refused to eat or drink these, Selma got very mad! She never let me leave. I could tell that she hated me. Brandon took the other kids down the hall, so I never saw if the food hurt them. Later, when they came back to the living room, I noticed Caleb, Mary, Hannah and Jacob were acting strange, like they didn't know what was going on. Some of them lay down and went to sleep."

After a pause, Jay looked right at their young son. "So, you're telling me that you never drank any apple juice or ate the candies?"

Teri could see that the question made Peter very uncomfortable. He glanced worriedly at his Dad, as if he might get into trouble if he said yes. Again, he would not meet Jay's eyes as he answered. "No, I didn't."

Paul could tell that his son wasn't telling the officer the truth. "Peter, you do know that if you did take the snacks, you were a victim, too. You wouldn't have done anything wrong. We just need to know if those guys forced you."

Peter gave a big sigh, "I only did that once over at the Haywoods. Selma had a big, sharp stick and said if I didn't take the apple juice I would be very sorry. After I drank it, I felt sleepy and confused. I can't remember what happened next." Tears trickled down his cheeks. "I don't want to talk about it. No matter what house we were in, she made the little kids eat her snacks.

Brandon and Selma were not alone when they hurt us. There were others."

Teri knew about Morris, but could there have been more? She wanted to ask, but Jay shot her a look which silenced her. Peter stood up, "I am finished talking to you about this." He walked quickly to his bedroom.

"OK," Jay sounded weary, " One to go." He asked Teri to fetch Jacob.

She wondered if her youngest would repeat what he had told her the day before. She didn't have long to find out. As soon as he walked into the kitchen, he went right up to Jay and repeated the disclosures he had told his mother. Teri almost blacked out as her world rocked with the words that came shakily out of her four- year- old's mouth. "Selma h-had a big, sharp s-s-stick. She hurt me with it. Lots and lots of people hurt me, t-t-too. I saw some mean big guys doing bad things to Hannah and Ali. They cried r-r-really h-hard."

Jacob started to cry quietly and the interview ended. Paul reached over and hugged his son, tenderly. After he left, Jay spoke softly to Paul and Teri. " Has he told you about other people before?"

Teri felt sick and weak as she answered, "No, he hasn't! This is becoming worse and worse every day! When is this all going to end? I don't know how much more we can take. What the kids just told us is completely overwhelming!"

Jay looked as bad as Teri felt. His clean cut face looked almost yellow. " It's not easy for me either, to hear all this. I am getting a longer list every day of children that I have to interview. Hard for me to go to sleep at nights!

I was thinking last night that it would be good for these children to do something fun with me for a change. My wife and I have a horse and buggy at home. Do you think the kids would like to ride in it? I'll mention it to some of the other parents whose kids have been interviewed. We'll let you know before we drive over. How does that sound?"

Paul smiled, "They would just love it. Could I let the other parents know, or do you want to ask them yourself?.

Jay gathered the papers and put the notes in his briefcase. "Sure, why don't you go ahead and arrange this. Saturday would be a good day for my wife and I."

He left with Sharon and backed his police car out of the driveway into the increasingly severe storm. "Looks like a bad one!" Paul commented, "I'd better go out and cover the boat."

Teri went to check on the three kids, before shutting herself in her bedroom. She sat on the bed as tears ran down her cheeks. *Lord, I think this is more than I can handle. You have promised that You 'will withhold no good thing from those who do what is right', and that You would be with us in trouble. Right now, I feel abandoned by You! I believe the promises of your Word, but this situation is completely overwhelming my heart. I need Your strength to even go on. I want to just bury myself in a blanket and pretend that it all hasn't happened. Please give me the peace and hope that only You can give! I can't go on without You.*

Her prayer ended abruptly by a loud cry from outside her door. "Mommy, Peter w-w-won't l-let me pl-play!" Teri felt weary to the point of exhaustion, but wiped her eyes and went out to help her children once again.

CHAPTER 23

"Ah, it's Saturday!" Teri whispered to her husband, who had just woken up. "Jay and his wife are bringing the horse and buggy over around eleven. Can you think of something else that's special we could do this afternoon?"

After rolling over to look her in the face, Paul huskily replied, "What I would like to do is go back to sleep for the day, so I don't have to think! How was your sleep?"

"Sleep? Maybe I got some. I don't know. But this I do know, we need to take the kids away from this house sometime today. We are all mentally and physically exhausted."

Paul was silent as he pondered various options. Teri waited somewhat impatiently, knowing that her husband was not impulsive like she was. He finally broke the quiet, "Well, I do need to work on my sermon for tomorrow. I was going to preach a message on forgiveness, but right now, I don't even want to think about it." His face had tightened as he grimaced. "I'll stick to the other sermon that I prepared a while back. This means that I do have time today to find something fun to do. So, maybe after Jay and his wife leave, we could go somewhere for a evening picnic. Maybe we'll take the boat and find a nice spot. I know a place where we can go through a tidal narrow to my favorite fishing ground. The kids will be able to fish there with success, as the area is full of rock fish and cod."

Later that morning, their three children, along with Caleb, Mary and Ali, waited by the side of the road, watching eagerly for the horse and buggy to come into view. All six children were jumping with excitement as they saw the buggy come around the corner. For the next hour, Jay and his wife drove them back and forth along a quiet street.

The kids would have liked the rides to continue all day, but Jay told them that the horse needed a rest. Teri and Diana thanked the drivers profusely. They all waved until the buggy went out of sight.

A few short hours later, Paul rolled the shiny white boat down the ramp into the lapping sea water. Peter ran eagerly beside the boat to help his dad. Hannah and Jacob gathered the stuffed animals they wanted to bring along. Soon they were off, flying through the waves. The sunny day and the happy waves splashing up the bow seemed to wash their tension away. The three children sat up on the bow. As they got sprayed by the waves, they laughed with glee. Jacob seemed like a bird set free. He, along with Hannah, held up the stuffies to watch.

After skirting some rocks, Paul found a quiet bay with a huge buoy floating not far from shore. He slowed down until he cut the motor beside it. "Peter and Hannah, come over here. I'll help you get out and stand on this buoy. Then, I'll back up away from it and take your picture. OK?"

To Teri's surprise, they both agreed. Hannah looked fearful at first. Then she saw Peter's eagerness and clambered on the buoy beside her brother. She often looked to her brother when she was uncertain about something. Carefully, they stood up and clung to the flag on top of the rocking buoy. Once secure, Hannah flashed a weak smile at her mom. Teri was thinking that she didn't much like her husband's idea. However, later, when she looked at the pictures that Paul had taken, she could see right away why he had them do this. They both looked triumphantly pleased that they had conquered that bobbing buoy.

"This is so fun, Mommy!" Hannah grinned as she caught another cod. Teri laughed as she thought of how she would have to dodge all those spikes to clean it for tomorrow's supper.

Finally they turned for home and back to face the fires of evil which seemed to stretch on forever.

Later that evening, Teri brought up a subject that she had been avoiding. "Paul, recently you mentioned letting our praying friends know about what is happening here. I hate the thought of troubling anyone with this horrible news, but I feel, more than ever these days, that it would be great to have their encouragement and prayer."

Paul looked at his hands, his face creased with stress. Teri quickly went on, "I realize that this is difficult and that we need to be tactful. I'll write it, if you agree to edit it to make sure that I haven't shared something I shouldn't."

He grudgingly agreed, but cautioned her on what they were able to write to insure confidentiality. Teri felt the same way. " I'll start putting it together tomorrow morning. I think it is important to send the letters off as soon as possible."

After breakfast, Teri went to work. She tried to write objectively about what had happened to them all. She imagined the shock and dismay their friends would feel as they read the letter. How she wanted to pour out her emotions on paper, but she knew that that wouldn't help anyone! It took her most of the morning to write the rough copy for Paul to edit. Together they finished it by that evening.

Finally, they were ready to send all the one-hundred letters. Paul read the final copy out loud.

"' Consider it all joy, my brothers, whenever you face trials of many kinds, because you know that the testing of your faith develops perseverance.' James 1:2,3

Dear friends,

Since the last time Teri and I wrote to you all, we have been involved in helping to investigate a major crime, and to minister to the victims. Knowledge of this crime has been rapidly increasing the last three months, and especially the past three weeks. We are now able to share some of the details with you, our prayer supporters.

We estimate that around twenty children, from nine Christian families here, including our own, have been systematically sexually abused. Two people have been charged, although only one has been arrested so far----a teenaged male babysitter and his mother. We hope that the mother will be arrested in the next week. Other abusers have also been implicated.

While the children (ages one to ten at the time) have not been able to disclose all that has happened to them, we know they (including our own three) have been repeatedly raped, sodomized, and even drugged, and used in even more bizarre deviant acts over a three year period. This has resulted in varying degrees of psychological trauma to the children, some of whom will apparently need years of counseling and help. They will also need to appear in court at least two times, starting next year.

This has resulted in several developments, including:

------ increased stress for all the families involved.

------ a drawing together of the Body of Christ here.

-----appointment, recently, of a special prosecutor by the Attorney General. This person is perhaps one of the best qualified in the country to handle to handle this case.

----- provision of excellent counselors to help both children and parents.

----- cancellation of our summer Bible camp for this summer, because so many of the local workers and supporters have been affected by this.

Because of the ongoing investigation of these crimes, you must keep this in confidence (not on bulletin boards or read in meetings). So far, we have been fortunate that the press has not found out about it. We do not want to burden you with this news, but know that you would want to know.

As you can imagine, our lives and ministry have been turned upside down by these circumstances. Please pray with us for:

The children's recovery. This has been very damaging to their self-esteem. They are dealing with a wide variety of emotions which really impact our families.

----- all the victims to be able to continue to tell us what has happened to them.

----- the parents to become excellent parents, so they can help with the healing of the broken hearts of these little victims.

----- justice, salvation/repentance, and help for all guilty persons.

----- grace for the children who will be testifying in court.

Thank you for your prayers.

Paul and Teri.

'Praise be to the Lord, to God our Savior, who daily bears our burdens.' Psalm 68: 19"

As Teri listened to this almost clinical description of the events of the past months, she started to tremble. This was the first time she had contemplated the reality of their present lives. Was this really their family? It seemed more like poor fiction. Many of the recipients of this newsletter had previously rejoiced at the fruit of their labours here in Echo Bay. Would they even believe this report? She braced herself for the onslaught of the various responses from these faithful friends.

CHAPTER 24

The 'case' doctor was coming to town in three days. Not time enough to prepare their children for this embarrassing and scary date with this professional! Doug had explained carefully to each child, that this was a very important part of the investigation. Because Peter had not described the specifics of what he had personally experienced, he did not have to be examined. This was a great relief to him! Hannah and Jacob were not exempt, however. Teri had a long talk with their daughter, while Paul talked to Jacob.

All this counselling did not appear to have helped their fears, as the day arrived. Jacob fussed and clung to his favorite stuffie, a bedraggled seal pup, from the moment he woke up until they walked into the clinic. Teri had been relieved to hear that their family nurse, Mary, would be there during the examination. Hannah was as white as the sea foam on the beach as she went in to see Dr. Crowley. Jacob fell into a shocked silence as he waited for his turn. Teri strained to hear any sound coming from the examining room, but she only heard the nurse talking in hushed tones.

Finally, Hannah returned with Mary. She looked as distressed as Teri felt. Jacob grabbed her arm as Mary approached him. He usually liked her, but now looked at her as if she were an executioner. Teri whispered in his ear, "Look, Hannah is doing OK. Mary will take care of you for me. Just go in with her to see the nice doctor! Remember, there will be no shots and this will go very quickly." Jacob reluctantly let go and held his hand out to Mary.

Teri thought of Doug's words, " *Try to avoid doing anything that takes away their control.*" Well, this was certainly an out of control situation! It made her sick at what these poor children continued to go through.

Suddenly, she heard Jacob yelling," No! N-n-no! Stop!" She felt heartbroken. It took all of her will not to burst into the examination room and yell the same words.

Hannah started to cry softly, which only increased Teri's distress. She pulled her daughter into her arms and comforted her. Just then, Jacob broke through the door and rushed up to her. Mary came through right after him and looked reassuringly at Teri. " It's all done now. The report will be given to the lawyers and counselors as soon as it is completed."

What Teri had not realized before, was that the reports would also go to the defence lawyer! Later, she found out that even all the notes she had handed over to their lawyer, would also, by law, go to the opposition as well.

This all came to light as they talked with their lawyer, Robin, last Wednesday. She already had the police reports, but was happy to receive Teri's careful log of disclosures. She went on to explain the details of how these kind of trials worked. Paul asked, " What does the defence lawyer get from you?"

Robin patiently taught them what they might expect from the opposing lawyers. She added, "There are pros and cons for parents taking notes like this." She paused, then looked up at Teri. "But be assured that there is also value in keeping track of everything, especially someone in your position."

Teri had mixed emotions on whether writing the journals had been a good or bad choice. She didn't want anything to hurt the prosecution's side of the court trials, but hated the thought of Selma and her lawyer reading them.

Oh, how much she wanted a conviction for Selma and Brandon! Finding those two guilty in court became the utmost thing on her mind, as the weeks drew them all closer to the first trial for Brandon. Teri wanted justice and vindication for the children. This became the main direction of her prayer times. She poured over Bible verses that spoke of triumph over their enemies. The Psalms reassured her. She read and re-read Psalm 32: 30 to 40. "But the salvation of the righteous is from the Lord; He is their strength in the time of trouble. And the Lord shall help them and deliver them; He shall deliver them from the wicked, and save them, because they trusted in Him." She memorized Psalm 27. She particularly liked the first few verses, "The Lord is my light and salvation; whom shall I fear? The Lord is the strength of my life; of whom shall I be afraid? When the wicked came against me to devour my flesh, my enemies and foes, they stumbled and fell." Throughout the days of the next month, these verses would take on a new perspective as more hideous information came out of the mouths of the children.

CHAPTER 25

Constable Jay had phoned to inform Teri that Selma was going to be arrested the next day. Word passed quickly around the group. Katie had a plan to watch the arrest from her kitchen window. There was a sense of vindication in the air. Several parents were thinking of joining Katie at the appointed time. Teri and Paul had decided to stay at home with the children.

That night, some strange things happened. Close to midnight, Teri had finally turned off her bedside light. Hannah was sleeping on a foam mattress near the door and Jacob tucked in beside Paul. Suddenly, Teri bolted upright! Her heart pounded as she heard a scraping sound at the side of the house. She frantically woke up her husband and cautioned him to be quiet. He jerked awake adrenalin pumping through his veins. He heard it, too. The noise sounded like a ladder being pushed against the outside of the house under Peter's bedroom window. Paul quietly got up, so he didn't wake the children, and reached for his shot gun lying under their window. He had planted it there to assure the three children that they were well- protected. Now he knew it had been the right thing to do! As soon as he pulled back the curtain, a figure on a ladder leaped down to the ground. Whoever it was grabbed the ladder and ran into the woods. Was this person trying to intimidate their children? How strange that this was happening the night before Selma's arrest! They had thought that only a few people knew about this. How could Selma have known this ahead of time?

After several hours had gone past with no more ladder attempts, Teri and Paul were able to go back to bed. "Thank you, Lord, that the children did not wake up!" Paul whispered.

As the two held hands under the blanket, they prayed again to the Lord for wisdom and continued protection. Paul decided that he would inform Jay in the morning about the incident. Teri finally went to sleep.

She awoke with the sound of the kitchen phone blaring incessantly. In a rush, Teri hurried to answer it before it woke the rest of the family. Before she could say, "Hello!" Ursula's panicky voice filled her ear.

"Teri, something scary happened last night. Someone tried to break in our front door! Before Don could get there to find out what was going on, the intruder ran away. Don looked around the trailer, but found nothing unusual." She took a deep breath. "What is going on here! Was someone trying to scare us or even hurt us? Maybe Selma sent someone to frighten us! I can't stop shaking and Don has gone to work. I'm not sending the kids to school today. They are too terrified."

"Oh no, Ursula! We had a similar thing happen to us last night." She explained about their intruder event last night. "So, did this wake your two?"

"Yes, I guess it was my screaming that did it."

Teri couldn't help but smile at her high strung friend, who often reacted instead of thinking first. "Well, no wonder they are so frightened! If it was a messenger from Selma, how could she know that she is about to be arrested?"

"That is what we want to know. This is getting weirder and weirder. What on earth is going on? I hate this town! Don is trying to get a transfer to somewhere else, but nothing is showing up. I can't handle this anymore. What should we do?"

As Ursula went rushing on, Teri realized that the group needed to get together to encourage and help each other. She reassured Ursula that after today, she would organize a meeting with all the families. Assured of support, Ursula finally relaxed and ended her call.

After breakfast, Teri glanced out the kitchen window and saw Diana heading towards their house. *Now what! Has the same thing happened to them?* It didn't take long for her to find out. She opened the door before Diana knocked and stepped outside to meet her. Her friend looked pale and tired. Teri spoke first, " Don't tell me that someone disturbed you guys last night!"

Diana quickly filled her in. Her voice was hushed, " Ya! It was two in the morning when Sam heard something outside of Caleb's bedroom. Someone was trying to open his window. Thank goodness that Caleb never woke up!

Sam opened our window to find out who it was, but the person ran behind the trailer out of sight. So what happened to you?"

"Well, a similar thing happened outside Peter's window, except a ladder was used. We never saw who it was, either."

They parted after agreeing to phone Jay individually. Paul checked the ground where the ladder was placed and found deep ruts. All this was conveyed to Jay later that morning. He was both shocked and upset by these reports, but told Paul that it was best for him to not investigate these threats until after Selma was arrested and flown to Hudson.

It was later that evening when Katie excitedly phoned to give the details." It's happened! Selma and Barry were outside in the front yard working in her garden. I've never seen them doing this, especially together! She didn't seem the least bit surprised when the police showed up. Selma glared at our house as she calmly climbed into the police car. Weird, eh?"

This verified that Selma did indeed know about this arrest ahead of time. As she and Katie talked, there was suddenly a funny click on their phone line as if someone had hung up.

"What was that? Did you do something on your end, Teri?"

She told Katie that she had not done anything but stand there. " Katie, do you think that our phones have been tapped?"

"What an awful thought, but I wouldn't put it past Selma to arrange this. I'm going to talk to Tony about this."

Tony was a friend of Katie's who was locally known as the' telephone man'. He worked for a local company and lived a few streets over from Katie and Joe's. Katie later reported, that he looked somewhat uncomfortable when she confronted him. " Well Teri, I think we are right. Tony is most likely involved in our phones being tapped. You know what he said to me; that it would be too difficult to do that! He looked so guilty, Teri! Then, he turned and walked out of his office, leaving me standing there."

They both agreed that Tony certainly knew something about this and left it at that. There was too many other things to deal with. Neither of them had any idea of the widening net of trouble about to descend on them.

CHAPTER 26

It was early September when the Nelsons drove to a small town one hundred miles south to visit their friend, Sophia. She was a sweet, generous, older lady whom they all loved. Her home sat on a gently sloping hill facing a sparkling, tiny lake. It was like a fresh breeze to visit her. Although she knew some of the details of 'the case', she never talked about it when the children were present. She welcomed them with open arms. Her white curls and kind blue eyes made her look like a picture-perfect grandmother.

She immediately gathered the three kids and disappeared into her quaint, cozy kitchen to make homemade ice cream. Paul and Teri settled back into a beige couch with a flowery throw rug draped over the back. Teri gave a big sigh of exhaustion and murmured to her husband, "At last, a break from all the stress! I hope we can take our minds off the nightmare back home for a few days."

Paul laid his head back with his eyes closed. "Sure hope so! It's been overwhelming this past month. I pray that we can relax and recover some before we return. Maybe, other than the court stuff, the worst is over."

Teri hoped with all her heart that this was true, but she had a dark feeling that there was more to come. Sadly, she didn't have long to wait.

The next day they drove through the town, just a bit bigger than Echo Bay, to visit the local native community that bordered a lovely ocean cove. As they stopped at the only stop sign in the village, a man staggered across the street in front of them. Hannah asked fearfully, "Mom, what is wrong with that man?"

Her dad explained that he had drunk too much alcohol, which made him act and walk funny. He went on to expound on the dangers of alcoholic drinks and the damage to lives it causes. Teri turned around and noticed that all three of the children looked tense. Peter twisted uncomfortably beside Hannah. Sophia, sitting beside Paul in the front seat, agreed with him and reported that there were so many alcoholics in her area that she was unable to give a number. Their voices faded into the background as Teri watched Hannah and Jacob behind her. Their faces had changed colour at the discussion in the front seat. Their faces were a shade too pale. Hannah licked her dry lips, while Jacob shuffled around in his car seat. Peter glanced at Teri with a startled expression, then quickly turned away to look out the window. *Now what! All three look like some awful memories were triggered.*

Her contentment faded away, leaving a bad taste in her mouth. As they entered the local museum, Teri tried to concentrate on the old Indian relics. Each child fiddled with some of the exhibits, but none of them looked like their usual inquisitive selves. Jacob attached himself to Teri's shirt as he looked around.

The rest of the visit went smoothly. The group went clam digging at a nearby beach and hiked a small hill to a lookout. The car bounced back to Sophia's house for their last night there. The car was filled with camp fire songs.

Jacob covered his ears most of the time. He hated his family singing as it brought back ugly memories. He had told his mom before of the way Selma had twisted some of these Christian songs into something evil. Teri tried not to think of this as she sang along with the others. *Why does everything fun turn into bad memories? Will we ever be able to enjoy normal activities again?*

That evening, as they enjoyed a supper of sea food and the ice cream that Sophia had made earlier, Teri was able to feel more at ease. Everyone seemed relaxed and happy! Even bedtime was easier than nights at home.

They drove back home the next afternoon. The peace they brought back with them didn't last long.

Katherine phoned Teri the very next morning. She had news. Although her two children had been witnessed by other victims as being abused by both Selma and Brandon, previously, only her oldest had talked about it. In a slow, measured voice, she spoke," Last night Drew and I heard unspeakable things from both Christina and Sue. It happened when Drew point- blank asked them if they knew anything bad about Selma. Teri, you should have seen their faces! I thought that Christina was going to be ill. After they finished telling us that both Selma and Brandon had hurt them at the Haywood's house, they both started to weep.

Teri, we are beyond shocked. I had to run to the bathroom, where I lost my supper. I guess that throws our whole family into the mix with the rest of you. I know that we need to phone the police, but right now, we both feel too sick to do it."

"I'm so sorry, Katherine! How horrible for you all! It's true, now this has happened, you will need to go through all the hoops of the legal system. There is also the possibility that they may have to testify in court. Of course this depends on our lawyer, Robin, who heads up the prosecution. This is such a shock, Katherine! I had hoped that your little ones had been spared. I know from experience how you guys are feeling."

Katherine's voice was tearful as she tried to explain her feelings, " As you know, Christina hasn't said much up till now, but this is the first time Selma has been mentioned. Drew looked terrible after she finished talking. I thought he might go storming out to confront Selma, until I told him that she had already been arrested and was out of town. I've never seen him so white and agitated. We met privately in our bedroom where I warned him that his reaction could hurt the children further and that it was important to remain calm. By God's grace we were both able to go back to the children and spend a lot of time comforting and loving them. I think Drew's understandable anger made him want to launch into immediate action against this unspeakable woman. Good thing she's been taken away!"

Teri felt as if she had been wacked across her head. *Oh Lord, has our whole church been violated by these unbelievably evil people? Done by the very people we were trying to reach! It makes me think that the whole of Echo Bay has been involved in one way or another.* She tried to comfort this broken woman. "Katherine, I think we need to organize a meeting in the next few days with all those involved. Not to share specific information, but just to spend some time with God. I'll talk to Paul and get back to you."

That was not all that happened that day. Teri had noticed that Hannah seemed distracted and looked like she wasn't feeling well. *I wonder if she has picked up a bug from our trip? I can always tell when she is getting sick.* She led her daughter into her bedroom and asked her if she was OK.

Her response was startling and made Teri feel even more sick than

Hannah looked. "Mom, can we go to our spot in the woods? I need to tell you something."

Teri knew this routine, oh so well. Hannah would remember something and then urgently ask her mom to go to her 'telling tree' right away. Teri was used to dropping everything and heading out to the place by the swamp to hear even more shocking things from the lips of her little girl. Sometimes she forgot that Hannah was only nine years old. At times like this she seemed so much older.

They no sooner had arrived at her tree, when the words came tumbling out. "Remember when we saw that drunk man? As I watched him, I had some bad memories."

"Oh, Hannah, I thought something was wrong after you looked at him!"

"Well, you were right. There were drunk parties at the Haywood's house. It was awful, Mom! They tried to make us drink some alcohol. Even Peter! They forced us! Does that make us bad, Mom?"

Lava flowed through her veins, but Teri managed to collect herself and responded calmly, "Hannah, none of you were bad at all! They were big adults who scared you so very much. What else could you and the others do? Nothing! These people were evil and forced you to do lots of things that you didn't want to do at all. I'm just so sorry that it happened to you, sweetheart. I wish we could take it all away."

Hannah looked out at the swamp and continued, "There were lots of others there. Teenagers like Brandon! They were mostly boys, but there were a few girls there. They put the kids in two rooms, the girls in Mary's room and the boys in Caleb's. Morris was one of the worst! Do you know him, Mom?"

"Yes, I do Hannah. He's got a brother. I-I forget his name." Teri faltered as she tried to comprehend what she was hearing. Her little girl went on to describe horrible things that Teri had never known. Hannah finished by saying,

"Morris hit me and said the same thing that Selma said, ' This is for being the pastor's daughter!' I prayed lots, Mom, but everything is blurry and weird."

Teri once again found herself fighting tears and trying not to show her anguish to her vulnerable child. Hannah's last words struck her heart and she was aware again of the wickedness of Satan reflected in these violators. *This has to be one of the worst day of my life!*

Back home, Paul and Teri followed their drill of praying and thinking through the multiple ramifications of this new information. This time they didn't phone Jay right away. They wanted to see if the other two had something to add.

With Selma detained in Hudson, it seemed to crack the door for other children to open up. Later that afternoon Diana called and asked if Teri could meet her outside her trailer in the next few minutes. Teri didn't think she could take any more but realized that this meeting was unavoidable.

Her neighbour met her behind their house. She was so white that her freckles stood out. "I need to sit down," Diana admitted shakily, "This is too much for me. I just want to take the kids and run away."

Teri felt exhausted and slumped down beside her friend. "I feel the same way. Hannah just told me some things this morning that are going to shake up the whole investigation."

Diana finally looked at Teri and said in halting sentences, " Caleb has just told me that once Selma took them all to her house. All three of your kids were there. Right in front of them, Selma did some rituals involving candles and a globe. Caleb had trouble describing every detail, but he did manage to say that Selma called out to Satan. Teri, this is pure evil and our kids witnessed all this. How do you think this will affect these poor children now and in the future?"

Both of the mothers sat in terrified silence. Teri wanted to clothe herself in sack cloth and throw ashes over them. When she was finally able to talk, she whispered, "Diana, this is too much to comprehend. One thing we must do is pray for spiritual protection for each child and for ourselves. We always knew that Satan was behind all this, but nothing as specific as this. Now we know that there is a dark, evil cloud over this whole town. Paul and I will plan a meeting of the parents at our house. I've already told Katherine that it would happen in the next day or so. We'll take turns looking after the kids downstairs."

Paul and she took turns calling all the families. Afterwards, they compared notes and found out that they were all eager to get together as soon as possible. The meeting was planned for the next evening at 7:00 pm.

The cars started to roll in well before the meeting time. The moms and dads crowded into the living room, while their children played downstairs. Wes, the father of Chris and Sue, took the first shift babysitting. The atmosphere was grim and silent. Ursula was close to tears and restlessly sat beside her husband Don. Paul started the meeting in prayer before anyone talked about 'the case'.

"The first thing we need to do is pray and ask the Father to comfort us and to give us wisdom. We want to share our hearts without giving information about our children's disclosures. I think you all know by now that any information about specifics need to wait until the police are updated. Let's pray!

'Dear Heavenly Father! We all ask that you would rule over this meeting. Comfort our hearts and pour Your Grace upon us! We especially ask for spiritual protection as we share together. You have said in Your Word that, 'Greater is Christ in us than the evil one that is in the world.' Help us be aware that You have all things under Your control! We do not understand all Your ways as You lead us through this path of overwhelming evil. You see our tears and persecutions and the unspeakable wrong that has been afflicted on Your little ones. We know that You have promised us the 'peace that surpasses all understanding' in the face of all this. Please cover us with Your presence as we share together! In Jesus precious name. Amen!"

At first, the parents were reluctant to speak. Ursula broke the silence as she stood up with tears streaming down her face. "What I want to know is why would God allow this to happen to us? Is this what we get for following Christ? We haven't done anything wrong. Why is He punishing us and allowing little children to be violated! I just don't understand." Don reached up to hold her hand, his face twisted with anxiety.

There it was; the big question of why God allowed His people to suffer. Paul's and Teri's minds raced through all the Bible verses they could share to bring some understanding to the group. However, this was not a time for sermons. Although this was the first time anyone in their fellowship had voiced the "Why, God?", Teri was sure that this had been thought of by many in these past months.

Paul answered, "Dear Ursula, this is a question that needs a thorough study of God's Word. I could give you some pat answers now, or we could wait for our Bible studies and respond better then. This is a hard thing to answer quickly, as some of you are such new Christians. Let me assure you, that as we grow to know God more, the easier it is to understand what people have grappled with for centuries. Even before Christ came to earth, this was something that some of the great followers of God asked, like Job and David."

Teri jumped in. "Ursula, and anyone else with this question, please do this. Read Job 38. This is God's response to Job's questioning His purposes. There are also some good chapters in the New Testament, like 1 Peter, chapters 1 and 2 and 2 Corinthians 4. I'll show you the passages after this meeting. I know how overwhelming this is for all of us, but right now let's concentrate on how we can help each other, and especially our children."

Everyone in the room nodded numbly in agreement. Ursula was sobbing quietly on her husband's shoulder. They decided to take turns around the circle, so that everyone had a chance to speak their hearts. Paul and Teri were pleased that a number of them talked about how the Lord was comforting their hearts and helping to keep their panic under His control. Others tried to explain how horrified they were and about their struggles at home.

Katie expressed how difficult it was for Joe and her, as every day they met people, at school and at stores mostly, who wanted to know what was going on. "As you guys know, I have many friends and acquaintances here. I'm under real pressure constantly to find a way to answer them. I just say something like, 'There's an investigation going on that I'm not able to tell you about right now.'"

Immediately, the others in the room agreed that this was a big problem for them. Sam agreed, "Ya! I want some ideas on how to handle this, too."

Just as Paul was ready to give some suggestions, there was a firm knock on the kitchen door. The room fell into shocked silence, as Teri jumped up to answer the door. To her surprise, Constable Jay was standing on the other side with a no nonsense expression on his face. For the first time since she met him, she saw anger in his eyes.

"What is going on here?" He moved past her and strode into the living room. "Do you all realize that you are risking your whole court case by meeting together like this? If the defence gets a hold of this information, they will accuse you all of conspiracy!"

Paul rose to meet him, "Jay, we are not talking about our children's disclosures. This time together is for the purpose of helping each other cope.

Don't we have the freedom of gathering together as friends to try and help each other out?"

"Not in this way! You would need to have a professional, like a counselor or myself, to witness that your meeting together is not a conspiracy to share information that you shouldn't. My visit here tonight is for your own protection."

After an awkward pause, Jackson, in a barely controlled voice asked sharply, "Do you mean to tell us that we are not going to be able to meet together as a Christian support group without permission? I just don't understand. I thought you were on our side."

"Right now, I am here as a policeman who is trying to protect your case against Brandon and Selma. You don't have much experience with this kind of thing. I have! Your own lawyer would agree that this smacks of a gathering where someone might break the confidentiality of their own brave children. Is this what you want?"

Teri felt chastised. She knew that he had made a good point, but what would this mean when they met as a church? She was about to ask Jay about this, when Paul replied, "We understand your concern, Jay. We never even thought of this angle. However, as a church we do need to be together, whether it's at the hall or in homes."

Jay thought for a moment before he said anything. The parents waited anxiously."OK, I see how you need to keep the church going here. I don't have an answer to this problem right now, but you must see the danger of meeting together like this. The community is already suspicious of what is going on. Word gets around this town very quickly about anything unusual that happens in our midst. When the defense lawyer comes sniffing around, the chances are good that if someone knows about your private meetings they will tell this lawyer. They will certainly use this against you in court."

Teri knew he was right, and felt guilty at not realizing this earlier. She was glad that Jay didn't know of all the times she and Paul had met with individual families and of the many phone calls they received every day from concerned parents.

Paul seemed to read her mind. "OK, Jay! Now we can see that this is a real concern. All of us want to see justice done and don't want anything to threaten that. We'll have to figure out something, though. You can understand our need for support. We never mention anything in a church service, but as a pastor I am called to shepherd the flock. I must continue with this, but will try and be much more discreet and aware of how closely we are being watched in this small town. Thanks for warning us about the possible implications! We will disperse after we have a time of prayer. You are welcome to stay."

"Thanks, Paul! Don't think I don't sympathize with you all. This is a terrible situation for you. Please don't hesitate to phone me anytime with concerns or new information! I'll wait out in the car until I see you leaving."

Teri turned to the group, "We will visit with you separately to help with some of the questions you brought up rather than take the time now. Ursula, I will try to get over to see you on Saturday. Katie, Paul and I will ask Jay about how we should respond to community folks who ask uncomfortable questions. I like what you shared about how you answered her friends. Is everyone OK with this?"

Several nodded in agreement. Nobody looked very happy. "Let's pray together before you leave," Paul encouraged.

After all had finished praying, Katherine went downstairs to tell Wes that the meeting was over. Teri could hear the others talking about what had happened, while the children scrambled up the stairs.

CHAPTER 27

Selma was back in town, released on bail. The authorities had asked her to move to a different town as soon as possible. A heavy weight fell on the families. Many wondered how she was able to pay bail. She had always complained about being so poor! They knew that they had to be extra careful about meeting together.

Selma's presence didn't stop the information from continuing to flow from the children. Hannah looked at school pictures from their last journal. She picked out seven more teens who had attended 'the parties'. This was corroborated by Katie's oldest, Kim, and Caleb next door. Susan had also opened up to her mother and described with chilling detail the same descriptions of the 'parties' that Hannah had shared the week before.

Paul and Teri interviewed Peter again. The three sat together in their son's bedroom. Peter did not look happy. Paul gently asked, "Son, we know that it is very hard for you to talk about what happened next door, but we just need to know who was there hurting kids with Selma and Brandon."

There was a long pause. At last he turned and fastened his eyes on his dad. "There were these drunk parties at the Haywood's trailer. A lot of teenagers came there after we arrived. Selma and Brandon gave them drinks of alcohol and some weird- smelling cigarettes. They got really loud and looked excited. Some teen girls tried to force me to drink, but I refused. Then I heard someone say that I would miss out on all the fun. They hated me, Mom, more than any other kid. They told me that. It really scared me. Once I tried to fight them off with a baseball bat. They got very angry at me. Some of the teenagers hit Hannah when she hid in the coats." He started to tremble and went more pale than usual. With a halting voice he continued, "I couldn't stop them, Dad. I tried."

Paul pulled his eleven year old son on to his lap and held him close. Peter continued, "Caleb and I tried to hide, as Brandon took the others to different rooms. Selma found us and said some really bad words. She hauled Caleb down the hall. Dad, what will happen if Selma finds out that I told you? Will Selma be there in court if I tell the judge what happened? I'm scared that a newspaper might report my name."

Both of his parents tried to comfort him. Teri explained confidently, "Robin assured me that there is a ban on publication of any of the names of kids. Reporters will not be allowed to print any names or even to give the name of where this all happened. We'll protect you at all times. Oh Peter, our precious son, this must have been unbelievably terrible for you! You are such a brave boy."

Teri could tell from his face that he disagreed with her. Instead, he looked as if he was ashamed of himself. Paul spoke up, "Son, you did absolutely nothing wrong! It's obvious that you did the best you could under the circumstances. I am so proud of you."

Peter whispered, "It is very scary for me to even tell you guys about these things. How am I ever going to be able to talk about it in court! I can't talk about lots of stuff. " Tears ran uncontrolled down his ashen face. His eyes were shut with fear and anxiety.

Paul hugged his son. "Let's pray about this, OK?"

Peter nodded silently. Paul bowed his head, "Our Father in Heaven, You know all things. You know how Peter is feeling right now and how our hearts are breaking for him. Please fill our wonderful son with comfort and strength in these really tough days! Give Peter the courage to tell the judge what happened! Help him know how much he is loved by You and by us! In Jesus Name, Amen."

Would life ever be normal again? Will our kids be able to live a good life after this overwhelming abuse? Teri would have thoughts like this for many years. She also knew that she would do everything she could to help their children recover.

Later, she showed Peter the school journal. Not surprisingly, he picked out the same teens that Hannah had recognized earlier.

An increased number of children also reported about other offenders involved at the 'parties'. This, of course, caused more outrage and panic.

CHAPTER 28

Sharon, Wes's wife, phoned Teri early one morning. Without giving a greeting, she blurted out, "Katie just phoned me to tell me that Sue and Chris were at one of these so- called parties! I thought they had been abused before, but now I know. What on earth am I supposed to do now! Neither of them will tell me anything! I can't stand this anymore! Katie and I are planning a meeting this afternoon at my house. I don't care about what Jay told us, we are meeting anyway!" Her voice was bordering on hysteria.

Teri responded quickly, "Oh no! Sharon, calm down for a minute and listen! There is nothing wrong with visiting our friends. We just need to be careful. We need to think this through calmly first. The most important thing right now is to protect our case. If we start getting together in a panic, word may spread into the community. Please, let's be careful! Let me talk to Paul first."

Teri was interrupted by Sharon's frantic voice, "It's no use, Teri. We've called the others too. If Paul and you want to come you're welcome, but we've had enough."

"What do you plan to do at this meeting, Sharon? " Teri was frightened that they might try to confront Selma themselves.

"Don't know yet! Maybe just to vent! I'm so angry I could spit! Don't try to stop us, either of you!" Sharon's tone had raised up several notches. "I'm sorry, Teri! I don't mean to be rude to you. We just have to get together now. I don't care if 'authorities' hear about it. They don't understand what we are going through here."

Teri sighed. She knew it was no use to try and change Sharon's mind at this point. Although she was a regular part of the church group, she had yet to put her trust in Christ. Therefore, she was missing out on the peace only God could give her.

"OK then, Paul and I will be there."

Teri and Paul dropped their kids off at Katherine's house later that afternoon. They noticed a number of kids playing 'Kick the Can' in the yard, as they entered Sharon and Wes's driveway. Utter confusion reigned inside!

The men had segregated into the kitchen, while the women milled about in the main room. Teri joined them and tried to figure out what they were planning to do. Katie was attempting to calm Sharon in one corner. Ursula restlessly moved from person to person. Diana was talking seriously with Tabitha on the couch. Teri sat with the latter two. She soon found out that they were both as concerned about the meeting as Teri was. "It is getting out of hand here," Tabitha spoke quietly. "What do you think we should do?"

Teri leaned forward, "I feel that I should try to get a hold of Doug, but I don't know his phone number. Do either of you have it?"

Neither of them did. She was about to continue, when the phone rang. Sharon ran to pick it up. "What! They have gone camping! Where? There sure is something fishy going on. Maybe they are hiding evidence! Thanks for letting us know!"

She hung up and turned to the group. The men had rejoined them to hear who had called. "That was my friend Tessa. She said that she saw Selma and son, Barry, drive by in their camper heading towards Reed Lake campground."

Tessa was Katie's sister. She seemed to know what everyone in Echo Bay was up to at any given moment.

Sharon continued to rant about this information. Out of the corner of her eye, Teri saw Paul and Sam slipping out of the house. To her horror, Sam was carrying a gun. All of her worse fears washed over her! For the first time she felt close to losing control. She hurried out after them. They were getting into Sam's car when she reached the pair. "What do you think you're doing!" She yelled. "Please stop! Don't do this!"

Paul responded with a sheepish smile, "It's OK. We are just going to spy on her to see if she is getting rid of important evidence. Sam's gun has scope on top which will help us see her more clearly."

With tears running down on to her shirt, Teri pleaded with them not to do this. She ran in front of Sam's truck, so they couldn't leave. Paul rolled down his window. "Get out of our way! Don't you trust us?"

At that moment, Teri thought, for the first time in their marriage, that she couldn't trust her husband with one-hundred percent certainty. She only felt terrified, that in the heat of the moment something would happen. As they drove past her she called after them, "It won't help the children if you end up in jail!"

She tore back into the house, wondering who she could call. *I can't call the police, that's for sure! I can't phone Robin either.* She didn't remember a time when she felt so helpless. Her stomach churned with anxiety. *Am I going to lose my greatest human support to prison?* She knew she was not being completely rational. Paralyzing anxiety gripped her! God seemed out of reach. Action was needed! She was stricken to the core of her being. Teri hurried up to Sharon and asked if there was another phone in the house. Sharon took one look at Teri's face and hurried to show her the one downstairs. Teri couldn't remember Doug's Hudson office number. As a last resort, she found Dr. Crowley's phone number and called him. He had assured her, when he was examining the victim children, that he was available to help at anytime. He also knew Doug and Robin well. After a long wait, he answered the phone.

"This is Teri Nelson calling. Sorry to trouble you, Doctor, but I don't know who to turn to. Things are going out of control up here." She blurted out. "I don't know what to do." She went on to explain the situation, purposely leaving out the part about guns. "I'm scared of what Paul and Sam are planning. Everyone is in a turmoil here! Some of us are trying to calm down the others and help them to not react in the wrong way. Do you have any suggestions? New information from some of the abused children has stirred up strong reactions. Some parents are distraught and feel completely helpless."

"I, personally, don't have any news of this new development." He answered calmly, "Please tell me again what is going on there!"

Teri, hurriedly, repeated her fear of the reaction of her friends to the new disclosures. "I think the main issue is that we all feel completely out of control. The town will be in an uproar if this information spreads. None of us had any idea that the number of these sex abusers would be so high. It's unbelievable!"

Dr. Crowley sounded worried. "This is a serious turn of events, Teri. I'm going to contact Doug and ask him to gather up all the help that he can. I think we should come up as soon as possible. In the meantime, try to calm the families with this news. Have you contacted the police?"

Teri had calmed down, but hesitated as she thought about what to say. She didn't want Jay to know about this gathering. At least this house was out of town. She would not tell any authority about the gun. Finally, she answered the doctor. "Constable Jay knows there are new developments and is interviewing some of the kids again in the next few days."

He seemed satisfied with her response. After she had ended the call, she rushed upstairs to see how the others were doing. Wes and Joe had gone outside to play with the kids. There was a sense of despair clouding the living room. Sharon had made more coffee and the mood had shifted to a somber silence. Teri told them what Dr.Crowley had said. Then she added, "We need to be calm with all this happening. We sure don't want our children to pick up on our fears! They may lose confidence in us as their protectors. I know how difficult this all is. I'm feeling awful, too."

Slowly, Teri's panic turned into the peace that only God can give. She asked, " Does anyone have a Bible handy?" Sharon picked up Wes's off the side table and passed it to her. Teri turned to Psalms 112. "We need to focus on the fact that God is still in control, even if we aren't. This is a chapter that I've read recently and it really hit home to me."

She quoted, "' Light arises in the darkness for the upright; He is gracious and compassionate and righteous. It is well with the man who is gracious and lends; he will conduct his affairs with justice, for he will never be shaken. The righteous will be remembered forever. He will not fear evil tidings; his heart is steadfast, trusting in the Lord. His heart is upheld, he will not fear, until he looks with satisfaction on his adversaries.'

Oh, look at this verse!" Her eyes had landed on verse 10." Listen to this!

'The wicked will see it and be grieved; he will gnash his teeth and melt away; the desire of the wicked shall perish.'

There are many Scriptures like this to give us hope and assurance that the Lord has our back. Nothing can separate us from the love of God! Do you guys believe this?"

Tabitha and Diana were quick to agree. Tabitha added firmly, "Thank you, Teri! This is where we need to focus, on reassuring verses like these! I remember something from one of our Bible studies, last year. Remember guys! We learned that God will keep us in perfect peace if we fix our minds on His Word. What Psalm was that again, Teri? The one you just read?"

"Yes!" Teri agreed. "This Psalm is 112 and I think it would be good for us to memorize it. Why don't we pray together about all this?"

She didn't tell them that her heart was beating irregularly from the deep stress she felt. She bowed her head in prayer, without even checking on who was joining her. She led off with thanking God for His safety net spread over them. "Please, Father, increase our faith in this battle! Give us courage as we work together to help our children in their pain! To do this we need Your help! This is Your battle against the powers of darkness."

Diana continued, " Also, Lord, please help us to turn to you when fear and uncertainty overcomes us. Please help Sam and Paul to do right and to not confront Selma!"

After a moment of silence, Teri closed in prayer. When she looked up, she noticed that Sharon was close to tears. She got to her feet to go over and comfort this friend, but Sharon got up and bolted from the room. The other moms went outside to collect their youngsters. Teri asked Diana if she would like a ride home, because Sam had driven away in their truck. Diana and Teri strapped in her three children and they drove over to Katherine's.

Peter and Hannah greeted her happily outside the front door. Teri gave them a big hug and moved inside the house to find Jacob. Katherine gazed at Teri with worry- filled eyes. She waited for Teri to say something about the meeting. Teri smiled at her friend, "I'll phone you later. OK?" Katherine understood why and nodded in agreement.

It was late in the afternoon when Paul and Sam returned. Teri went out to greet them. She was weak with trepidation. However, Paul came toward her with a smile, "It's alright dear. Nothing happened! We just watched her for awhile from a distance. There is no doubt that she is up to something. We think she is getting rid of evidence. Can you even imagine her camping just for the fun of it?"

She spoke with a rebuke in her tone, "What a relief! I really thought that you and Sam were caught up in the moment and could have done something that we all would have regretted."

Paul looked a bit hurt, "I thought you knew me better than that. We only wanted to spy on her."

"What was I supposed to think!" Teri retorted, "The atmosphere at the house was frantic and seemed out of control. Then out of that chaos, I watched as you guys went off w-with a gun. I ended up phoning Dr. Crowley for advice. I didn't mention the gun."

At this point, she never told him that she had asked the doctor for help. The look of frustration on her husband's face was enough to silence her. She turned and walked into the house before he said anything else. She couldn't remember a time when she was this angry with Paul. They entered the house through different doors. He went to his office. She went into the bedroom and shut the door, needing time to compose herself.

Supper that night was tense and silent. Teri knew that the kids had picked up on this, as they quietly ate the chicken and rice. Teri realized that Paul and she needed to talk this out. Soon! After Teri had done the dishes and made sure the kids were occupied, she went down to the office. Paul was ready to talk. "I think we have both done wrong today. I admit that it was impulsive for Sam and I to go out with the gun to watch Selma, and you should not have phoned Dr. Crowley."

Teri defended herself, " If anyone had seen you and Sam with a gun pointing at Selma, it would have gotten you in big trouble. Not only with the law, but also greatly affect our case against this woman. I may have panicked when I phoned Dr. Crowley, but I felt that I needed some reassurance from a professional."

Paul looked deflated and admitted that it did indeed have an appearance of wrong doing. Teri finally confessed that she had acted out of fear and in ways she regretted her phone call. "I am glad that the doctor and Doug will arrive soon to help us all." She went on to explain how she had tried to encourage the others with Scripture and prayer before she had left.

"So, are we just going to wait until Doug and crew arrive?" Paul wondered.

"Well, I figure that as soon as Doug gives us a date, I'll phone around and let people know"

CHAPTER 29

They were all surprised when not only Doug showed up, but also Robin, Dr.Crowley and Doug's co-worker, Wanda. A meeting for next day at the local clinic was planned.

It was a much larger group of parents that met this time. Teri counted three new families who had recently heard about their own children's abuse by Brandon and others. They sat in gloomy silence as these professionals, one by one, assured the families of their ongoing support and availability.

Doug made a strong point, " All of you need to focus on your children and not worry too much about the future. We are all working together to help you. How you react will affect the children a great deal!"

Robin pleaded, "Please keep calm! I realize that you have recently received the worst news of your lives. However, it is imperative that you don't act on impulse! I can't emphasis enough how important this is. I know you all want justice done here. Therefore, you must be extra careful to keep everything confidential. Doug's right, your focus needs to be on your children. They need your full attention. Remember, if you give them comfort and are careful to not over react, they will be better able to speak to me with confidence and accuracy about what happened to them. We are working hard to keep court appearances to the minimum. Right now, we are trying to eliminate the preliminary hearing, so that none of you need to have yet another court experience. So much is going on that I realize you don't understand, or even know about. So we ask for your patience. We will be in close communication to let you know details about dates.

Those of you who have children who have recently given new information, we are able to meet with you in the next two days. Please speak with me at the end of the meeting so we can make an appointment!"

The gathering ended with a promise from Doug that he would also meet with them all individually in the next few days. He pointed, "I'll be over at that table. So, come over and make appointments."

After making appointments, Paul and Teri walked out to their van. They agreed that this meeting had been just right to calm them all down. "I liked the focus they gave of us helping our children and leaving the offenders and court issues up to them." Teri commented, "It'll still be difficult, for all of us, to keep our minds from being affected by all these offenders who we see almost daily."

Paul agreed, " I know that this will be a hard time, but one thing I'm thankful for, is how God put together an awesome group to help us. I'm relieved that they will be taking some of the pressure off us, so that we can help our friends spiritually. Hopefully, this limits the number of phone calls we get every day. It's exhausting!"

Teri added sadly, " Jacob especially needs both of us. I never, ever thought that he would change so drastically. He's turning from a happy, fun guy into a super- traumatized, stressed little boy. Some days I just don't know how to help his pain."

Paul replied, "We definitely need more help from Doug, alright!"

Early the next morning, Teri had just finished clearing the breakfast dishes when she heard the heavy steps of Paul coming up from the basement. "Teri! Can I bounce something off you? I have spent a long time praying and thinking about this .You see, I think it's time for me to preach on forgiveness. I feel that this is a critical time to bring this subject up. I'm not going to stress a blanket of forgiveness for all these perverts. I realize that Sam and I gave an impression of vengeance the other day, but I need to assure the others that any kind of vengeance would be disobedience to God. What do you think about the timing of this? I was thinking of giving this sermon next Sunday."

Teri put the last plate into the sink and turned to her husband. "Hmmm! I think I agree with you. The timing does seems right for this. People are so angry right now. Even for me, this is a difficult issue. I'm not sure I'm ready to forgive, although I know that I need to start praying about this. Still, I think we all need to start the ball rolling in that direction. I doubt that any of us are ready, right now, to forgive these abusers, even though I know that it's God's will to do this. We all need to be aware that, ultimately, we need to forgive these awful people to obey our Lord."

Paul looked at Teri thoughtfully. "I know that it will take a work of God to bring us to the place of forgiveness. What that will look like, I don't yet know!"

He trudged back down the stairs, leaving Teri with a lot to think about. *In ways, I can't even imagine forgiving Selma to her face. Of course that may never happen! I can't forgive what she did to our children, but I can work on coming to the place of forgiving her in other ways. It seems like a process to give up my right of responding naturally and instead choosing to obey what God has said. I'm kinda thinking of tackling this more after court. Well, guess I'll wait to see what Paul says on Sunday!*

Sunday after church, Teri sat alone staring out at the waves rolling up the sand. Paul had delivered a strong sermon on the subject of forgiveness. The congregation had left the building with thoughtful, quiet faces. No chattering this time. Now, Teri had a chance to think it through. There was one part that echoed in her brain.

"What is included in the forgiveness of others? First, it means to take no vengeance on a personal level. Some of us here today have struggled with this. Romans 12:19 says, 'Beloved, do not avenge yourselves, but rather give way for God's wrath. *Vengeance is mine, I will repay, says the Lord'.* Verse 21 states,' *Do not be overcome with evil, but overcome evil with good'.* We don't want to become like ones who do evil. Instead, we need to hand it over to God. In doing so, we free ourselves from trying to forgive in our own strength.

The result of forgiveness is that you will experience the rewarding grace of God in your life, as He gives you peace and healing."

Later that day, she talked with Paul about this. "That was a very thought-provoking message you gave today. You are right, it's never too soon to apply this truth. The Lord knows that I want to please Him, but I'm just not at the point of being able to do this. If I feel this way, I wonder how the others are handling this?"

"I understand, Teri, cause I'm in the same boat. It wasn't easy to preach this. I truly felt the Lord leading me this morning. Because this is a priority of God's, we all need to work on this. Even though it may take time!" He grudgingly admitted.

CHAPTER 30

Peter, Caleb and Hannah were clearing a trail near the swamp. They chatted away happily as they swung their axes and knives to clear the new trail. After a pause in the chatter, Peter cautiously stopped his work and turned to the others. "Hey, are you guys scared if we have to go court?"

The question was so unlike Peter, as he never talked about the case, ever. Caleb and Hannah exchanged worried looks. "Are we allowed to talk about this?" Caleb asked. "Remember what Constable Jay told us?"

Hannah answered firmly, "You know we never talk about what happened. I mean, who wants to anyway! But yes, I am quite scared about going to court. How about you, Peter?"

"Well, I hate the thought of seeing Brandon and Selma up close again. Sometimes I feel sick about the whole thing."

Caleb reluctantly added, "I feel the same way. Do you think Selma would hurt us if we tell about her in court? What if she burns our house down!"

"I don't think she'll try. It's too close to her having to go to court.

I really don't want to let Mom and Dad down, or Robin either. So, I will try to do my best in court" Hannah continued. "I know our parents will keep us safe. I hope Selma goes away soon and stays away!"

Peter swept the sweat off his forehead with his hand. His bright blue eyes hardened. "I think Dad will shoot her if she comes near us. Caleb, did you hear that your dad and mine went looking for her with a gun?"

"I overheard Mom and Dad talking about it. Dad said it was only to use the binoculars on the gun." Caleb said uncertainly.

Peter corrected him sharply, "It's called a scope, Caleb. Anyway, Dad has a gun propped up near the bedroom window. I know he would use it if we are threatened."

"But what about out here? We are NOT safe away from home." Hannah blurted. "Maybe we should go home."

"No, it's OK, Hannah. I have an axe and you both have knives. They wouldn't dare try to come near out here!"

Hannah felt a growing sense of panic. "Well, I feel really scared! Can you take me home, Peter?"

Peter never said no to his beloved sister. Without a word, they picked up their tools, with Cricket leading the way, and headed home.

Teri watched the kids come back from the woods. She always breathed a sigh of relief when she saw them return. Although she had some misgiving about letting them go on their wood treks, she wanted to give them at least a little bit of freedom.

She sat down suddenly, feeling overwhelmed. It seemed like everything was on hold until their first court appearance. This had become the focal point of her life. It was a continual burden weighing her down. She urgently wanted a conviction of all the perpetrators, especially Brandon and Selma. However, Robin had warned them that a conviction was not a done deal. It greatly depended on the children being able to stand before their abusers and testify accurately.

The next day, Robin's secretary phoned Tabitha. She had news." Word has come to our office, informing us that Brandon's pretrial, in Fort Smith, has been waived. Instead, the case will be held in a higher court at a later time. I will let you know the date as soon as we know. This is good news, as it reduces the times your children need to appear."

Tabitha gave a big sigh of relief. "Thank you so much for this! I'll let the others know. You guys are doing such a good job!"

She hung up, but quickly picked it up again to phone Teri. After telling her the good news, she let her friend know that Robin was coming to Echo cove, the next week, to interview all the children who were lined up to appear in the trials.

A few days later, the entire Nelson family arrived at the hall to meet with their lawyer. Her assistant, Sharon, asked Paul and Teri to fill out individual questionnaires about how much time they thought the kids needed to spend with the lawyer. She explained, " Robin needs to spend time with each child witness to clarify what they remember, who they have told and what to expect in the court sessions. Robin will answer any questions you may have. Sound OK?"

Before they could answer, Robin came over and sat down opposite the family. She drew a picture of the court room and where the different participants would be seated. After showing them the diagram, she looked at them seriously. "For your information, there will be a judge presiding at Brandon's trial, but a jury in Selma's."

Teri looked at the children to see if they understood want that meant. "Robin, could you explain this to Peter and Hannah?"

While Robin went on to explain this, Teri got up to try and distract Jacob. She reached for him as he ran around making funny noises. Robin noticed and smiled at Teri. "Don't worry! Jacob will not be appearing in any trial. Did you bring any toys for him to play with?"

"Yes! Paul, can you hand me the toy bag?"

Teri understood that because he was only five- years- old, with severe speech problems, he would not do well, at all, in court. She rummaged through the toy bag and found some Legos. Paul took them from her and went over to calm Jacob. Jacob finally listened and found a place on the floor to build something.

Robin had the rest of the family play different roles in a court skit. They took turns being lawyers, judges, witnesses and even the accused. Peter did an exceptional job as the judge. Hannah was a good witness. Everyone enjoyed this! The crime was Paul's robbery of a rabbit. Teri's prosecution position was put in jeopardy, as the defendant, Paul, denied owning a rabbit. Teri responded with glee, "You are misleading this court. I have photos of rabbit hutches in your yard!" This caused uproarious laughter as Peter smashed his hammer down and declared a mistrial.

Jacob had stopped playing. Instead, he started to run around tipping chairs over and bothering his siblings. Embarrassed, Teri apologized to Robin and Sharon ."I'm so sorry. He acts worse when he knows it's about Selma and Brandon. He seems beyond our control at these times."

Robin gently assured the parents, "This behavior is quite typical of a lot of young children who have been abused. Jacob is too young to understand what has happened to him. If it's any reassurance to you, these greatly affected kids slowly recover over time. He has an excellent counselor who will help him greatly."

Paul, finally, had to take him out of the room. Robin continued with her interviews of Peter and Hannah

Teri hoped that the older two felt better about court after their time with Robin. She certainly did, but couldn't get rid of the butterflies in her gut every time she thought about it. Robin had told her that she would be a key witness. She had also warned Teri that the defense lawyer would try her best to mess her testimony up. This certainly didn't help her stress level.

The next few days were particularly difficult. They had five phone calls, a visit from Constable Jay with more information and, finally, another disclosure from Jacob. Teri anguished that nine months after he had first told her about Brandon, information was still turning up!

Despite all this, she was aware that God was sustaining her and holding her up. She loved memorizing key passages in the Bible. They reinforced her knowledge that her Heavenly Father was loving and caring for them all. She found His peace and grace easing her fears, especially on her frequent jogs along the beaches. The sound of the waves and wind soothed her as she listened to music and prayed. Often she would stand looking across the waters and weep with grief and anguish.

CHAPTER 31

The defense lawyer, Gladys, was coming to town. She was going to interview all the accused offenders. It was only later, that Paul and Teri found out the damage done by her visit. For one thing, the abusers now had the opportunity to deny the children's accusations and to heap lies upon lies to deny their own involvement. In turn, Gladys had apparently told them how little evidence the prosecution had and that they had nothing to worry about. It was through Gladys that the entire community came to know about the abuse case. This resulted in an intense division of the town into those who did not believe the children and those who did.

The next week, Constable Jay warned Paul and Teri that there was going to be a community meeting. The attendees were going to discuss the allegations that had been made against many of the town's teens and adults. Gladys's visit had stirred up many of the teen's parents and friends who were outraged at these accusations. When Paul asked Jay about possible outcomes of this meeting, he answered, "I really don't know, Paul. There is no doubt that it will stir up a lot of anger towards the allegations that so many in town have been involved with abusing children. I'm very sorry that this is happening. I'll do my best to keep this meeting under control. Meanwhile, please watch your kids particularly carefully, until things calm down. By the way, there's a possibility that the ringleader is a member of your church. I haven't found who that is yet."

Teri looked at Paul in shock! "That can't be Selma, so who could it be?" Her heart started to beat irregularly as she thought of the ramifications of the meeting and who could be the organizer.

"I have my suspicions," Paul muttered, "But I won't mention any names."

"Jay, do you know when this meeting is taking place?" Teri asked.

He answered that he thought it was in two days at the school. His look was sympathetic as he waved goodbye.

Teri and Paul dragged their feet into the basement for a discussion. They sat down silently and looked at each other sadly for a minute. Paul broke the silence, "I hate to say this, but in many ways I want you and the kids out of here for awhile. One idea I have is this. You know the island where we're working to create a site for future Bible camps? Well, I think this would be a safe place to hide out for awhile with the children. I would set you and the kids up with a big tent and provisions to last awhile. I'd take you over in the boat, then come back here and carry on as if nothing were wrong. Nobody would have clue where you are! What do you think?"

Teri couldn't help feeling a bit panicky, but slowly nodded her head in agreement. "As you know, I don't mind roughing it, but this sounds quite nerve racking. I'll have no way to contact you. You're right though, it's a pretty good place to camp. I know the kids would find this a big adventure. Guess it's best to not tell anyone where we're going!"

Paul looked thoughtful, "Yes, it is best that no one knows. We have no idea how this community meeting will go, but it's possible it could get out of control. I think it would be best if you left as soon as possible, like tomorrow morning. We won't tell the kids why, just that you want to have some fun time with them before it gets too wintery."

"Ok! You tell the kids and I'll start putting things together."

She heard Jacob calling for her upstairs. She slowly got up and paused before she headed out the door, "I'll get ready as quickly as I can. Can you go to the grocery store and buy some food? I'll give you a list. I'll be cooking over both the camp stove and the fire, so I need a grill and enough propane to last me. I would feel safer if you gave me the gun with ammunition. Do you agree?"

Paul responded quickly, "Oh yes, I was going to suggest it. I'll get all these things done by tonight."

While Teri made supper, Paul called all three into the living room. She heard her husband start to tell them about the camping trip. As Paul had predicted, they were ecstatic and immediately hurried away to get ready for the expedition. Hannah lingered behind and whispered to her mother, "Mom, I'm a bit scared! Are there bears over there? What if bad people hear that we are on the island?"

Teri hid her own anxiety and assured her, "There are no bears on this island, sweetie. I promise that no one will find out where we are. We aren't even telling our friends!"

Paul returned from the store with no incident to report, and began to load the boxes. By bedtime, Teri and the children were all packed up. Paul had given her their Coleman lantern and several flashlights. Peter and Hannah brought books and some toys. Teri made sure that there were plenty of Legos for Jacob. Paul prepared the little row boat to tow over to the island, so that they had a way to escape, if needed.

Early the next morning they packed the boat, making sure that no one was watching, and headed over to the boat launch. It was quiet and private as they pulled away. Soon the island came into view. The kids began to shout in excitement.

They arrived at a tiny dock sticking out among the trees. They carried supplies up the hill to a perfect tent site. Teri was an experienced camper. She had no concern about living in the rustic, isolated location, but still felt the occasional tingle of fear about their safety. The gun gave her some relief. Paul seemed relaxed and confident that they would be fine. "I'll return later this week with more supplies."

He kissed Teri goodbye and gave a big hug to each child. She watched with some trepidation as the boat putted out of view.

Teri turned her energy and focus on feeding and entertaining the children, but her mind often wandered to the awful turn of events in Echo Bay. *What are we going to do? Will we have to move from the area like some of the others? I don't sense that God is leading us away from town just yet. When we return from this island, could we be physically attacked? I never had time to discuss this with Paul.*

It took a few days to settle in. She had to agree with herself that it had its moments of fun. The four spent time exploring, gathering mint for tea, rowing across the channel to explore an old ship wreck, looking for fossils and planning fun games. The one the kids liked best was a cross country jumping event through the forest.

Early one morning, she set out alone to set the course. When she finished, it was over a mile long with multiple jumps. She marked the trail with toilet paper. Satisfied, she returned to camp to find all three eagerly waiting. She sent Peter off first and timed him. After fifteen minutes, he returned puffing up the hill. He told Teri that his legs were shaking and he was out of breath. Teri realized that the children had had very little exercise other than playing floor hockey. Hannah took off without fear and jumped the course with glee. She was a little faster than her brother, but Teri never told him that. Finally, she ran with Jacob around the course. To her joy, he laughed as he jumped. She also laughed at his noble efforts to clear each obstacle.

The next day, Paul boated over to see them and bring more supplies. The group raced down to the dock to meet him. After the excitement wore down some, she was able to take a short walk alone with him. She asked the question burning in her mind. "Is it time for us to consider leaving Echo Bay?"

Paul took some time to answer, "It seems to me that the Lord wants us to stay to help the remaining Christian families. Until they are ready to leave, we need to stay and care for them. I don't really want to think about leaving. I know it won't be easy at all for us to remain here, at least for awhile longer. I believe that we haven't finished all that God wants us to accomplish here. Are you able to trust God for this?"

Teri nodded thoughtfully.

"I'm hoping that the community unrest and opposition will blow over in awhile. Certainly hope so! I haven't seen any trouble developing this past week, anyway. Christmas is nearly here, so I think that will distract the community some.

Jay is watching our back all the time. By the way, he told me who the ringleader is. You won't be very surprised to hear that it is Cathy. She is a close friend of Selma, so it makes some sense."

Teri felt a stab of fear. This woman had always intimidated her. She sighed, "No, I guess I'm not surprised. She is an over- powering woman who has the ability to get others stirred up. We need to alert our friends to this!"

She went on tearfully, " To tell the truth, I want to leave! The stress of living here has become almost unbearable. Who knows what will happen next! I think we are in danger. Maybe I have too much time to think about all this. Please don't remind me that God is sovereign. I know He is in control, but He is certainly allowing Satan to try and crush us all."

"I know not to preach at you, Teri! I have struggles myself about what's going on and what to do."

Paul joined them for a supper of hot dogs cooked in rice, then motored away. Teri lit the lantern as darkness fell. They all snuggled into their sleeping bags, while Teri read to them from one of the many books she had gathered before they had left home. Jacob curled up beside her. Several hours later, she turned off the light and tried to sleep. She wasn't sure if she had slipped into a restless sleep, until she was startled awake by the sound of men's voices over the water. She sat up in terror. The rain pounding on the tent roof did not hide the put-put sound of a boat landing at the little dock. She quickly calculated. The dock was only about fifty feet from their tent. Now she could hear the loud voices of two men echoing around her. Curse words pierced the darkness! Teri could hardly breathe. *Are they going to come up the beaten track to our camp site?*

She quietly got out of her bag and reached for the gun. She shook with alarm at the thought that she would actually use this, if the children were threatened. What if they were angry men sent from Echo Bay to get them! She waited silently, not wanting to turn on a flashlight. She slipped out of the tent and hid behind a tree. The only thing she could see through the trees were the boat lights. Was she imagining that the voices were getting closer? She could tell they had been drinking. She prayed that the children would stay asleep.

"Well," one grumbled, "I hate this rain! It's going to be hard to see anything. I guess we should make some attempt to see if they're here. This might not even be the island we heard they were camping on, but we better check it out."

The other voice responded quietly, "OK, but remember that we are just supposed to scare them. She's paying us good money to do this, otherwise, I wouldn't be doing this little deed at all!"

Teri heard them move through the clearing below the tent. *Please Lord, keep us hidden from these men! Blind them, so they can't see our trail! I'm trusting you to help us.*

It seemed like countless hours before she heard them stomping back through the long grass. "How does she expect us to find them in the dark and pouring rain! I don't think anyone is here. Do you? Who would be crazy enough to camp on a remote island like this anyway! She probably got wrong information. We'll tell her that they are not where she thinks they are."

She heard branches break as they groped their way back to the boat. Their angry mutterings filled the air. She held her breath as she waited for the motor to start. When they finally pulled away, she collapsed against the tree in relief. *Thank you, Heavenly Father!*

There was no sleep for her that night. As she tossed and turned, frantic thoughts filled her. *How on earth did they find out we were camping on an island! Unbelievable! Obviously it was Selma who sent them here!* Finally, she was able to calm down when she realized that they were not likely to come back. Was this awful woman trying again to intimidate the children into not testifying? She knew that they would probably never find out.

She never said a word about it to the kids the next morning. No games today! She felt too exhausted to get out of bed. The three got their own breakfast, as Teri sat up and opened her Bible. She turned to Romans 8:31-39, meditating on the wonderful passage: "Yet in all these things, we are more than conquerors through Him who loved us. For I am persuaded that that neither death or life, nor angels nor principalities nor powers, nor things present nor things to come, nor height nor depth, nor any other created thing, shall be able to separate us from the love of God which is in Christ Jesus our Lord."

Suddenly, she felt a rush as the love of Jesus flowed deeply into her heart. Grateful that He had protected them last night, Teri realized, more fully, that she could trust her Lord for whatever lay ahead. God was with her family and would lead them through the rough waters ahead. Her eyes fell on verse 28. "And we know that all things work together for good to those who love God, to those who are called according to His purpose." Trust! That was the key. This verse stayed close to her heart for many years.

October had changed to November. Paul came to pick them up. He was horrified to hear of their close call and was only too glad to bring them all home. Teri felt all camped out and was ready to face her foes again.

Paul filled her in on the latest news. Apparently, while Gladys, the defense lawyer, was interviewing her witnesses, she spread the word that the abused children were liars. This stirred up the community even more than before. Obviously, the defense was trying to build their case against them all. Time would tell if this strategy would have any effect on the trial. Teri and Paul were both shocked at these tactics.

Later, Robin told them that what Selma's lawyer had done was extremely unethical. She assured them that she would do her best to refute these claims in court. Her assurances did little to comfort the pair.

CHAPTER 32

Teri was organizing a special Christmas program for the church. She was glad to find something to distract her from their troubles. The focus would be on the children participating. Katherine and Ursula were making costumes for the skit that Teri had found in one of her books. It was mostly serious, but had some funny parts in it. Even Peter started to show some interest, so Teri had given him the main role. She longed to see him more relaxed and able to enjoy himself again.

Paul had been right. It seemed as if the town had calmed down. Even the teens kept their distance. *Is this temporary,* Teri wondered, *or is it merely a lull in the storm?*

Finally, it was Christmas Eve and many spectators had arrived at the hall to watch the Christmas program. Teri was surprised to see some from the community in the congregation. Katie and Diana had decorated the building. As well, they had built a makeshift stage with a curtain. The children, with their costumes on, were ready in the back room They had been excited for days! Their parents were relieved to have something good to distract them all from the stress.

The play was a great success, other than Jasper, Ursula and Don's son, tripping over his long 'wise man' robe and falling into Caleb. This little wise man promptly dropped his 'incense' which rolled off the platform into the audience. Holding back giggles, the actors continued with their lines. Peter stole the show with his funny portrayal as Herod. Laughter filled the room as the kids performed.

To close the evening, Paul, Straps, Drew and Sam went on stage to sing their special number of "Good Christian Men Rejoice". All four sang off tune with serious expressions, as they tried hard to remember the words.

Teri thought she was doing a good job of not laughing out loud, until she saw Peter and a friend almost rolling in their seats with hysterical glee. All the tension of the past days slipped away, as Teri lost control. Tears poured down her cheeks as she tried to hide her face from view. Soon, the whole room was desperately trying to keep straight faces while shaking with silent laughter. The only ones not laughing were the four performers who were deep into the moment.

The joy didn't last long. In the following days, Jacob was back to constantly acting out. He was not the only child in the group behaving badly. Teri heard almost daily of other very young children who were, seemingly, out of control. This, despite the help of the counselors! At the end of a particularly tough day, Teri wrote in her diary:

This month is going poorly with Jacob. He is so angry, that there are many times when he does not have any self-control. He continually baits Peter and vents his wrath on him. Peter is not coping well. I sometimes wonder if we will ever forget these days. When Jacob is not testing us every moment, he howls, screams, slams into doors and walls. He cuts his clothes, scribbles on books, and breaks toys. All these acts are punctuated with, 'I love you, Mom.' and 'Do you love me?' Occasionally, he will draw a picture of an angry person, or of a fat body with no head and a huge belly button. His fists are clenched a lot of the time, as if he is ready to hit. If we send him to his room, he is scared. He resists doing anything we say. It's only when he is asleep do we have any peace. At these times, I especially resent what these evil people have done. Is it worse now that court is nearing? Or will this go on for years?

Sometimes, we see a glimpse of the real Jacob. Then, he is loving, expressive and enthusiastic. He is still sleeping in our room on a makeshift bed on the floor, close to my side. I know that sometimes Paul resents this loss of privacy.

On a legal note, some of the children Robin picked to testify have become emotional and resistant. Peter doesn't want to talk to her these days. He recently said to me that he is so scared of court that he refused to give any more details to his lawyer. Hannah and Susan are more eager, but sometimes their description of events conflict. Robin told me that she thinks it is because they were not always at the same 'party'. I feel so completely overwhelmed by this. If only the judge and jury could see a day in our household!

Then, yesterday, Robin told us some upsetting news. As a result of this lack of corroboration in the girls' testimonies, there is 99% chance she will use Susan a witness at Selma's trial and not Hannah. Nothing could upset me more! Here is our little girl, so accurate, willing and able to tell all the truth, and she may not be able to testify.

As a result of this, I've struggled with trusting God. I know intellectually that He is in control, but my heart trembles thinking about the future. Finally, I had an opportunity to go for a long walk by myself. I went about a mile into the woods and found a quiet spot. It was so peaceful! Birds and frogs broke the silence with their beautiful songs. I felt so totally overwhelmed and worn out. I spent nearly an hour talking to the Lord. I asked Him again to take over everything- the court sessions, the children and even the results. This was hard to do. The Savior gently pointed out to me, that He, Paul and the kids are far more important than what could happen in the upcoming trials. Even so, I will not stop praying for justice and affirmation of all these dear children so deeply affected by this awful abuse.

CHAPTER 33

It was March and the time of Brandon's trial had finally arrived. Jackson, Tabitha and the three children were preparing to travel to Fort Smith, where this trial would take place. The Nelsons were scheduled to be the last to go to court. Robin had phoned to say that it would take another week or so before they were needed.

Teri's efforts to remain relaxed were overcome by anxiety. Her stomach was in turmoil and her heart beat erratically throughout the day. Tensions were rising again in the community. The end result was that Paul and Teri decided it was best for her and the children to go away from Echo Bay until court time.

Drew had a small camper trailer that he hauled up to some friends of theirs in Morristown, a small community about eighty miles away. Teri and the children moved in the next day. Paul drove back to Echo Bay to guard the house. The kids seemed to enjoy this temporary move. It helped that Jacob's behavior settled down as soon as they got out of Echo Bay. Teri worked hard to organize activities to keep the children all busy and to distract them from their coming ordeal

One morning, Peter and Teri biked to a far beach. The younger two were being watched by their friends. Teri was secretly concerned that her irregular heart beat might affect this long ride. She was afraid to mention it to anyone in case they insisted she see a doctor. Nothing must get in the way of the justice they were all seeking! Not even this! After an hour of travelling on the dirt road, both of them felt too tired to continue. Even though they could smell the fresh, salty air of the ocean, Teri knew that they were only half way there. They pulled off into a shady grove of windswept trees. Teri knew this was a good time to ask her withdrawn son how he was feeling about being a witness for the prosecution next week. His response was slow in coming. Finally, his intelligent blue eyes fastened on to her face. *I wish he had more colour,* Teri thought. She tried to imagine how difficult this was for her shy son.

He confessed, "Mom, I don't want to let everyone down, but deep inside I really don't want to do this." His eyes brimmed with tears. "I feel as if I have no other choice."

Teri worked at being calm and managed to keep her face relaxed. "Aww, sweetie! This is all so hard for you, especially right now. What do you think will be the worst part of going to court?"

He sniffed, "All of it, I guess. The worst part is telling what happened in front of others. I don't want anybody to know what happened to me and the other kids, much less strangers."

"Are you afraid to see Brandon there?"

"No! I'm more afraid of Selma. I'm glad Brandon has to hear me tell on him."

"Peter, I know how you have tried to protect the others, especially Hannah and Jacob. I understand your fears. I'm nervous, too. Can you see, that by telling the court the truth, you will help find the justice you deserve? Remember, the Lord will strengthen you when you face Brandon. We know this because the Bible teaches it. There's one verse I've memorized. It's from Luke, chapter 12. It says, 'Now when they bring you to the synagogues and magistrates and authorities, do not worry about how or what you should answer, or what you should say. For the Holy Spirit will teach you in that very hour what you ought to say.'

Please think about this and pray! I'm sure that you will find His strength when the time comes." She paused, "Does this help you?"

Her son smiled weakly, "I think so."

Teri prayed that the Lord would comfort her precious son. She gave him a hug and kissed his thick dark hair. "I love you, Peter!"

Back at the trailer at last, Teri felt exhausted. She laid down and closed her eyes. Peter went to find the others. She had started to drift into sleep, when the door whipped open and all three crowded through.

"Mom!" Hannah shouted, "Mrs. Morrison is on the phone and wants to talk to you."

Teri hurried over to their friend's house and picked up the phone to talk with Tabitha.

"Hi, Teri! I just wanted to tell you that Susan will be the first witness. They think she will be called early next week. The rest of us won't be testifying until later. I hear that you are flying here sometime before we are finished, so can we get together and have a time of prayer the night you arrive?"

"Yes, Tabitha, we would love to do that. Our flight will arrive in Fort Smith next Friday at about two in the afternoon, so that will give us time to settle in first. How is it going?"

"Oh, not bad, I guess! The kids seem fairly relaxed, which is more than I can say for myself. Robin and Doug have done a great job preparing them. I'm the only one who seems stressed, but I can't let the kids see that."

"Please pray for Peter, Tabitha! He is pretty upset about going to court, but I think he'll do better once we're there."

"OK, we will do that. Look forward to seeing you next week! Well, bye for now!"

All three children stood around their mom, waiting to hear what Tabitha had said. Teri could feel their tension as they intently stared at her. She quickly updated them, emphasizing how relaxed their friends were, now that they were there. "I think you will all feel better once we join them in Fort Smith next weekend."

Peter nodded and went outside with Jacob. Hannah came over and took her Mom's hand in hers. She spoke quietly, "Can we talk somewhere alone?"

Teri sat with her at the picnic bench outside on the lawn. Her daughter leaned against her and sighed. "I feel so frustrated, Mom. I'm angry and sad at the same time. Sometimes, I feel overwhelmed. I just can't sort out my feelings. It's hard for me to think of standing in front of Brandon and telling others what he has done to us."

Teri put her arm around her. "It's very hard, Hannah! I try to remember that God has promised that He will always be with us."

After quoting the verse she had given to Peter, she asked. "Do you believe this? I know that you will feel His strength when you are in the court room."

Hannah looked up at her mom and nodded. "Yes! I do believe this, but will you be there, too?"

Teri smiled lovingly at her beautiful child. "I'll be there when you enter the court room. I'll pray for you the whole time! Let's pray now!"

Quietly Hannah prayed. "Dear Heavenly Father, I know you see my anger and sadness. This is not how You want me to feel. Please help me change this, so that I can tell in court! Help there to be no danger to the kids in court and to not be scared! Amen!"

Teri was amazed at the maturity of her little girl. "Lord, I am also mad and sad, just like Hannah. Please change our hearts and comfort my girl, so that she will be able to face her fears! We know this is an important job you have given us to do. You have promised in Your Word that you would help us and give us the right words to say. Thank you for hearing our prayers! Encourage us to trust You! In Jesus Name, Amen!"

They snuggled together until the rain sent them running to the camper. Jacob was playing with Lego pieces, while Peter lay on his bed immersed in his book. *If only these two could always be this peaceful. It would be a huge relief*! Teri turned on the music player, finding a soothing worship song for Hannah, who smiled at her mother and picked up her latest horse book and sat beside her on the roll- out bed.

That night, when Teri tried to sleep, thoughts lingered of what she might have done if she had walked in on these monsters abusing her beloved children. Devastating sadness permeated her heart! Now, however, she wanted to focus on justice and helping her precious children.

Paul was planning to pick them up on Wednesday. This would give them time to pack and be ready to fly out on Friday. To Teri's amazement, her nerves relaxed and her heart stopped its fluctuations. She found herself calm and focussed on the journey ahead. Despite continued spats between Peter and Jacob, the three were as composed as possible.

CHAPTER 34

Teri woke up early. As awareness set in, she sat up quickly. Today they were flying to Fort Smith! Hearing rain lashing against the window, Teri stood and looked out the bedroom window. Strong winds were bending the trees. It was raining so hard, she could hardly see across the yard. Paul came to stand beside her, "It's a good thing that we are travelling by jet and not by a smaller plane today."

They had been told earlier by prosecution staff, that they would fly to Fort Smith in a Cessna, but changed their minds yesterday. Peter and Hannah wanted Cricket, their beloved pet, to go to court with them. Although the dog wouldn't be able to attend the actual sessions, she was allowed to be with them, to help them be calm, when they visited the court room with Doug and Robin. A borrowed rabbit cage would be her home in the jet.

After a turbulent flight, they landed at their destination in the wind and fog. A taxi awaited to whisk the family over to a motel the prosecution had arranged for them. Teri watched the crowd of happy travellers who bustled about them, eager to visit the historic fort. She wished that her family were tourists on holiday like them.

Their family had been given a roomy double suite with a kitchen. The kids rushed around exploring every corner. They were delighted to see that there was a TV; a luxury they didn't have at home. After a late snack, they all walked over to visit the Morrison family at a nearby motel. Their suite was a bit smaller than their motel rooms, but comfortable, with a living room to relax in. There was also a swimming pool. The youngsters were jumping up and down in excitement. "Can we go now, Mom?" "Where are the swim suits?" "Let's go!" Teri suddenly realized that this would be their first swimming pool experience.

She asked Paul, "Do you and Jackson want to take them? Then Tabitha and I can visit in peace." She hoped they would say yes.

Jackson looked with amusement at the women. "I'll go with Paul, but you won't catch me in a swimming suit." This was outside this logger's comfort zone.

The women spent their time talking and praying. The group was gone for two hours. The six children hurried through the door shivering and looking like prunes. The men looked like they had enough of that entertainment!

"OK," Tabitha raised her voice, "Everyone get dried off and dressed, then we'll take you to McDonalds for supper!"

The kids yelled with glee and hurried of to get ready. Teri glanced at her friend with a smile. "What a treat! Nothing like that in Echo Bay for sure!"

Doug had rented a downstairs suite at the Morrison's motel to counsel the children. He had asked the two families to meet him there after McDonalds.

Later, as they entered the suite, Teri noticed a big drawing on the wall that displayed the interior of the court building. With a felt pen, Doug had drawn where the judge, lawyers and Brandon would all sit. A large TV with a video attachment sat against the other wall.

The subdued children crowded together on one large couch facing the TV. Doug pulled up a chair and sat in front of them. "Hi kids! You all look great! First of all, I'm going to show you what the Court here looks like.

I know you have already testified, Susan. This is mainly for the others. I was so pleased at how well you did in court today. Robin was very happy with your testimony. This will, no doubt, encourage the other kids . Now, the rest of you, do you see the chart on the wall over there?"

All eyes looked over at it miserably. As Doug observed their body language, he quickly added, " The good news, for tonight, is that I have a really fun video you can watch when I'm finished."

Susan looked at Hannah with a happy smile, while the others started to noticeably relax. Doug gently described the Court building, especially the room where the court case would be held. At the end of the session, he started a funny movie of a talking dog. The children were instantly riveted. Doug motioned for the parents to meet him in an adjoining room."So here we are at last! How are you doing, now that court time has finally arrived?"

One by one they expressed their concerns.

"Peter has not been doing well the last two days," Teri confided, "He's been critical and demanding. We think he is acting this way out of stress and fear. Do you have any suggestions?"

"I think he will feel better after going through the court visit tomorrow." His light brown eyes looked at her intently. "I will try to spend some private time with him afterwards. You did tell me, last week I think it was, that he was quite upset about appearing in court."

"Yes, but I thought I had encouraged him at the time."

Doug paused, then said thoughtfully, "You and I know that Peter has not disclosed what happened to him personally during the abuse. He has only told of what was done to the younger kids. Robin will be careful not to push him to answer questions about himself, but will focus on what he witnessed. I'll make sure to tell him that, when I talk to him. Does that sound OK to you?"

"Yes! Thank you so much for being here with us. It means so much!"

Tabitha confessed that her nerves were pretty raw and hoped that the children had not picked up on it. "Susan and Jamie seem a lot more relaxed than me!"

"Tabitha," Doug responded, "I think once you're in the witness chair, you will find that you really want to tell the judge what has happened to your children. Remember, you will be asked lots of dates and times of when your children were babysat by Brandon. You are very well spoken and strong in your faith. I really think you will do fine."

"Thank you, Doug! You are very reassuring."

"That's what I'm here for." He smiled at them all. "OK! I hear the movie nearly ending out there. Teri and Paul, I'll meet you with your children, at the front doors of the court at 9:30 am."

The kids sat enraptured. Teri tried to watch the end of the movie with them, but found that her nerves were too rattled. Hannah was sitting close to Susan, her curly blond hair contrasting with her friend's long black hair. They had drawn even closer to each other as they faced the trial together. Her daughter was reassured by Susan's positive experience after her testimony earlier that day.

Tabitha had earlier described to Paul and Teri, that when the defense lawyer for Brandon had cross-examined Susan, he had been respectful and gentle. Teri thought, *What a difference from Selma's lawyer, Gladys, who sounds like she is as similar in temperament as her client!* Teri was, once again, thankful that she had kept Gladys's visit to Echo Bay a secret from her children.

Now, adding to her anxiety, was what Tabitha had confessed to her earlier. She had shared that she felt tense and insecure about what she would be like under cross-examination. As she shared this with her friend, Tabitha had started to cry. This was not like her at all. She usually kept her emotions to herself. Teri wondered if she, too, would feel this way just before she testified.

Morning came, with the sun shining through the windows. This was a rare happening in this rainy coastal town. The sun failed to cheer Teri up, as she poured the kid's favorite cereal into bowls. The children came out of the bedroom, and silently milled aimlessly around the kitchen area. When they finally sat down, Peter just picked at his meal. He looked solemn beyond his years. Teri really hoped that the tour of the court building would help him feel more assured. After breakfast, she lead Peter into his bedroom and tried to encourage him. She reminded him of the promise in the Bible that the Holy Spirit would help him testify. As they bowed in prayer, she fervently asked their Heavenly Father that He would comfort and strengthen her son. Peter looked somewhat stronger as they all left the motel with Cricket in tow.

Teri wondered why the door into the back entrance of the building was propped open. Peter, with his faithful dog by his side, went into an office with another prosecutor. Hannah and Jacob sat down in the hall reading cartoons from a newspaper. Robin beckoned to Paul and Teri to join her at the back door. Wordlessly, she pulled the heavy door to a place where they could see the outside part of it. Teri gasped, as her eyes fell on the painted message there. In bold print was written, '666' and a satanic symbol.

"What does '666' mean?" Robin asked.

Paul replied, "It's found in the book of Revelations. Theologically, it usually refers to the name of the future anti-Christ that is prophesized in the Bible. It's used by some satanic groups to represent Satan."

Robin looked shocked, "This was written in the night. I suppose they are trying to intimidate the children." She sighed heavily, "That's why we left the door opened, when we knew you were arriving. We certainly did not want the kids to see this. We will have someone paint over it today."

Teri immediately asked, "Can we use this as evidence?"

"No! Maybe I didn't tell you that all aspects of Satanism must be left out of these trials. The defense would pounce all over it to discredit the witnesses."

Teri glanced at Paul who returned a knowing look. They both knew that they would need to pray with Jackson and Tabitha for the power of Christ to over-rule the enemy. Immediately, the Scripture came to Teri's mind from 1 John 4:4, *"You are of God, little children, and have overcome them, because greater is He who is in you, than he who is in the world."* Although assured by this verse, Teri's stomach turned upside down by the audacity of these people.

Robin left them in the hall and went in to talk with Peter. It was a long, tense wait, as the interviews with both of the children took one hour each. Before they all went up to see the actual court room, Teri took Cricket out to have a break. Interestingly, their sharp nosed small dog got agitated by something on the ground just outside the door. It made Teri wonder if she had picked up the scent of someone she knew. This staggered her imagination. She knew that Selma had moved to Fort Smith with Brandon and Barry. Was she lurking around this area trying to find an opportunity to scare the children? They would all have to be extra diligent.

Robin made the court rehearsal as fun as possible. She showed them where the judge sat and pretended that she was presiding the case. She acted seriously, but twisted in some humour as well. After that, she sat in the defendant's chair and tried to look remorseful. The kids chuckled at some of her antics. Cricket busied herself sniffing around them. Once, Peter called her to his side and snuggled her closely. He seemed much more relaxed. Teri thought again how glad she was that they brought this little dog was with them.

Later that day, Tabitha and Jackson were called to testify. Paul went over to the court with them. Because he was not testifying, he was able to sit in the room. Teri stayed behind to babysit the children at the Morrison's motel room. The children hurriedly slipped into their bathing suits. They couldn't get into the pool fast enough. Teri watched the kids play, happily splashing water in every direction. She relaxed back in the pool chair and continued to pray. *Heavenly Father, I beseech you to help all of us as we tell what we know about Brandon's abuse. Give Tabitha, Jackson and the rest of us the right answers to the lawyer's questions. Fill us with Your Spirit so that we can speak boldly before our enemies, just as You promised in Your Word! Please encourage*

Tabitha right now, as she prepares to go in! Her testimony is important, as You know, Lord. Thank You for the strength You've given us so far. Amen!

After an hour, she brought them back to the rooms to dress. They had another appointment with Doug in the downstairs' play room. After a short talk, Doug put on a funny movie about a playful Volkswagen called Herbie. It seemed to be just the right movie for the children. All went well, until the little car fell off a bank and was abandoned. It's plaintive beeping for help upset both Hannah and Jacob, so much, that Teri had to take them out. "What's wrong Hannah, I thought you were happy watching this movie!"

Both children sobbed about the poor little car that was left to the enemies, who were racing towards it. Hannah wailed, "It reminds me of, of Brandon chasing us and you were gone."

Teri was horrified, "Oh no, I'm so sorry! You don't need this before trial. Shall I peek in to see if this bad part is over?" They both nodded their heads sadly. Teri quickly returned and told them that the car had motored away from the bad guys. The two crept back into the room with moist eyes. Did this mean that Hannah was scared of seeing Brandon? She needed to talk to her daughter later.

Jackson returned in the afternoon. Tabitha was still on the stand. After giving Jackson a hug, Teri left with the kids and returned to their own motel. On the way, they stopped to get a pizza, which was a big treat. Back at their motel, they ate in front of the TV.

It was at bedtime that the two oldest opened up about going to court the next morning. Peter was resigned to his fate, but asked for prayer that he would be able to look at Brandon as he testified. He wanted to tell the judge what Brandon had done. Teri felt confident that her articulate son would do a good job. She knew that he would be both honest and descriptive. She kissed him good night and went into Hannah's room. Hannah was waiting for her and sat up when Teri entered.

"Mom, I think I'm doing better. I just prayed and asked God to take away my fears. It also really helped talking to Robin today. She seemed to know already that I would do OK in court." She smiled up at her mom.

This sent a thrill through her mother's heart. *She is leaning on the Lord all on her own. What a special little girl! Sometimes she seems more mature than I am.* She bent over and kissed the top of Hannah's head. "I love you, sweetheart. You are a special child of God."

Teri went to bed feeling a bit more relaxed. After a while she glanced over to see if Paul was awake. He rolled over to peer into her eyes. "Well, what do you think about tomorrow? Are both of them doing OK?"

"Yes," she replied, "They seem way better than they did earlier. Hannah is really turning to Jesus to help her. It's amazing to see such faith in a ten- year- old. Peter is pretty matter- of- fact about it all now. Much more confident than he has ever been. How did Tabitha do?"

"So well! She never missed a beat. She is phoning you in the morning."

After they prayed, Teri was able to sleep. Just before she dozed off, she reminded herself that many people were praying for them. She could feel her soul resting in her Savior's Hands as she trusted Him who knows all things.

The moment had finally arrived! Peter was about to enter the court room. Teri held her precious son and reminded him about their special Bible verses. With his head held high, in he went. Teri felt about to collapse. Dizziness overwhelmed her. She quickly sat down outside the room with Hannah. *I must get rid of this feeling, for Hannah's sake! Please Lord! Help! I can't fall now, just when Hannah needs my strength and courage.* She took a few deep breaths, then turned to her young daughter.

"I have something for you to take into court. Every time you feel scared or upset, you can feel it inside your pocket and remember that God is with you." She handed a note to her. "Read it to me, Hannah!"

Softly, Hannah read, "Psalm 91:1-4. 'He who dwells in the shelter of the Most High will rest in the shadow of the Almighty. I will say of the Lord, He is my refuge and my fortress, my God in whom I trust. Surely He will save you from the deadly pestilence. He will cover you with His feathers, and under His wings you will find refuge; His faithfulness will be your shield and rampart.'"

"Remember when we memorized this! God will be with you as you sit and tell the lawyers what happened to you. Don't take it out of your pocket, though! Just know it's there as a comfort from the Lord and His Word. OK?"

Hannah snuggled against her mom. "Yes, I won't forget. I have these words in my heart. I love you Mom!"

Teri fought back tears at the faith of her little girl. An hour later, the Court door opened and Peter followed by Robin came out.

"Peter did great! Now it's Hannah's turn." Robin smiled and gave Teri an OK sign.

After Hannah walked in, Teri rushed with Peter down to Paul, who was looking after Jacob and Cricket in a playroom. "There you go, son. All done!"

She turned to Paul, "Peter did very well, according to Robin. Hannah just went in. She may be an hour or so. Are you going to wait here for us?"

"I may take the boys over to the Morrisons. They aren't flying home until tomorrow morning."

She looked back at her husband with a shaky smile, then raced back up the stairs to the waiting area. She couldn't sit and she couldn't pray. Pacing back and forth during her agonizing wait for Hannah, she felt awful and teary. *I'm so glad that I'm not going in this afternoon. I would probably burst into tears.* Time moved slowly by for the next hour. Just when she thought she would go crazy with waiting, the door opened. Hannah was smiling as Robin told her how well she did. The lawyer looked at Teri and reported, "They both did an excellent job. Hannah narrated all the facts clearly, as did Peter. This will go a long way to convict Brandon. You need to be back here, at 9:30 am. to have your turn."

Teri had just enough strength to reply, "OK! Sounds good."

With her arm around Hannah, they walked out to wait for a taxi to take them to the Morrison's motel.

While Hannah ran in to see what the other kids were doing, Tabitha stepped out into the empty hall to talk to her friend. "So, how did it go for the kids?" she asked.

"I'll tell you all about it, after you tell me what happened yesterday." She answered with a smile.

"Oh, OK! Remember what I told you before I testified? I thought I just might blow it and cry, but I didn't. The Lord helped me to answer calmly to every question. The lawyers spent a lot of time asking me dates and times of everything relevant. I was glad they let me look at my notebook that they had in evidence. They also asked me what my relationship was with you, the Haywoods and even Selma. Robin told me that she was very pleased with how I did. I am incredibly relieved that this is over for us for now. Did you hear that Selma's trial will be sometime early next year?"

"Man, I can't even think about that now. I'm gearing up for my day in court tomorrow. Do you know if the Haywoods have arrived yet?"

Tabitha answered quickly, "Yes, they flew in this morning. I don't actually know where they are staying. Robin told them to stay separate from all of us for now. I hear that Caleb is testifying in the afternoon right after you finish."

"Oh, I wanted to hear how they are doing!" Teri was disappointed.

"So, now it's your turn to tell me how the kids did today," Tabitha continued.

Teri spent some time telling her what she knew. Tabitha's eyes shone with relief. She turned and opened the door to go in to the others. Teri felt completely drained as she followed.

The family returned to their own motel before six pm. Paul had bought some chicken for supper from a nearby fast food restaurant. Peter and Hannah were different children. Although they didn't talk about the court proceedings, they gobbled up their feast with laughter. They were so ramped up, Paul took them all for a walk to a small park a short distance away.

He reported later that as he watched the youngsters run around playing their own version of tag, he suddenly had an uneasy feeling that someone was watching. them.

"I looked around, but didn't see anyone. There were several parked cars across the street. I know I saw a person duck down behind a steering wheel. The hair on the back of my neck prickled, so I rounded up the kids and came home. That's why I'm back so soon. You know I'm not easily scared. I would have walked over to that car, but I had the safety of the children to consider."

Teri knew he was right. She had never known him to react like that. "That's a bit weird alright! I think I'll phone Robin at her hotel and ask her to warn the Haywoods. I guess it's possible that you imagined all this, but knowing you, it's very unlikely."

It seemed to Teri that neither of them slept at all. Getting up early, she looked out of the window and saw that it was raining hard. *A typical day in Fort Smith. Sure adds to my own feelings of gloom!*

The Morrisons were flying home later that morning. Teri felt a twinge of envy at the thought. Paul was going to stay with the children while she testified. She had no idea how long her court appearance would be.

She took a taxi to the court. The driver was the quiet sort, so she spent the time in prayer. When she looked up, the taxi was entering the drop off place. She suddenly felt a strong sense of confidence. Silently, she thanked the Lord for His loving response. Robin was already in the court room, so her assistant told her to go straight up to wait outside the door.

Finally, the door opened and a clerk invited her in. As Teri entered into court, her eyes swept the room. Everyone was in their place. Her glance stopped where Brandon sat. He never looked up. Did he look ashamed? No! Teri tried to read his expressionless face. He looked more zoned out than guilty.

She was sworn in and sat opposite Robin who was standing in front of her. Her questions seemed almost boring to begin with. Teri patiently answered them, explaining who she was, where they lived and what her children's names and ages were. Robin asked her to elaborate on how she knew the various families involved with this case and how long she had known each. She carefully described how she knew Selma and why she had Brandon babysit the group's children. Meticulously, Robin took her through which children he had looked after and at what locations. Then, the questions got much more difficult.

"Mrs. Nelson, I want to ask you for more details on the times that Brandon looked after the children, including your own. In other words, I'm going to ask you specific dates and times when this occurred."

"May I refer to my calendar which is already in evidence?" Teri asked the judge.

He responded, "Yes, go ahead, Mrs. Nelson."

Teri referred to the dates on her calendar one by one. Teri silently thanked the Lord that she had kept such careful records. The lawyer also asked who would have attended each event. Teri spoke slowly and thoughtfully, as she tried to be as accurate as possible. As Robin's questioned got more and more detailed, it became difficult for her to remember who was at each event. She realized where the prosecution was heading and how very important this was to their case.

In conclusion, Robin asked her witness for details about the beach swing, where some abuse had taken place." What did the swing look like three years ago? Was it visible from the road if you drove or walked by it?"

Teri was thankful that she had checked the view of the swing from the road earlier. "No, you can't see the beach or swing from the road. You need to walk on a short trail through the tall grass."

Robin nodded at the Judge. "That is all, your Honour."

The defence lawyer for Brandon started his cross examination of Teri. He made a big effort to discredit Teri's statements, to no avail. She did not back down or contradict herself as he fired questions at her. Teri was amazed at how calm she felt in the face of this. Finally, the lawyer said, "No more questions, your Honour."

The Judge dismissed her. Teri felt weak as she arose and walked to the exit. In her heart, she knew she had done her best. Behind her, she heard the Judge adjourn the session until after lunch. She heard Robin's quick steps behind her. Outside the room, Teri turned to her with questioning eyes, "Did I do OK, Robin?"

"Yes, I was very pleased with all of your family's testimonies. Your responses and demeanor on the stand were excellent. You did a particularly good job with the dates and times. This will all help the prosecution win this case. I'll be in touch at a later time."

"Oh, just a reminder." Robin continued, " The Haywoods have arrived here. Please don't contact Diana and Sam until after they are finished here."

Teri nodded in agreement, "I won't. We are flying out early tomorrow morning anyway."

She took the taxi back to the motel. All of them got up eagerly when she entered the room. Surrounded, she reassured them that everything had gone very well. She told them what Robin had said after court. The faces around her beamed with relief. Teri had never felt so optimistic about the outcome of the trial. She could almost feel that justice was right around the corner. She smiled and said, " Let's get ready to go home, everyone!"

CHAPTER 35

It seemed like years ago since they had testified. However, it had only been two weeks. Teri was horrified to receive some nasty letters from Selma supporters. All had varying degrees of condemnation of the victim families. Apparently, Selma had continued her deceptive ways at a church in Fort Smith. She had proclaimed her and Brandon's innocence to members of the congregation. She had persuaded many to believe her story. Teri had been heartbroken to realize that their family had been betrayed by this church. Not one had showed any interest in asking them their side of the case! Teri pondered. *This makes some sense, I guess! One of the names of the devil is 'accuser of the righteous'.* This fact didn't comfort her.

Paul and Teri tried to distract themselves by organizing a family camp to be held at the beachside Bible camp site. They found two volunteer cooks and a special speaker from Hudson. Seven families attended. The children were all relaxed and happy. The sand castle contest was great fun. Teri rejoiced to see the families focussed on the most creative scene they could make from a Bible story. The winner was Drew and Katherine's family, who had formed a giant fish with what looked like a man being swallowed. The parents all tried not to talk about the case, but around the nightly campfires concerns were shared.

A few days after returning from camp, Doug phoned with the trial verdict. Teri held her breath, her heart racing, as she waited to hear. "I am happy to tell you that the outcome was more than favourable. Brandon was found guilty of six out of the eight charges of violent sexual assault by the judge."

"Praise the Lord!" She burst out. She knew that this was an answer to many prayers. God had arisen as Judge over this offender.

Doug continued, sharing in Teri's happiness. "Please pass this on to all the others. I'll answer questions from any of you, but at this time, I only have this information. Robin will also be in touch. The verdict was only reached a few minutes ago. You are the first to know. They believed the children over the other witnesses of the defense. You probably already know that some of the accused teens were subpoenaed. However, they lacked credibility. Robin was even able to get them to confess to their lifestyle of drugs, alcohol and parties.

I do know that Brandon is being held in custody and will soon be transferred to a psychiatric hospital for another assessment. He will then be sentenced later in October."

Teri hurried to write his information down. She felt enormously grateful for his work with the families. "Thank you so much for helping us with the children! You made it possible for the children to testify as well as they did. I will pass this information on right away. Will you be seeing us as often as before? We need a lot of help before Selma's trial."

"Yes, I will be coming up every two weeks until the next trial. This guilty verdict will certainly help in the children's recovery."

"Paul and I are quite concerned about Jacob's worsening speech problems. Why is it becoming worse for him to talk?"

Doug paused and sighed, "There is no doubt he is seriously affected by this trial. This has possibly triggered his speech to be even worse than before. Eventually, you will need to find a speech pathologist. I will assess him again after I arrive there next time."

As soon as she hung up, Teri raced outside where Paul was playing with the kids. She yelled for everyone to come quickly. She was dancing with excitement. "What is it, Mom?" three voices echoed in the backyard. Paul looked with expectation filling his eyes. She couldn't hold it in any longer, "Brandon has been found guilty! The judge believed the children, not the defense."

All four opened their mouths in unison, then rushed at Teri. Peter, ever practical, piped up, "When will Brandon be sentenced?"

"I don't know, sweetheart. Doug said sometime in October. Brandon has to spend some time in a special hospital for a psychiatric examination."

Peter spoke quietly, "He is not crazy! He's just bad."

Teri was surprised at her sudden pang of sadness for Brandon. She realized that he had been a pawn in the hands of a very evil mother. However, it did not diminish her tremendous feeling of joy over his 'guilty' verdict. What a vindication of the victims! "Let's go out for Chinese food to celebrate!"

Paul nodded in agreement. "First, let's tell the others. I'll go over and tell Diana, so we can both spread the good news to the others."

Later, as they walked to the Inn, they received many stares from the people they passed by. Some even smiled at them, while others looked miserably away. *Boy, news travels fast in this town!* Teri thought. She looked at Paul, who returned her glance. His expression said that he had the same thought.

Later, after the kids had all been settled in bed, Paul and Teri snuggled together and discussed the day's events. They both felt a great release of tension. Paul whispered into his wife's ear, "Now, we can finally let the children join the Floor Hockey club at the school gym." He added, "We will still have to watch the children very carefully."

A week later, Wes, Sharon, Paul and Teri sat in the stands at school and cheered for the floor hockey teams that their kids played on. They were louder than the whole crowd put together. Teri didn't mind that they were drawing attention. What a feeling of released tension! When Jacob shot the final goal of the game, they all leaped to their feet yelling. Jacob looked up from the game at them, with the biggest smile she had seen in years.

The next morning, Teri sat reading her Bible. She turned to Psalm 37 that she had been memorizing and read, ' Do not fret because of evil doers. Nor be envious of the workers of iniquity. For they shall soon be cut down like grass, and wither as the green herb. Trust in the Lord and do good; dwell in the land and feed on His faithfulness. Delight yourself also in the Lord, and He shall give you the desires of your heart. Commit your way to the Lord, trust also in Him.'

Did she dare believe that her Heavenly Father would also see Selma convicted? This was her deep desire! The second trial was set for four months from now. Oh, how she yearned for justice to be done! She wondered about the teen offenders. Hannah had recently told her that she was especially scared of them. Tears had flowed unchecked down her pretty, little face. Teri's heart broke all over again. Would these teens ever be charged? Robin had warned Paul and her that it depended on the outcome of Selma's trial.

Their lawyer was also concerned about multiple court cases the children would have to testify in, if Selma was found guilty. This was hard to hear, but in her heart Teri knew it was true. These young people would never be held accountable for what they participated in.

CHAPTER 36

Teri was wrong if she thought that their world would continue as before. Katie and Joe, Wes and Sharon and their families, were moving. How she would miss them! There were so few of these young believers left. On the plus side, their friends from the remote logging camp Paul visited weekly had moved to Echo Bay. Jean and her husband, Rob, with their two girls, Leona and Melanie had arrived several weeks ago. Rob had a new job in town. They were only too happy to be moving out of the secluded, little camp. Teri was thrilled to have a good friend in town who was not involved with the sexual abuse case.

The town itself was proving to be more and more unfriendly, as Selma's trial approached. Many of the offending teen's parents were spreading rumours; telling their friends and neighbours that the victims had been lying and their parents had conspired against Selma. Persecution against them had intensified.

After floor hockey one night, they had gone outside to drive home and saw with dismay that not only had their tires been slashed, but also, the van's back door had messages written with chalk. They had many references to Satan.

Many times on the weekends, youths gathered outside their house and yelled blasphemies and obscenities. Usually it was when Paul was away. Thankfully, her children had never heard them! Every time, Teri had found them all mercifully asleep. Whenever this happened, Teri peeked out to see if she could identify any of the individuals. It was always too dark to tell who they were, but Teri could guess. She was grateful for her Lord's grace and peace at these times.

Weird things continued. At the Christmas Sunday service, Cathy,

Selma's friend, walked in dressed in white. She wore white shoes, white nylons, white dress, a white hat with a veil, and an expensive shawl made up of white fox, wrapped around her angry face. Nearly everyone there shared later, that they had felt the presence of evil after this woman entered the room. Paul managed to fit in Revelations 12:11 during his message. He read, "Then I heard a loud voice saying in Heaven, 'Now salvation and strength and the Kingdom of our God, and the power of His Christ have come, for the accuser of our brethren, who accused them day and night before our God, has been cast down. And they overcame him by the blood of the Lamb, and by the word of their testimony.'" As soon as Paul had read the words, 'blood of the Lamb', Cathy left in a fury. Before she stormed out the door, she turned and faced the congregation and glared at each person in the room. She bellowed, "You'll all be sorry!"In the silence that followed, Paul bowed his head and thanked the Lord for His powerful Word. He asked for mercy for Cathy and that she would repent. Straps leapt to his feet and looked around for affirmation as he shouted, "And thank you, Lord, for protecting us from this evil woman!"

A few weeks later, some parents travelled down to the sentencing hearing for Brandon. Sam, Ursula and Tabitha gave impact statements. Katie phoned the Nelsons from court, "Everyone did so well and told the court how very impacted their children were as a result of the abuse done by Brandon!

Selma was there, " Katie continued breathlessly, "She was with some people from the Fort Smith church. You should have seen the way Selma played with them. She acted like an outraged victim of false accusations. I'll phone you right away after the judge sentences Brandon. OK?"

Teri almost waited by the phone. Two days later, Katie finally phoned. Teri grabbed up the phone. She could hear her heart racing as she waited for the results. "It's good news, I think," Katie spoke quickly, "He was sentenced to nine years less a day. I don't quite understand this. The Judge said that it was eighteen months for each child. So that roughly works out to 9 years. That's all I know. You are the first to hear this news."

Katie lowered her voice, " Something else happened. My two sisters confronted Selma and her supporters outside the court building. I overheard some of what they said. Tessa shouted, 'You Satan worshipper! We know exactly who you are! You have apparently done a good job deceiving these so- called Christians you are spending time with. Why are we not surprised!'

My other sister, Thelma, turned on the church people. when they tried to pull Selma away. 'What kind of Christians are you guys? You have believed this deceiver, but have not listened to the other side. They are your brothers and sisters, but you don't care. Do you! You choose to believe this woman. What about the victims?'

I finally dragged my sisters away and told them that they could damage the next trial if they took this any further."

Teri added, sadly, "Well, maybe that was wrong, but I'm glad they confronted her and her followers. You would think that Selma's supporters would have been shaken by the impact statements they heard. I do hope that Selma won't dare bring this incident to her lawyer's attention."

She had just updated her family with this good news, when the phone rang again. This time it was Sam with a more assurances. He started by telling Paul what the judge had said about Brandon. "The judge was hard on Brandon. She emphasised the awfulness of his crimes. She also mentioned that his mother was a terrible influence on his life. Boy! She even told Brandon that he deceives and manipulates others. She continued by saying that she didn't think psychiatric treatment would cure him. She drew attention to his use of sticks during the abuse, concluding that it revealed that he had deeper problems. Looking straight at Brandon, she said that until he stops denying his crimes, he will be capable of further offences.

So, that's all I know. I'm coming home tomorrow."

Paul thanked Sam for the information and promised that he would pass it around to the others. "How are you holding up, Sam? We have been praying for you all. Is Caleb OK? We hope it wasn't too hard on him being there with you."

Sam laughed, "Can you believe this? He was relaxed about it all. I had to stop him cheering when the sentence came down. I think this experience has strengthened him for the next trial."

They signed off and Paul took his family into the living room to tell them what Sam had told him. For the first time, Peter looked thoroughly happy. Teri embraced Hannah and reached for Peter. "Did you guys know that you are heroes? Well, you are! So many other children would not have had your courage. Dad and I are so proud of you!"

The next week, Robin and Doug arrived in Echo Bay. Teri, Paul and the three children spent two hours with Robin. She explained in detail about the court hearings and sentences. "Brandon's trial went very well." She told the family, "Justice has been done in this case. The children's testimonies were all believed verbatim, although there were a few inconsistencies noted. This is possibly because the children described their own experience at the so-called, different 'parties', where another child testifying may not have been present. It was amazing to me, how accurately each child described what had happened to them. You all should be proud of your children; they were a delight to work with."

The families all settled in for the wait till Selma's trial. With this stress increasing, the children reacted. Katie's daughter opened up once again and told her mother many of the things that the abusers had done to her. Katie phoned up in tears. Teri had never heard her cry. "I'm so overwhelmed," Katie confessed." Today Kim dropped a bomb shell on us. She described some of the others who were hurting kids alongside Brandon and Selma. Teri, some of these people are my friends! I've known them for years. It would be unbelievable to me, except Kim gave me details that I could not deny. I never knew, all these years, that this town is full of deceit and downright evil. As you know, we are planning to move south just as soon as Joe finds a good job. We can no longer stay here."

Teri could hardly find the words to console her friend. She knew how she felt. "I'm so very sorry, Katie. Kim corroborates with what Hannah has said. You need to contact Robin and prepare Kim to be able to talk with Constable Jay. This is such a sick town! I want to move away, too, but we need to wait until after Selma's trial. Our children are upset enough as it is, without adding a big move just now. However, I see that it has now become necessary for you guys to leave. So far, Kim doesn't have to testify and you all need to get away from this scene. I will miss you so much!"

The Nelson children were in chaos. They were arguing and fighting daily. Peter would get mad at Jacob for almost no reason. Jacob would react by crying and screaming. Hannah tried in vain to bring peace to each situation, but usually ended up entering the fray.

One night it reached a new height. It was hockey night at the school. Jacob shot a goal and Hannah's team beat Peter's. Teens who had been named by the kids were everywhere glaring at the family. Teri was glad that Constable Jay was there. He was a coach, so was in full view of everyone there.

Peter came home in a foul mood and wanted the first shower. When Paul told him that the youngest were to go first, he flipped out. They had never seen him this angry. He stormed into his room and slammed the door. While Hannah was having her shower, the water suddenly stopped flowing. It started up almost immediately, but then went from icy cold to burning hot. She screamed in terror. Teri ran in and found her weeping, shivering and absolutely terrified. She could not move, so Teri pulled her out and wrapped her in a towel. Teri hugged her as she shook with sobs and fear. This started a nose bleed. "Mom, I think I'm going to faint!"she whimpered. Teri started to tremble, too, and put Hannah's head between her knees. Soon they were both covered in tears, blood and water.

Teri yelled for her husband, who rushed in and carried Hannah to the couch. Finally, their little girl calmed down, but her eyes were filled with dread. She tried to tell her parents why she was so scared. "Why did that happen? Who made the shower get weird? It gave me terrible thoughts!"

After helping Hannah get into her pajamas, Teri went to check on Jacob. To her horror, Jacob was staring straight ahead and curled in a fetal position on his bed. She quickly picked him up and held him tightly on her lap. "M-my tummy hu-hurts and I'm having b-b-bad thoughts."

Teri kept her frustrating thoughts to herself. *It's been over a year! All this pain, stress and tension still fill our lives! Tonight I want to leave this sick, sick town full of child abusers and evil. Lord, please help us cope!"*

Teri realized that these episodes were darts from their greatest enemy, Satan. Fear was one of his greatest weapons! After Teri had carried Jacob to their bed, Paul sat beside her on the living room couch. She shared her thoughts with him, knowing that he would understand. They both took turns praying for their family. Paul finished by asking the Father to cast out the powers of darkness from their midst and surround them instead with His army.

Teri went into Hannah's bedroom. Her keen- eared daughter had overheard her dad praying. Mom asked Hannah if she understood the prayers. She answered slowly "Sort of! Dad was praying about God's protection over us . Did these weird things come from the devil to scare us?"

"We think so, Hannah. That's why we prayed for the Almighty to help us. Let me read something to you."

Teri quickly found her Bible and went back to her girl. "I'm reading from

1 John, chapter 4, 'You are of God, little children, and have overcome them, because He who is in you is greater than he who is in the world.' Do you understand what it means?"

Peter answered from his bedroom, "It's talking about the devil. God is on our side!"

Teri felt a rush of love for her brave son. She was impressed that he understood the Bible passage. "That's right Peter. Good job! So you see, Hannah, that when strange things happen or bad thoughts come, know that you can always call upon the Lord to protect you. He is far more powerful than the devil. Remember this and it will help you face Selma in the court." Even as these words came out of her mouth, she realized that she was speaking to herself as well.

Slowly, it seemed like the peace of God flowed over their home. Hannah sighed and leaned against her mom. Peter went back to bed. For once, he went to sleep before Teri came in to check on him.

CHAPTER 37

Court was two months away. Teri was looking forward to Jacob's birthday in a couple of days. She decided to take all three to the grocery store to get birthday treats. She sat Jacob in the grocery basket and headed towards the fruit section. She kept a close watch for any of the accused teens or adults. She saw Hannah jerk her head up when a black haired woman came smiling towards them. Hannah whispered, "I'm scared of that woman. She is really bad."

Robin had warned them all to not confront any of the accused offenders. All Teri could do was bite her tongue from spilling out what she was thinking. Teri was astonished to see this woman reach out her hand to pat Hannah's head and say, "Such beautiful children! "

Oh, she was being so 'nice' to them! It didn't work. Peter expressed is anger by glaring at this phony woman. His face went red with fury. His reaction certainly confirmed Hannah's fear. Teri tried to smile, but it was more like a grimace. Teri ignored her grocery list and, instead, raced towards the birthday aisle.

When they got back to the car, Teri sighed in relief and hugged Peter." You did a good job of not kicking her in the shins. I could tell that you sure felt like doing it." She smiled sadly, "Did you remember what Robin told us about these people? She warned us to not respond to them."

Peter looked down at his shoes. He had not said much about the other individuals involved with the abuse. He knew that he had just given himself away.

Jacob's birthday was a wonderful day. Everyone was happy and relaxed. His friends all played together without the tension that often occurred when the victim children were together. Jacob's speech improved so that could actually form complete sentences. Teri wondered about this unexpected peace. *God is so amazing! Right now, we have peace in the midst of the storm. I know in my heart that my Father is merciful and kind, but some days it is so difficult to focus on this.*

The days stretched on. Everywhere they went, they saw some of the offenders. Some looked angry, some glared with hatred, while others pretended to be innocent. One of the teens, named by some of the children, gestured with his middle finger at Teri when she went for a jog by the ocean one day. Recently, this older teen had been in the group that had verbally attacked the family outside their house at night. Angered, she phoned Constable Jay and reported him. The next evening, to her shock and dismay, she saw this offender come up to the kitchen door. She had been able to get the kids downstairs, before he knocked. Paul opened the door, as this youth took off his cap. He instantly blurted out, "I'm sorry that I was rude to your wife yesterday. I won't do it again."

He fearfully looked up to see what Paul would say. Teri came upstairs asked, "Did Constable Jay ask you to do this?"

Reluctantly, he looked down and answered with what sounded like belligerence, "Ya! He did, but I didn't have to come."

Teri stopped herself from saying, "So will you stay away from us from now on?" Instead she replied with a terse, "OK, thanks for coming."

Paul shut the door behind him and looked at Teri, " Do you understand why Robin told us to not confront these people?"

Teri knew how he felt. "I think it's because she is protecting us from possible repercussions at court. If this guy said to the defense that he was troubled by any of us, it might come back on us. I actually don't understand all this myself, but we must trust that Robin knows a lot more than we do."

The Nelsons tried to spend as much time as they could out of town, exploring logging roads and going for boat rides. For some reason, the town seemed to have quieted down. There were no more incidents. A friend who lived near Hudson phoned one day. She encouraged Teri by saying, "I wanted you to be aware of how many of us are praying for you all. Did you know that large groups are meeting in various places to pray for you? My group had ten or more come, just to pray for your family last night."

Overwhelmed by emotion, Teri managed to say, "Oh, that is so wonderful. I wondered why Jacob's birthday was filled with such peace. It was amazing! Jacob could speak without any problem for the first time since he originally told us what had happened to him. It makes me realize that God is still on His Throne! Some days it is hard to focus on His promises to us. I know that I'm spending too much time thinking about Selma's trial and all the ramifications. Please thank as many as you can for us! We continue to need lots of prayer as the time for court approaches."

Her good friend continued to comfort Teri. "Some of the women from our group are planning to come up when you testify. We will be standing with you, knowing how important this is."

After they hung up, Teri went into her bedroom and wept with gratitude. She prayed, "Thank you, Lord, for your people standing with us in these awful times. This confirms Your love and care through these scary and dark days. Please forgive me for my lack of faith and for being so caught up with our circumstances that my mind wanders away from You!"

CHAPTER 38

Paul thought that it would be a good time for Peter to have break. He made plans for Peter and Teri to fly out to see her parents. It turned out to be just what he needed. He enjoyed visiting with his cousins, aunts and grandparents. Teri heard him laughing as he played a game with some of the family. As he happily talked to the others, she realized once again how smart and articulate her son was. He astounded the others with his knowledge of world events and history. He seemed to remember everything he had read in his encyclopaedias.

As she meditated on this, she realized that he must also remember every detail of what had happened to him. She had heard the term 'blocking away' memories. Could it be that this was already happening? How then, would he be able to testify at Selma's trial? She knew that honesty was very important to her son. This must be putting a great deal of pressure on him. She decided to talk to him on the flight home.

The morning of their departure, Nan had taken them out to lunch. She continued to plead with them to leave Echo Bay. "I hate the thought of you still living there. You are surrounded by terrible memories and those awful people. Please consider leaving as soon as possible!"

Teri tried to comfort her distraught mother by promising that they were planning to leave the community, but not until after the trial. She realized that this was very difficult for family members to understand, especially her mother.

After the plane took off and they were well settled, she started the difficult conversation with her son. The whole time she talked, Peter kept his head turned away. First she praised him for his courage. Then she assured him that no matter what happened, she would always love and support him. "Peter, please look at me! Sometimes our minds help us to forget awful things that happen to us. I think that this may be happening to you, but at the same time, I think that you remember much more than you are able to say. Perhaps you think you're guilty of something to do with the awful things you and the others suffered. Think about this! They were adults and had power over you. We know that you tried to protect the kids.

I also know that you are feeling worried about court. Just remember, all you have to do is try your best. No one thinks otherwise!"

Sadly, she leaned over and put her arm around her downcast son.

Teri continued, "Remember, most of the people in Brandon's trial believed your testimony. The judge believed you and said so. You need to think about this. We wouldn't have won the case if the children had not been believed."

Peter didn't appear very happy, but gave a slight nod. At least he didn't contradict her. Teri had no idea how else to help her distraught son. Last week, he had told Doug that he didn't feel as afraid of court anymore. However, his behavior at home did not back this up.

A few days after they had returned, Teri phoned Tabitha. She shared with her friend, "Some days are so overwhelming! One thing after another! How is your family doing?"

Tabitha gave a sad chuckle, "Same thing here! Our three are forever at it. Sometimes I feel like getting away from the house just to get some relief and personal time."

"Yes, I know exactly how you feel! I can't wait for all this court stuff to be over! I'm hoping we will be able to move on afterwards. You know that we are planning to leave Echo Bay after court. We still have no idea where."

Before they hung up, Teri encouraged her friend to take a break without children every other day. "It sure helps me keep my sanity!"

She was furious! Her mind raced in anger. I've tried everything I can think of to stop these wretched children and their stupid parents. Guilty! Brandon was found guilty! Why would anyone believe those snotty, little brats? She had given them drugs, tried to confuse them and terrify them! Why are they still talking? My god is greater than theirs! I must keep remembering this . I must not doubt that my own court case will win. I'm sure I'll be acquitted! My lawyer, Gladys, promised that she would make mincemeat out of all the child witnesses. She has a good plan. Best of all she believes me, not the kids! She chuckled. No, I'm not scared at all! When Gladys calls me up to testify on my own behalf, I will blow the jury away with my power and acting ability!

CHAPTER 39

Information continued to pour out of some of the children. Teri was thankful that she hadn't heard anything more from her own. In her quiet moments, she wondered how these new Christians were able to cope. So far, it seemed that they were victorious in continuing to live for Christ despite the horror they were experiencing. Paul and Teri were thankful for the good Bible teaching they had given these friends.

Day after day the Nelson's phone rang. Today it was Katie. " Hey, I've just found out from my sister, Tessa, that one of our nephews used to live in Echo Bay before you guys came. He became a good friend of Brandon." Sadly, she lamented, "Now this young man is involved with the occult, heavy drugs and kiddy porn."

Teri grieved with her friend. Teri knew that this information would not help their case in court, but it made both of them aware of the widespread impact this abusive family had on their community.

"That news was bad enough!" Katie continued, "But now, Joe and I are very disturbed by what happened at school this morning. Kim came home early in tears. She told us that some children at school had squirted ketchup all over the class window next to her desk and had written 666 in it. She knew that this number was referring to something satanic. She was too scared to stay in her classroom and got permission to come home. We're thinking of not sending her back. Honestly Teri, it's time for us to leave. The sooner the better! Please pray that Joe will find a job somewhere else soon, so that we can move."

Teri quickly replied, "Yes, we will pray about this. It certainly looks like it is getting far too difficult for you guys to be here anymore."

"Oh, for sure we've had enough! I think your family must move soon, as well."

"Yes, I totally agree, Katie. We won't be able to stay here much longer, either."

Paul had just received news from their Mission Board. They had unanimously agreed that their family needed to relocate, so that they could start the healing process. Teri had asked eagerly, "How soon can we pack!"

Paul had thought this through and replied, "You know as well as I do, that we have to wait until this court business is over. The Mission Board has given us two alternatives. One is that we continue church planting in a different area, or another is to be directors at a new Bible camp opening up. We need to pray and seek God's leading in this. For now, we have way too much on our plate to deal with this now. Right?"

Reluctantly, Teri agreed. She found herself feeling anxious about living in Echo Bay for even one more day. She knew that she needed to try and not worry about this, especially for the children's sake.

Her anxiety was heightened by a sudden visit from Katie. She had come over after her daughter, Kim, had shared some horrific news about her abuse. With her hair dishevelled and her face white through her tanned skin, her friend looked almost panic-stricken. Pulling a chair out from the table, she sat down in silence. Teri hurriedly placed a cup of fresh, hot coffee in front of Katie and sat down facing her. Not a word was spoken for ten minutes! Finally, Katie's expression relaxed and she looked up and stared intently in front of her.

"Last night, Kim shared something so scary that I don't know what to do! She was shaking so hard, that she could hardly speak. I have no idea what triggered this memory.

Apparently, one day, Selma had gathered the children Brandon was babysitting to a hidden spot behind Sam and Diane's home. I can hardly tell you this, Teri! Selma had lifted a little black dog with curly hair out of a box, and tied it down with ropes. Then, right in front of them, she killed it! Kim said that she would show me the spot. After this, Selma told the children that if they said anything to their mothers, she would do the same thing to their own pets. Teri, you know how much she loves her cat, Slink! This was why she hadn't said anything about this before.

Oh, Teri, I know this stretches the imagination, but I know it's true.

Everything she has told me so far fits into what other children have said! How can the kids recover from these unspeakable traumas?"

Teri felt her stomach turn and groaned out loud as Katie relayed this.

Katie managed to whisper, "Kim was so scared that Selma would hear that she had told me this. I couldn't stop her crying for nearly an hour. Finally, I got through to her that she was safe and that we would always protect her and Slink. Although I promised this to her, I know that I can't guarantee it for sure. She is not always with us at home."

Teri was almost speechless. She was as appalled as Katie. "I've heard of some other kids mentioning something about hurting dogs. These kids are certainly not making this up!"

The next day, Teri found Hannah playing alone with her stuffies. She hated to break the peace, but desperately wanted to hear from her daughter. "Do you remember if Selma or others have done anything bad with animals?"

Teri nearly fell over backwards with Hannah's reply, "Do you mean killing dogs?"

Her mother hid her alarm and tried to speak calmly, "I can't answer that, Hannah, because I don't want to put thoughts in your head."

"You're not, Mom! Sometimes I have flashes of things like that happening. But I don't have to remember cause I'm not going to court, remember?"

Teri tried to think of how her little girl had concluded that. "Well, we don't know that for sure yet. You don't have to tell me about this, OK?"

Hiding her tears, Teri put her running shoes on to go for her jog. She needed time alone.

CHAPTER 40

Hannah woke up with a little yawn. She heard Mommy getting breakfast ready in the kitchen. Her tummy tensed with anxiety, as she remembered that this was a morning she'd been dreading! Today was the day she had to go to the dentist. *Yuk! I know that I need my tooth taken out. I don't like the needles, but I really like our dentist.* Slowly, she got up and dressed. A thought crossed her mind. *At least it's a safe place. What could possibly happen at a dentist's office!*

After an hour of driving, Mom walked with her into the dentist's waiting area and sat down next to her. Hannah saw her mom look carefully around the lounge. She whispered, "Looks like everything is all right here! I know you like Dr. Emory and there is no one else waiting. Is it OK if I slip into town to grab a few groceries?"

Hannah replied with confidence, "That's OK, Mom! I trust Dr. Emory. What could go wrong? I just don't like the needles, but I can handle it."

"I'll wait until you are called in, just to be sure."

Hannah knew that her mom was concerned that someone she feared might suddenly turn up. Nevertheless, she answered, "OK!"

After a short wait, Dr. Emory called her into his office."Well, how is my pretty little patient doing today? I remember that you don't enjoy the freezing, but you're always brave. Shall we get started?"

Mom informed the doctor that she was going to slip out for a few groceries. He smiled and replied that this was a short appointment and would take about twenty minutes. After Mom left, Dr. Emory put in the needle. She shut her eyes and tried to think good thoughts. When she opened them, he was done. "That went well, Hannah. I will be back soon to pull that nasty tooth out."

Alone in the office, she noticed a little book shelf within reach. As she started to bend forward to get a book that looked like fun, she felt a presence behind her. Startled, Hannah started to turn to see if it was Dr. Emory, but it wasn't! She had a glimpse of a thin, tall man she had never seen before. He kept behind her so she could not see him. She felt his face close to her. He had bad breath like cigarette smoke. "You are in big trouble, kid! You had better keep your mouth shut from now on."

She heard quick steps as he slipped out of the room. She sat frozen in terror and squeezed her eyes shut. Right away, she remembered all the threats Selma had given her. Shaking, she thought of Selma's trial. *If I go to court and tell them about Selma, maybe she will kill Cricket.* She was too scared to say anything to Dr. Emory when he returned. *I think I'd better tell Mom, but I don't want her to tell anyone else about this.*

"You look a bit pale, Hannah. Are you feeling all right?" The dentist asked with concern.

She quickly tried to hide her fear, "I'm fine," she lied.

After he finished pulling her tooth out, Mom walked in. They both thanked the dentist, then went out to the car.

Hannah shut the door of the car, then reached for her mother. It was impossible for her to hide her tears any longer. She tried to talk, but sobs kept getting in the way. Mom looked alarmed and hugged her daughter to herself. "What is it, Hannah? What happened?"

Hannah looked around to see if the thin man was gone, then told her mom what had just happened. Mom looked close to tears. "It doesn't seem to matter how careful I am trying to protect you from these awful people. I'm so sorry, Hannah! I feel like wrapping you in cotton- batten and standing guard over you. You're sure you don't want me to let Constable Jay know?"

"No, Mom, please don't tell anyone! Selma will find out. Then something worse could happen." She didn't feel like saying any more.

CHAPTER 41

Court was just around the corner. The stress increased every day. Paul and Teri had been very shaken by what happened to their daughter at the dentist's office. Obviously, Selma and crew were looking for any opportunity to harass the child witnesses!

Life continued to be unsettling in Echo Bay. Robin still hadn't made up her mind about which children were going to appear in court to testify. She wanted to spend more time with Hannah. Jacob kept remembering some awful encounters with Selma. Most of the children involved were acting out anger, resentment and fear. Some of them had never spoken of what had happened, even though they had been babysat by Brandon many times. They were either too young or too scared. Teri wondered if even worse things had happened to these children that would never be revealed. She had to remind herself, over and over again, that Jesus was the Burden Bearer. No one had followed up on little Kim's disclosures! Did the police think that they didn't need any more information from these victims?

A week before Selma's trial, Robin talked with Hannah once again. "I wanted to ask you if you remember being babysat at the Haywood's house while your parents were attending a wedding. Apparently, Brandon was babysitting you all. Do you remember Jamie being there?"

"Yes, I remember being there with the others, but I don't think Jamie was."

"Previously, you told me he was there with the others."

Hannah looked away. "Maybe he was, but I don't remember now."

Robin looked disappointed, but asked no more questions.

As a result of this interview, Robin told Teri that she had decided that Susan would be the better witness. She had remembered details that Hannah hadn't.

"Another reason, Teri, is that Hannah has a tendency to smile under examination." Robin tried to comfort Teri, "I know why she smiles. It is just her way of displaying embarrassment, but the jury may not see it that way. Otherwise, I want you to know that I believe every word she has shared. Hannah is so open and honest about the abuse. I'm sorry that she will not be able to testify."

Teri didn't find out until after the trial, that Hannah had purposely lied to Robin so she wouldn't have to face Selma. However, at this time, she felt only anguish that Hannah's testimony of her terrible abuse would never be heard at this trial. She reflected with some anger. *I can't believe this is happening! Hannah has told more than all the other kids put together. She is brave and articulate. It just doesn't seem right. After all she's been through! I bet that Selma will gloat and think that her threats worked! Lord, please rain down your vengeance on these wicked people!*

It turned out that just Peter and Teri would testify from the Nelson family. Paul would stay with them in a nearby hotel, while Nan would look after Hannah and Jacob. The younger two were only too happy to go to their grandparents. They were looking forward to having fun with relatives.

There were a total of six children who had been selected by Robin to go to court for the Prosecution. These were Jamie, Susan, Caleb, Mary, Ursula's son Jasper, and Peter. Four adults would also need to appear: Tabitha, Diana, Ursula and Teri.

Finally, after the long wait, Selma's trial started. Before the first family arrived, it had been in progress for days. Robin had already called to the stand some expert witnesses, including doctors, child psychologists and members of the RCMP.

Jackson had phoned from Hudson to inform them that their family were staying at a large hotel near the Supreme Court building. They had already been escorted through the court building, so that they would be familiar with it. Selma had not been seen yet, for which they were all thankful. Teri could hear Jackson's voice as he talked to Paul. "Now that we are here, it seems almost anti-climatic to me. We are busy trying to keep the kids occupied so they aren't sitting around thinking about things. Man, I'll be glad when this is over!"

Robin's secretary, Heather, phoned the Nelsons a few days later to tell them to be down in Hudson in a week's time. Teri felt a huge adrenalin rush as she helped the kids get ready.

Before they knew it, they were unpacking at the hotel. Nan met them there to pick up Jacob and Hannah. They had just started to settle into their rooms, when Heather phoned. "Robin asked me to call you and let you know that because of a number of delays, you two won't be testifying until next week. six more days. She would like you to come to the court building tomorrow at 9:30 am for orientation. I'll be there to show you around." Teri felt a dart of fear shoot through her at the thought of seeing Selma again.

The next morning, Heather met them at the entrance. As they approached the closed door of the room where Selma's trial was being held, Teri felt sick. The assistant opened the door and asked that they look in briefly. Yes, there was Selma! She turned to look at them as they stood in the entrance. Teri was stunned that Peter boldly looked in, made a face at Selma and gave a small mocking wave. As soon as they went back downstairs, his alarmed mom asked him, "Why did you do that Peter?"

He smiled at her and told her, as the assistant listened, "I did it because it looked great seeing Selma on trial. You know I was just mocking her, don't you?"

The assistant spoke up. "Just watch! This will come back on you somehow. The defense will try and twist this in court and, perhaps, say that you waved in a friendly manner. I would suggest that you don't do that again."

Peter looked downcast as he walked with Teri to the hotel. "It's OK Peter, I understand why you waved, but others could misunderstand. If they ask you why in court, just tell them what you just told us."

Although Robin was trying to keep the case a low profile in the media, a few reporters were attending each day. There was a publication ban on the names of children. Nevertheless, later that morning, they heard on the news that a child psychologist, Dr. Dave Miller, had spoken to the media after his deposition on the first day of the trial. He told the reporter that even with no physical injury, abused children could have psychological symptoms that would last the rest of their lives. Apparently, this doctor had been one of the psychologists who had examined Brandon. He also told the reporter that Selma had treated Brandon in an abusive fashion.

"This sounds like a good beginning for the prosecution." Paul commented. Teri started to feel more optimistic.

Soon after they turned off the radio, the phone rang at their suite. Teri answered. She was not surprised to hear Tabitha on the line. She sounded quite stressed, "Did you just hear the news? I'm glad Dr. Miller said those things, but it makes me very scared of what the future holds for our kids. Right now, they are all behaving miserably. Susan is the worst. She is very emotional and apathetic about court. I don't have a clue as to how to help her. Any suggestions?"

"We better keep this conversation private. I'm not sure you should have phoned, but I'm so glad you did! Did you know that we have a prayer chain with many people praying for all of us? They are following the trial carefully. I will ask them to pray especially for Susan. Is she going in first?"

"Yes, unfortunately she is!" Tabitha moaned.

Teri thought carefully. "I think she needs to lean on some reassurances from God's Word. How about Luke 12:11-12? Remember that Jesus said, 'When you are brought before synagogues, rulers and authorities, do not worry about how you will defend yourselves or what you will say, for the Holy Spirit will teach you at that time what you should say'. I'm planning to remind Peter, again, of these verses. Last time, it seemed to encourage him."

"Oh, that's a good one. I'll share it with her right now. Thanks Teri! I'll probably be in touch again soon."

The next day Paul attended some of the court sessions because he wasn't on the roster to appear. He returned about four-thirty that afternoon. He looked fatigued as he explained to his wife a little of what was going on. "It seems to drag on and on! I was stunned to hear that Gladys is calling around thirty witnesses. One piece of good news is that the youngest child witness, Mary, may not have to be in the court to tell her part. If she is scared to be in the same room as Selma, the prosecution are planning to do her testimony by video in a separate room. I think that Susan will be called in either this Thursday or Friday. They have more expert witnesses to go through. I'm sure that Doug will be one of them. Sadly, I think we have quite a wait ahead of us. When's supper?"

Teri suggested that they feed Cricket then take the bus to McDonalds. It turned out to be a bad choice. The place was full of unkempt people, some of whom looked drunk. Out front some bedraggled men asked for money. Peter had never seen anything like this and had many questions. Paul gave a long explanation as to why people acted like this to their inquisitive boy. It didn't help anyone feel better. They went to bed early. City life was not for them!

Their mission director, Drew Costello, phoned them early the next morning. Last night had been their monthly board meeting. There they had all agreed that the Nelsons should plan on moving soon after they had returned home to Echo Bay. He told Paul, "We will meet after the trial. Soon, you need to think about the two options we gave you awhile back. You guys will have to decide which of the locations you are interested in relocating to. Of course you don't need to think of this now. All your time and energy is taken up with the court case. We want to help and support you in every way we can. All of us here are praying fervently that justice will be served."

After he signed off, Paul and Teri looked at each other sadly. Teri reminded her husband that Joe and Katie were making plans to move away from Echo Bay as soon as possible. Paul looked grim, "This means that only a couple of our families are left there. I heard that they both are also planning to move as soon as possible. Conditions there have become unbearable! We'll tackle this after Selma's trial. I was thinking recently that even if Selma is found guilty, there are many in the community who could react with anger towards us. I think we will start packing as soon as we get home."

Teri turned to Peter who was reading on the couch. "What do you think about us moving?"

His face lit up, "How soon? I'll miss our fort and the beach, but I really want to live somewhere else."

CHAPTER 42

The expert witnesses were finally done and Susan was having her turn in court. Tabitha gave Teri a quick call. "Well, she's in the court room. Please pray for her testimony and my nerves! I sort of regret that I didn't excuse her from testifying. I can't stand the thought of her facing that horrible woman! I'll phone after she's finished. I think Jamie is going in right after her. I'm a wreck! I'm testifying after Jamie. If I feel this way, how on earth can the children do this, Teri?"

"I sure understand how you are feeling! Don't you wish that that the trial only needed adults to give evidence! I'm finding that this trial is more stressful than Brandon's.

But, remember how well Susan and Jamie did in Fort Smith. I think they will do just as well here. Why don't we pray about it right now! " Teri suggested.

They did just that. "We are in God's Hands," Tabitha concluded.

Paul returned later that afternoon with a smile on his face. "Susan did fantastically! She didn't appear afraid of Selma at all. Instead, she told of some incidences that I hadn't heard about. Gladys sure tried to confuse her with stupid little details that had nothing to do with anything. She's working hard to show the court that the kids are unsure and inconsistent."

With her face wrinkled with concern, Teri replied, "Well, it was what we expected. Gladys has already proved to be utterly ruthless."

Paul smiled, "Well, we are seeing answers to prayer right before our eyes. This sure encourages me that God's promises are proving true, even in these impossible circumstances! Aren't you relieved that we have so many people praying for us all?"

Teri reached for her Bible. "Yes, I certainly am! I sense these prayers upholding us every day. Found something in Psalm 37 the other day that I loved! Let's see! Oh, here it is in verses 5 and 6! 'Commit your way to the Lord, trust in Him and He will do this: He will make your righteousness shine like the dawn, the justice of your cause like the noon day sun.'"

"Yes, so true! Very applicable to our lives right now. I'm going into Peter's room to encourage him with what happened today."

Teri overheard them talking, the father encouraging his son! She was so grateful to have such a strong and loving husband.

A few hours later, Tabitha phoned with her update on Susan's day in court. " Oh Teri! I feel way better than earlier. According to Robin, Susan's continuing to do well on the stand. I'm so proud of her! She certainly is happy to be nearly finished. But she told me something kinda weird! I don't know if we should be worried or not. She noticed some things about one of the jurors. This woman, dressed all in black, keeps watching Selma. Susan saw them exchanging looks and once she saw this juror smile at her. Teri, something is very wrong here and there is nothing we can do about it!"

"Yikes! That is scary. She could really influence the jury if she is for Selma. I'll ask Paul if he has noticed her."

They hung up and Teri went to find Paul. He was watching TV in the small living room. She sat down beside him and tried to keep her voice down. "Have you, by any chance, noticed a woman in the jury dressed all in black?"

He answered quietly, "Yes! She seems to appreciate Selma's theatrics. I'm wondering if she is involved in the occult too. I mean, why is she dressed from top to bottom in black? I definitely have a bad feeling about this woman."

Teri's went to bed with a heavy heart. She realized once again that the outcome of this trial may not be what they had hoped.

The next day, Ms. Cotton smoothed out her best black dress and confidentially walked into the court room with the other jurors. She sat in her accustomed seat and looked around. Yes, there was Selma reading something! She suddenly looked up from her papers and fixed her eyes on her friend. Ms. Cotton gave her a quick nod after she checked to see if the judge was looking their way. Selma gave a brief smile back before going back to her reading.

That's good, Selma understands! Yesterday she had contacted, by phone, the secret group she was part of. The size and network of these underground believers was intricate and close knit. Ms. Cotton conjured up memories of these meetings. She wished she had been there. Last night as she was trying to sleep, a short phone call came from the ritual leader, Salem. He had reassured her that they all felt that Selma would have the victory over their enemies.

These Christians will be decimated by the defense. She just knew it! She had tried to phone Selma from her room, but her noisy roommate was always there. So she had tried mental telepathy. Selma's return smile to her this morning told her that they had connected.

Ms. Cotton turned her concentration to the first witness. Oh, she detested the confident way this snivelling little girl testified against her friend. She found the expressions and gesturing of Selma to be a consolation to her. Keep it up, my friend! Maybe you'll turn some of the other jurors your way. I don't want to be the only one standing up for you.

⚬━━━━━━⚬

As Paul entered the court the next morning, he had a strange sense of spiritual warfare permeating the air. The juror in black seemed to be enjoying Selma's pretence to be the innocent victim. A dark- skinned man, who seemed to be a friend of Selma's, sat on the row behind the defense. He had a badge saying 'reporter' on his blazer. Paul whispered to Jackson beside him, " I don't know about you, but that so-called reporter looks evil to me."

Jackson turned to Paul, with a grim look on his face, and nodded.

Meanwhile, Teri at the hotel room felt more burdened than ever. Her heart fluttered with anxiety; her voice had became husky. As a result of having too much time on her hands, she knew she was agonizing way too much on what was happening at court.

I can't believe this depth of anxiety! I didn't expect it to be this bad! I know that God is faithful. It's almost as if there's a cloud of protection around those testifying. I know that if I pray, instead of all this worrying, the Lord will gently remove much of this stress. Sometimes I just don't feel like praying! It's hard to concentrate! Please God, help me pray and praise You for Your mighty power over our enemy!

That night Tabitha phoned again. "Jackson and Susan just got back from court. I just want to update you on how well Susan did today. Apparently, Gladys didn't shake her! Boy, I'm impressed with her and how God is helping! So grateful for all the people praying! I guess it's not over for Susan yet. She's been called back tomorrow to continue with the defense's cross examination. Jackson told me that she has testified of even more details of the abuse than ever before . Because of this, Gladys is trying to show the court that there are inconsistencies, especially regarding the 'parties'. Of course, this doesn't match her Fort Smith testimony! Jackson hadn't even heard this new information!"

"Thank you, Lord!" Teri exclaimed. "I will update the prayer group."

Paul had missed the court session that day. He had taken Peter to the docks to watch the fishing boats. Teri had spent the day alone for a change. She had had a long talk with her mother that afternoon. Nan was planning on coming over in a few days to sit in at court. Teri was relieved that her mother had only sympathy for them. She had lost her, 'I told you so' attitude. She only had praise for Hannah and Jacob. "They are being wonderful about this whole situation. Your brother, James, is spending a lot of time entertaining them. Today he's taking them to the beach."

Teri was grateful that her mother was so much more supportive. *Maybe the Lord will use all this to bring her to Himself!*

The next morning, Susan continued to kept her composure and consistency. Gladys tried, to no avail, to frustrate the prosecution, by constantly baiting this young witness. Susan was eventually dismissed without satisfying the defense. The Judge had decided to stop Gladys's endless trivial questioning. Shortly after, Jamie was called to the stand.

CHAPTER 43

Tabitha and Jackson had done everything they could to encourage their young son for this day. Jamie had come a long way from the first time he had told his parents what Brandon had done to him. He was ready to tell the Judge as much as he could about Selma.

Now the time had come! The nine- year- old brushed his wavy black hair back from his forehead and opened the door into court. His bravado collapsed when he saw how packed the court room was. So many people! Suddenly he felt like turning and running away. Then, he remembered that God wanted him to do this and that He would be with him. This is what his parents had told him just before he came in!

He entered the witness box and turned to face Selma. At first he quailed as she glared at him. Then, Robin stood in front of him. She smiled at him reassuringly as she blocked his view of the accused. The questions began. He started out well until Robin moved. He caught a glimpse of Selma turning around and gestured to the jury in disbelief at what he had just said. His nerve dropped like a stone. What was the question Robin had just asked? He looked down at his lap and muttered that he didn't remember. Would his lawyers be mad at him? He was overcome by embarrassment. When Robin asked him the next question, his memory flew out the window. At that point, the judge declared that there would be a recess until they resumed after the weekend.

Tabitha urgently phoned Teri, after the kids went to bed. Fear colored her voice as she described Jamie's dilemma.

"Don't worry Tabitha, I'll get a hold of the prayer team." Teri reassured her friend, feeling like a hypocrite as her heart fluttered and waves of fear washed over her.

She quickly phoned one of the prayer group leaders. Her calm, loving friend asked Teri to pray with her on the phone. Her faltering faith slowly returning as they prayed. Teri beseeched the Lord to give this child witness the courage he needed to finish his testimony. Her prayer partner promised to contact all prayer groups with this emergency request.

Monday morning, little Jamie woke up refreshed and relaxed. He remembered the kind words that Robin had encouraged him with last night. He remembered Mom and Dad praying with him at bedtime. He ate a big breakfast and got ready for court. He dreaded having to apologize to the Court. Robin said that it was very important. She promised to help him.

Jamie felt almost like a grown-up, despite his age. Marching up to the witness stand, he turned confidently towards Robin. She asked him if he wanted to tell the Court something first. Reluctantly, he twisted in his seat to face the judge. To his surprise, the man winked at him with a smile. His face red with embarrassment, Jamie tried to look into his eyes. Slowly, he apologized for not telling what he remembered on Friday. The judge accepted his confession and motioned Robin to continue.

The lawyer repeated the questions she had asked him before. This time Jamie answered as accurately as he could. He knew he must not lie or exaggerate. Instead, he searched his memory for details of the different 'parties'. He was even able to ignore the smirks and glares that Selma sent his way.

The next day, Jamie continued with his evidence. Then, it was the defence lawyer's turn. Gladys took over. Her angry questions reminded him of Selma. He lifted his chin in determination to endure this part of the trial. Then, Gladys asked him if he had lied in Brandon's trial about a stick. It hurt so much to be called a liar. Tears started down his cheeks. He broke down on the stand, but managed to utter, "No!"

The judge asked him if he wanted a break. Jamie thought for a minute. If he had a break, the trial would go on longer. He just wanted it over with. Jamie told the judge that he wanted to keep on going. Gladys continued to besiege him with her trivial cross- examination. What was Selma wearing at one of the 'parties' at Morrison's house? Who else was there? Where was Brandon standing? Was he sure that he was telling the truth? What about this, what about that? Jamie considered her every question and answered as best he could. All the memories flooded back. His biggest terror at these' parties', had been trying to survive. Could this lawyer not understand what it was like for a six year old to be surrounded by so many awful people? He understood that she was trying hard to mix him up. Finally, the judge brought it to a close. He declared that Jamie's evidence was accepted as 'sworn testimony'. His ordeal was over.

There was rejoicing in the Christian camp that evening, as word of Jamie's victory in court spread. Teri praised God for the fulfillment of His Word in Psalm 8: 2, "Out of the mouths of children and infants You have ordained strength. Because of Your enemies, that you may silence the enemy and the avenger."

After supper, Paul phoned the prayer group co-ordinator with this praise item. This dear friend responded, "Paul, could you please tell Teri that some of us are coming up to Hudson when she testifies. We will sit at the back and pray."

Paul turned to Teri and repeated what he had just heard. Astounded by the love and faithfulness of these prayer warriors, she grabbed the phone. "Wow! Thank you so much! This is so encouraging!"

CHAPTER 44

Today was Tabitha's turn. As she entered the court, her fears vanished. She felt strong in the Lord and was confident that the Holy Spirit was filling her with courage. Sure enough, as Robin asked the questions, she knew just what to say. "Did you have your children looked after at the Haywood's house in the Spring of 1985?" "Were you friends with the accused?"" How often did you visit with her?" "Can you give me specific dates when your children were babysat by Selma's son, Brandon?"

Tabitha was surprised at how accurate her memory was as she recalled the many times her three were looked after by Brandon. She described the behavior changes in the children that began after Brandon had started to babysit them. Dates and times were remembered. She was grateful that she had kept track of these meetings in her notebook.

Before she knew it, Gladys was standing in front of her. Right away she tried to confuse Tabitha with questions about the dates she had given. Then she stated, "You didn't like Selma, did you? You were neighbors, but you didn't communicate with her much, did you!"

Robin stood up, "Where are the relevant questions here? These are accusations."

The judge agreed, "Sustained!"

Tabitha was grateful that she didn't need to answer Gladys's aggressive question. Before she knew it, her appearance was over. "Thank you, Lord!" She murmured, as she went out of court.

The next morning Ursula was to be called to the stand. That night, Tabitha shared her concern for this new Christian with Teri. "As you know, Ursula is quite high-strung and reactive. In light of what I went through today, I'm wondering how she will react to the defense when pressed."

Teri replied thoughtfully, "Hmm! I haven't talked with her, for awhile, about court. I have no idea what her state of mind is these days. Let's continue to pray that she will be calm and accurate! Our prayer- answering God will strengthen her, too."

The next day after Ursula's rather short time on the stand, Paul reported to Teri that she had done fairly well. "She did lose her composure once, though. She lost her temper under cross-examination. Although I don't blame her for reacting to Gladys's endless questions, we need to pray that it doesn't damage the case. Let's do that right now!"

Nothing was planned with Robin the next day, so the Nelson family decided to drive to Nan's house. This was a great distraction for Peter. Teri watched him visibly relax. With his aunts and cousins there as well, it was a fun time. She even was able to turn her mind away from their impending court appearances. Hannah and Jacob were happy to see them and joined in with hilarity. They were especially glad to see Cricket again. The dog had been a good comfort for Peter, who had spent a lot of time lying on the couch reading. Cricket always curled up to him and never left his side. The only place the little dog couldn't go was into court with him.

As they turned their rented car back towards Hudson, Teri felt the return of dread. Teri had found out earlier that she was to be the last witness for the Prosecution. It was the sitting around at the hotel that worried her the most. She had to plan for more outings for them all.

CHAPTER 45

Jasper watched his mother pace back and forth in their hotel room. He knew that she was worried about him. It made him feel shaky inside. Oh, how he wished she would stop and talk to him! Finally, his dad returned after getting some groceries. Mom stopped pacing and told Dad she needed to talk with him privately right away. He joined Ursula in the small living area. "Jasper," he asked quietly, "Please go into your room and work some more on the homework Mrs. Madden gave you! Shut your door, OK?"

Their son went obediently to do what his dad had asked. Jasper opened his math's book, but no way could he concentrate. He could hear his mother's high pitched voice breaking the silence, but couldn't hear what she was saying. He felt sure that she was telling Dad how upset she was from her time in the court room today. His heart sank. Could it be that scary? His turn was tomorrow morning. How could he even sleep? Just before bedtime, Dad came into his cramped room. "Can you get ready for bed, son? Your mom has calmed down now. I thought it was better that I came to talk with you. You know she is worried about you. I--"

Jasper interrupted, "Dad, I know that. She's made me pretty scared. Was it really that awful? I don't want to go to court tomorrow. Please!"

Dad replied soothingly, "There are many, many people praying for you right now. I don't know much about the Bible yet, but I do know that God gives us peace and bravery when we ask Him to. I am certain that the Lord Himself will give you this. Do you believe this?"

In a trembling voice Jasper answered, "Yes, I think so."

"Then you can sleep OK now, can't you?"

Daddy prayed with his nine year old son, then clicked off the lamp by the bed. "Goodnight Jasper! Try to think of happy things as you go to sleep. You'll feel better after a good sleep."

Dad was right, he did feel better in the morning. Mom was kinda quiet at breakfast. Occasionally, she smiled weakly at her only son. She kissed him goodbye. "I think it would be best if I don't come, Jasper. I know you will do a good job today. All you have to do is tell the truth. Don't let the defense lawyer trick you! You are a smart boy, so I know that you can figure her out. I'll be praying for you here at our hotel room."

Jasper stepped into the court session. His first reaction was how strange it all looked. His eyes riveted on Selma face. *She is sitting too close to the box at front where I'm supposed to sit! Her face is still really scary, but now is my only chance to tell what she did to me and my sister.*

Robin asked some easy questions first. Jasper answered quickly to each one. His lawyer reminded him to think carefully before he gave his answers. He did what she told him to do. He found remembering quite easy and replied with confidence. Even Gladys couldn't trip him up. He had always been articulate, even from a very early age. He described his memories well. Jasper had been at different places with Brandon than some of the other witnesses. Using this information, Gladys tried to show inconsistencies to the jury. By the end of his session, Jasper was pleased that he had done all that he was able to do. Robin met him outside after the court was dismissed. She smiled warmly at young Jasper, "You did a very good job in court today. I am proud of you." Jasper felt warm all over as he went out to his dad in the waiting area.

Next in line was Caleb Haywood. He had recently celebrated his eighth birthday. Diana phoned to describe her

worries to Teri. "I don't know how Caleb will do. He seems very nervous one minute and optimistic the next. You already know that Mary may be allowed to be videotaped in a separate room. Now he wants the same! Robin has already explained that Caleb has showed every ability to be able go into the court room to testify. He cried himself to sleep last night just thinking about it."

"Awww! Diana, that's just awful! These poor kids! If even adults are scared of being witnesses, what about these small children? It's a lot to ask.

If God were not on our side, we would all fail. Our faithful prayer warriors are praying constantly for us all. I'm phoning to update them tonight."

Diana thanked Teri, then abruptly hung up . Paul was taking Teri and Peter to the park this evening. He found a good restaurant there. Once again they were momentarily distracted from thinking of court.

CHAPTER 46

Caleb knew what to expect, cause Robin had shown him. Still, it seemed unreal as he walked into the court room alone. Selma tried to stare him down. All she accomplished was to encourage him even more to tell on her! Caleb knew that this was his time to talk to these important people about what she had done. He felt ready!

When the time came to disclose the worst things that had ever happened to him, he looked down in embarrassment. It was terrible telling these strangers about such private things. He carefully answered all of Robin's questions. Just when he thought he was nearly done, the scary defense lawyer stood up to take her turn. Caleb felt like crying! He quickly wiped his eyes before she looked at him. With her every question, he tried not to break down. His chin wobbled as he carefully answered her weird questions. Towards the end of her questioning, he knew that he had not lied once to the court; even though she said he did. It was the truth! He had never talked to the other kids about Selma and Brandon! Why was she so mean? She reminded him of Selma. Suddenly, it struck him. *She is a friend of Selma! That's why she's so mad!* He stopped being scared, and looked her straight in the eye. She and Selma could not hurt him anymore. It was safe to tell the court all of the terrible times she had hurt him.

Nan had decided to attend court that day. After court was adjoined, Teri met her mom at the stairs coming down from the Supreme Court building. When Teri saw her white, distressed face, she hurried up to meet her. Nan didn't even look up as she mumbled about the horrible things she had just heard. She stopped and asked her daughter. "Did these people do this to my grandchildren, too? I never thought it was that bad!"

"Yes!" Teri said, "It was way worse than all the things that you heard in there."

The pair went into a colorful little sidewalk restaurant. As they waited for the snack, Nan read the newspaper while Teri had a chance to think about her mom's response to what she had just heard in court. She appreciated that her mom had never tried to say, "I told you so!" Nan had certainly, always, thought that Echo Bay was a bad place for their family to live, so Teri was especially grateful for this. But, it caused Teri to think about what they would have done if they had, somehow, known before hand what was going to happen to them in Echo Bay. They would have never have moved there. She suddenly realized how much God loved the souls of the people who lived there. They would not have heard the good news of Jesus, if the Nelsons hadn't gone to them. Teri thought to herself how very high the cost of a soul was. The truth was that Jesus had paid the supreme price to save these very ones and had given their family the privilege to bring this good news to this needy community.

Teri sat across from her distraught mother, who was uncharacteristically silent. She looked much older. Finally, she looked up from her paper, "That little boy is so cute! I couldn't believe what came out of his mouth! I've never heard of anything so awful. Those poor children! I wonder if they will ever be normal again?"

Teri considered her question. Even though she felt angry that her mother didn't think their kids were 'normal', she grasped the fact that she was worried about this same thing. Would their three ever be able to recover from this? She rested in the thought that God was able to bring good out of all the evil that happened to them. She thought of the Bible passage in Romans 8, "And we know that all things work together for good to those who love God, to those who are called according to His purpose." Oh, how she needed to believe that now!

"Mom, you know that Paul and I believe what God says in His Word, the Bible. There are many promises there that reassure us that He is in control. Yes, He allowed this unspeakable horror to happen to our family, but we know that He is more powerful then evil. I realize that you may not believe this, but we do with all our hearts. This is why we, as well as the other families who are going through this, are able to keep our sanity." Teri tried to keep her voice calm and relaxed. "He will also comfort and heal our children, eventually. I guess it depends on what you call 'normal'. I think you mean healthy, happily functioning adults."

Nan replied genuinely, "Well, I can see that you are all very close and have done well to get this far, but I do worry about the children. I will never forget what that little boy said. He was very brave! Your faith has helped you so much. Sometimes I wish that I had a faith like yours!"

Teri's heart leapt at this opportunity to share the salvation message to her mother. How many years had she prayed for this! Gently, she explained about all that Christ had done for her mother. Because He loved her so much, He had sacrificed Himself so that she could have her sins forgiven and gain eternal life.

Nan looked seriously at her daughter, "So, what do I have to do to have this salvation you're talking about?"

"Way back in the Old Testament, it says that if you seek the Lord your God with all your heart and with all your soul, you will find Him. He loves you so much that when you do this He will always answer you. Read the book of John in the New Testament with a seeking heart and you will find the answer to your question! Really, He is only a prayer away."

Nan answered slowly, "You make it sound so easy. I've lived a long time, but have never heard this before. Because I've seen the way you are going through this unspeakable time in your life, I'm going to look into this. I have a Bible tucked away on my bookcase, so I'll dig it out and read it. I know I've done lots of wrong things in my day, but I've always just put it all behind me. God's forgiveness sounds very appealing."

Teri encouraged her, "Inviting Jesus into my life was the best and greatest decision I've ever made. Talk about life changing! I use to be terrified of dying, but now I know where I'm going."

Nan left for home, while Teri returned to the hotel. She found that the guys were out. Paul left a note saying that he, Peter and Cricket had gone to a nearby park. *Good, maybe I can have a time to myself for awhile!* She put on some Christian music and reviewed the notes from Brandon's trial. *Heavenly Father, please help me to remember these facts and to have your strength in the coming days.*

CHAPTER 47

Diana was called to testify next. She had reported to Teri earlier that she was actually excited to testify against Selma. As she talked, Teri could tell that underneath, she was quietly seething with anger. She expressed this by whispering into the phone, "Apparently, Selma sits in court shaking her head and acting astonished at the kid's answers. What a liar! She is just trying to impress the jury with her disbelieving antics. Just wait until she's behind bars! Then she can have her own pity party."

Diana couldn't wait to see Selma put away for a long time. Teri was surprised that she was so confident that Selma would be found guilty. She tried not to think of the possibility of Selma being acquitted. How would they all cope?

Later, Paul recounted how well Diana had answered both lawyers. Apparently Robin was very pleased with her responses. Diana had refused to be moved by Gladys's feeble attempt to trip her up. Paul snickered as he recounted how she had the audacity to confront this lawyer about her manipulation techniques. The judge had brought down his gavel and warned Diana to stop accusing an honoured member of the law society.

Now it was time for Mary, Caleb's six year old sister, to go in. Mary was a shy and quiet little girl. She had a number of counsellors, besides Doug, who were helping her prepare for this court appearance. They had all assembled outside the court room in the waiting area. When Robin's assistant came out to get her, Mary shook her head and said, "No!"

Sam had to finally pick her up and take her to the open door, where she started to cry in distress. The whole courtroom turned a collective ear to this disturbance. Robin immediately came out to check what was happening. Sam had retreated to a chair with Mary clinging to him. Diana and Robin tried to talk her into going to court. Her little round face wrinkled up as she used her long hair to wipe the tears. "I want to go into the room, but I'm scared of Selma. She will make faces at me and make me cry."

Robin gently asked, "Would you be able to tell the court what happened to you, if you didn't have to see Selma?"

"Yes, Mary whimpered. "I think so."

Court was adjourned till the afternoon.

After lunch, Robin asked the judge if she could call two witnesses who would testify to what Mary had said about her fear of the defendant. After the judge agreed, Sam and one of counselors, Laura, explained Mary's state of mind. They both emphasized that Mary would testify if she could not see Selma.

After they were dismissed, Robin asked the court if Mary could be screened, or even better, answer questions from an adjoining room and be recorded using an in court TV. This was followed by a heated debate between the two lawyers. The judge listened carefully, then declared that this was an unprecedented request by the prosecution. Considering the circumstances, however, he ordered Robin to move forward with the TV testimony for Mary. There was a sense of relief in the prosecution quarters that afternoon, as Robin went to organize setting up the equipment.

The next morning, the court watched the large TV screen as Mary quietly answered Robin's questions from a nearby room. Gladys kept interrupting by asking for Mary's previous disclosure reports to show inconsistencies. Teri heard later how very petty these requests were. Through it all, Mary held up well. She talked about what happened without being confused by the defense lawyer. She did not break down once and stuck to her testimony. *How amazing!* Teri thought, as she listened to Paul's description. *A six year old girl standing up to the monsters who violated her!*

Paul glowed, "These kids will go down in Christ's record as heroes!"

Teri knew that some Christian friends had traveled for over two hours to sit in court and pray. The encouragement of their presence there could not be emphasized enough. Teri felt her heart swell with peace and joy as she meditated on how much God's people loved them. Enough to actually join them in their quest for justice!

The next morning, Peter waited outside the court room. The dark cloud that filled his mind kept popping up. He had not told his parents what was said to him by Robin's assistant, Jay. It was difficult to forget his threat. At a recent meeting he had told Peter in no uncertain terms, that if he didn't repeat exactly what he had testified at Brandon's trial, than he would be exposed as a liar. Peter quailed at the thought. This was almost the worst thing that could happen to him. He had always tried to be truthful and to be called a liar publically was horrifying. He broke into a sweat just thinking about it. He had spent hours trying to remember his previous testimony. He knew he was blocking out many of the things that had happened to him, just as his mom had suggested. He had to search the deep recesses of his mind to remember. He tried to focus on the Bible verses that Mom had shared with him more than once. They filtered through the fear, as he remembered that God Himself was on his side.

Robin walked down the hall towards him. "Well Peter, now it's your time to go in. How are you doing?"

Peter responded, "I'm ready now."

She smiled reassuringly at him. "Mary did so well yesterday. I know you can do a good job, too. I'll come out to get you after I check in here."

Soon she came back, and Peter entered the court. To his shock, Selma looked over her shoulder than waved at him. Peter set his face towards the witness seat. After he was sworn in, Robin asked right away about the time when he waved at Selma through the court door. Peter was grateful that his lawyer had asked him this before Selma's lawyer did. He replied, "It was a mocking wave. It made me happy to see that Selma was finally in court."

Gladys turned and frowned at her client and mouthed something that no one could hear.

The early questions were easy. He only had to give his name, where he lived and who was in his family. Peter had just started to relax, when Robin asked him if he recognized the accused and where he had seen this person. Selma had a grim face as Peter pointed her out. Seeing her face to face made him feel in control. The questions got more difficult and he concentrated on answering as truthfully as he could. Sometimes, he found it difficult to recall exact events. He hadn't thought of them for awhile and had tried so hard to forget. He was thankful that Robin did not ask if he had been assaulted by Selma. Peter started to sweat when she repeated a question that she had asked him at the trial in Fort Smith. He described what he saw at the parties, but sometimes they blurred into a maze of confusing memories.

Time rolled on. finally, at 4:30pm, Judge Carlson brought it all to a close. "We will recess until 9:00 a.m tomorrow. Thank you Peter, we will see you again in the morning."

Mom met him at the door and scrutinized his face. "Are you OK, Peter? Let's go straight to the hotel. Can you believe that Dad is cooking supper tonight!" Her face reflected her amazement. Peter smiled back.

When they arrived, Cricket ran up to Peter and wiggled around in excitement. Their exhausted son threw himself on the couch and cuddled their dog. Mom sat opposite him, relaxing in the stuffed chair. "Well, how was it? Were you scared? I'm not allowed to ask what you said. Was it as bad as you thought it was going to be?"

Peter did not feel like talking about it, but told his mom that it was alright. Teri could tell that he was not happy and worried that it had gone badly. "I just want to know if it went OK, Peter. Other than that, you certainly don't have to talk about it."

It was a quiet evening at the supper table. Teri was grateful that Paul had made supper. She knew that it was not easy for him to do. She was concerned for their son. He had hardly said a word since he got back from court. After he finished eating, he went to his room with the dog to read. Teri started to stew. She imagined that Peter's experience had been traumatic. With a sigh, she went to pray in the living room. This decision to pray was more difficult then she thought it would be. With an effort of her will, she bowed her head. The words poured through her mind as she turned to her Heavenly Father. Paul came to join her after doing the dishes. Their heads almost touched as they prayed in whispers. They knew that God was in control as they beseeched Him to help their son.

Peter's gut twisted as he entered the court room once again. He was scared of what Gladys would ask him. Sure enough, she tried to tear apart all that he had said yesterday.

Although Robin interceded from time to time, he was on his own. Gladys paced from side to side as she sarcastically asked, "Now, tell us again, Peter, who you saw at these so called 'parties'."

His mind froze! *What did he say at Brandon's trial? There were so many parties. They all mingled together.* Suddenly, he felt very frustrated and blurted out, "How do expect me to remember all the details, when it happened so long ago!"

Gladys glanced at the jury and smirked. The lady in black nodded in satisfaction. *Now we are getting somewhere! The other brats did too well. Keep at it Gladys!*

Robin stood up and spoke to the Judge, "Your Honour, this line of questioning is out of order. Peter's testimony at Fort Smith was entered as sworn evidence. According to the previous witnesses, there were a number of different gatherings at different homes. The defense cannot expect this witness to remember who attended all these different events."

The judge said firmly, "The jury will discount this question. The defense will try another line of questioning."

Peter sat bowed over in the witness box and tried to settle his racing mind. He felt that he was on trial instead of his persecutor. He looked up as Judge Carlson asked him if he felt ready to continue. With an effort, he answered, "Yes!"

A couple of times Gladys asked Peter questions he was not allowed to answer. "Peter," she said smoothly with a short smile, "Can you recount the times you saw the accused participate in any spiritual rituals?"

Before Peter spoke, Robin jumped up from her seat to object. "Objection! My honoured friend seems to forget that this is a sexual assault trial. This question is inappropriate in light of the charges before the court."

Peter breathed a quiet sigh of relief. A flash of a terrifying memory hurled across his brain. He quickly thrust it aside.

The defense lawyer finally finished up her cross examination and sauntered her stocky frame back to her chair. Her body movement spoke of her satisfaction with her cross examination. She turned and gave her client a knowing look as Robin escorted Peter back to sit with his dad. She whispered reassuringly, "Good job, Peter! You did fine."

The court adjoined for a short break.

Teri had just come out of the shower and had started to dry her hair, when the phone rang. She raced to answer it. Robin's assistant was on the line, "It's time for you to appear at the Court. Can you please come as soon as possible!"

Teri threw on her clothes and had one final look in the mirror. She looked a little dishevelled, so quickly straightened her outfit and brushed her unruly curls into a semblance of order. She grabbed her bag full of notes and calendars and headed down to court. She failed to notice a man, standing at the court entrance, who seemed to show great interest in her arrival at court. As soon as Teri had entered the building, he disappeared into a crowd of people.

The court clerk held an open Bible as Teri was sworn in. "Do you swear to tell the truth and nothing but the truth, so help you God?"

Teri answered with conviction, "Yes, I do!"

All her previous fears and anxiety left her. She only felt courage and peace. Amazingly, her mind was clear and uncluttered from unwanted emotions.

The questioning began. Right away, she felt a connection between Robin and herself. It was like they were the only two people in the room. Teri was able to look at her calendar when Robin asked her about the different dates that Brandon had babysat the children. She confidently gave dates, locations and who she remembered at each group gathering at the different homes.

The cross-examination by Gladys went on and on. It was nearing the end of the day, when Gladys asked a bomb shell of a question. She asked Teri, "Do you consider that Selma was involved with witchcraft?"

Robin leaped to her feet, "Objection, your Honour. May we approach the bench?"

Judge Carlson dismissed the jury and Teri was asked to recess until tomorrow. As she walked towards the door, she glanced to where her friends sat. Jenny, a close friend, smiled with a slight nod and mouthed the words," We are staying!"

Exhaustion swept over Teri like she had never felt before. She dragged herself to the hotel rooms and lay down on the couch. She was emotionally spent from the intense cross examination. She had given it all she had.

She didn't have much time to rest. Her mother, brother James, Peter and Cricket surged into the room. They had gone for a walk at a nearby park. Nan exclaimed, "Oh my, Teri, you look awful! You are so pale. That defense lawyer must have raked you over the coals!"

Nan had earlier decided that she had enough of court. She said that she was so horrified that it made her sick. Teri was glad for this, as it made her relax knowing that her mom was not in the room when she testified. "It was difficult", she explained to her mother, "but our lawyer said that it went very well. Selma's lawyer is trying to stir things up. Both of them are talking to the judge about it right now. I don't know what exactly is going on, but I think it's serious. Paul's still there."

Teri's family didn't stay long. James wrapped his arm around Peter's shoulder. "Let's go! Do you have everything you need." Teri was relieved that Peter could finally leave the hotel. Of course, Cricket went with them.

That evening, she found out some of what happened after she had left court. Just before supper, their supporting friends arrived at the hotel room. Grace, an older woman who had mentored Paul and herself when they were new Christians, was bursting with news. Her usual happy face was grim underneath her full, white hair. She said intently, "I'm not allowed to say much, but we have experienced a wonderful answer to prayer. The judge decided in favour of the prosecution. Praise God! The defense is not allowed to bring up anything to do with the witchcraft side of the case. This was a crucial decision. I'll tell you more once you've finished testifying. Coming up to support you has turned out to be more upsetting than I thought! We're all so glad that we came, because now we can pray together for all of you. What a dreadful trial! God has truly helped you survive this far."

"I can't tell you what a comfort and joy it is to know you prayer warriors are actually in the court, seeing for yourselves what we have gone through and what we still face." Paul passionately agreed.

Their friends surrounded Teri and Paul and started to pray. Once again, Teri felt peace flood her aching heart. She knew that as a result of this prayer time, she had courage to face tomorrow.

Selma looked at herself in the mirror. She brushed back her messy locks and looked critically at her image. She glared at herself and muttered, "Yes, I need more lipstick!" She did look pretty scary, alright! Her small blue-green eyes narrowed as she thought about yesterday's decision made by the judge. It should have gone our way, she thought bitterly. As if anyone would believe the stupid witnesses' stories about witches and satanic rituals! She snorted in amusement. We sure had fun while it lasted! I know Satan will mess up Teri this morning, especially when Gladys asks her about not inviting me to anything after stupid Brandon got caught. I sure am looking forward to that.

As Teri hurried over to the court building early the next morning, she desperately hoped this would be the last time. Wearily, she dragged herself up the court stairs. She had gotten tired of the smoky, thick air of this city. It reeked of thousands of vehicles racing up and down the streets. The steep, wide steps at the entrance seemed twice as high compared to the other times. Her trim body felt like a ton. She slumped to an outside bench to catch her breath. Briefly bowing her head, she prayed that her Heavenly Father would strengthen her and give her clarity.

The court room seemed packed with chattering people as Teri entered. She heard later that a high school group was trying to enter to learn more about court proceedings. An official met them at the door and demanded that they move on to a different case. Teri looked around just as Robin and her team marched through the door. Gladys came in from another side door. All of them looked serious and tense. She was relieved when Robin flashed her a quick smile.

Right after the judge entered, Gladys moved forward to question Teri. She had a peculiar look on her face. Teri thought that she looked like an owl as she cocked her head. "You're a Christian." she stated sarcastically. "Your religion teaches you to be kind and to think of others. Then, why is it that when you organized events for the church, you did not invite my client? That doesn't sound very 'Christian' now, does it! Tell the court why you didn't invite her, especially after you found out about her son's criminal activities!"

Teri replied quietly, trying to keep herself from responding in anger, "I invited Selma to every church event, even after we found out about Brandon. I can prove it to you."

Gladys looked shocked as Teri turned to look at the judge. "May I fetch a calendar from my bag? My husband, Paul, has got it with him. "

He gave her a subdued smile, "Yes, Mrs. Nelson, you can do that."

Teri hurried back to Paul, who had already opened the bag for her. Quickly she found the calendar of eighteen months ago. She flipped the pages to find where she had written in, 'phoned Selma'. Calmly she strode back to the witness stand.

After Teri had read her notations out loud to the court, Gladys snatched the calendar from her hands. She glared at Robin."I didn't see this before!"

In a clear voice, Robin asked the judge if she could clarify the last statement. He readily gave the answer, "Yes!"

Robin's assistant, Jay, handed over a file from the prosecution's desk. Robin held it up for all to see. "This is a copy of all the information we gave the defense. If you look at page 106, you will notice a copy of the calendar to which the witness has referred. It reads, 'June 21, 1987. Phoned Selma for potluck'. This evidence stands for itself."

Gladys's face was a picture of a mixture of embarrassment and rage. Selma sat in solemn silence. Finally, the defense lawyer declared, "I'm finished with this witness."

Robin stood up, saying, "The prosecution rests, your Honour."

Court was dismissed for the day. Robin met Teri outside with a huge smile, "You did really, really well, Teri. You came across as a self-controlled, organized and well spoken witness. This has helped our case a good deal."

Teri felt a rush of gratitude, "You were perfect, Robin. You really out shone Gladys."

She gave a big hug to her lawyer, who spoke into her ear. "We're a good team!"

Teri couldn't think anymore. She staggered as she walked out of the Court. Dizziness and exhaustion once again overcame her. This time Paul met her at the entrance and helped her back to the hotel.

Relief swept over her small frame. Teri experienced optimism, hope and joy all at the same time. As they entered the room, Teri was finally able to say, " At last! We are finally done with court. Let's go and pick up the kids at Nan's!"

A celebration was happening as they pulled into Nan's driveway. Music was pouring out of the house. Hannah ran out, "Surprise! We are having an early birthday party for Peter. You won't believe the fun we had getting ready!"

Their oldest son looked like the happy little boy he had been years ago. He looked much younger than his twelve years. He rushed into the house after Hannah.

Balloons and streamers filled the air, and the sweet smell of cake wafted around the large living room. Teri's entire family shouted "Happy Birthday Peter!!" Besides Nan, she saw her sisters and her brother, James, with his wife and children. Peter was radiant. You could no longer tell what he had been through in the past two weeks. Jacob came into his mom's arms and crushed her with his hugs. With no stutter, he shouted, "You're home, Mom. I missed you so much!"

His parents looked at each other with wonder. What had just happened? Had Jacob changed overnight into a happy, loveable six year old? Suddenly, Teri felt ten years younger as realization hit her. *Maybe this is the beginning of a new life for our family! Wow! Court is over for us!* Then, with a shot of dismay, she remembered that court was actually only half way over. *What was the defense going to do? Would they bring any evidence that will hurt our case? There are so many defense witnesses being called to the stand!* With an effort, Teri pushed these disturbing facts out of her mind and allowed herself to give into the party mood.

CHAPTER 48

The defense was putting on quite a show. Gladys put on the stand one witness after another to testify against the prosecution. Diana and Katie sat through day after day of useless testimony. Gladys tried to draw out statements from reluctant teens and some of their parents to prove Selma's innocence.

Teri had daily phone conversations with Diana. Although Teri and family were visiting with Paul's mother in Arizona, her thoughts were often thrust into the court room at Hudson.

Diana tried to describe what was going on. "Well, first of all, everyone who has been called to the stand for the defense has failed, in my opinion. They not only contradict each other, but even their own testimonies! One of the worst liars was Morris, who was so nervous he couldn't sit still. When Robin cross examined him, he even admitted to being a drug and alcohol user and said he couldn't remember anything about Selma. Ha! Then Robin quoted from his testimony in Fort Smith, which was the opposite to the one he had just given. Robin had him there! Finally, Morris in his frustration and panic, blurted out that he had lied at the last Court hearing." Laughing out loud, Diana concluded, "That, of course, threw his whole testimony out the door! Honestly, they are a pathetic bunch and have certainly done Selma no favours!"

Diana went on. "The only one who had any credibility was Edith."

This woman was a disgruntled attendee of the Echo Bay congregation. Her oldest son had been exposed, by several of the children, as being involved with the abusive teens at one of Selma's parties. Diana thought that she was fighting more for her son's innocence than for Selma's. Edith spoke harshly of the Nelsons and twisted events that made Paul look badly.

Diana added, "Did you know that earlier Edith tried to get some church minutes from our church secretary, before she was to testify? Of course Jean refused and told Edith that she needed the pastor's permission. Sadly, Katie and I realized, as we listened to her ranting, that it seems like she's been one of Selma's agents in Echo Bay to find evidence against us. Without anything to support her claims, she resorted to lying in court. Drawing from her own imagination, she tried to smear you guys. You should have been here when she was cross-examined! Did Robin ever confuse Edith's previous statements! No other witness has confirmed her lies! Edith even told the court that she was not the only one with this opinion! That fell flat! Because she couldn't give any evidence to back this up, it kinda wrecked her whole testimony. Still waiting for one person who actually helps Selma's case!"

After she signed off, Teri shared the information with the others. "This makes me feel more confident than ever that Selma and crew will go down in flames. Aren't you glad that we are far away from the action going on in Hudson? Diana has promised to continue to update us."

Later that week, Katie and Diana watched Selma's younger son, Barry, enter. He was so pale his freckles stood out in brown contrasts. He seemed confused and very nervous. He kept glancing with anxiety at his mother. Selma looked like a frowning cold statue as she listened to him. He stammered as he tried to convince the court he was telling the truth. He would make one statement, then turn around and say something that contradicted it. Katie turned to Diana and whispered, "He's trying to remember what his mother told him to say. Pretty obvious, eh?"

Robin asked Barry what the initials SP stood for on his cap. Reluctantly, he admitted that it meant 'sexual pervert' . Katie told Teri later that he was an abysmal failure on the stand. "Selma must be fuming!"

What a dolt!! I told him what to say! Now he has messed everything up. Again!! Why can't I even trust my own sons! They are so stupid! They certainly didn't get their brains from me. I'll take care of him later. He was no help at all. I'm surrounded by idiots. I could have done a better job than Gladys. That's for sure! Every juror will find me innocent after I've testified. Robin, that disgusting lawyer, will not be able to trip me up. Not like all these fools! Not a chance!

———————✦————••••••••••————✦———————

    The next day, Diana and Katie arrived early to the court. After the room had settled, Gladys called Selma to the stand. They watched as Selma charged over to the witness chair. She looked around the court with as sad a demeanor as she could muster. Her small eyes gleamed with confidence as she looked at her lawyer. With each question fielded by Gladys, she tried to be a sweet, harmless victim, falsely accused. Katie noticed how frequently she glanced at the jury. She was trying to woo them into her world with every word.

    Diana phoned Teri at the end of the day to tell her of Selma's cross-examination. "So, Selma's testimony did her no good today. I can't believe what she said! Not only that, but we watched as she turned into her true self when she was cross- examined. She snapped at Robin and told her in no uncertain terms that the lawyer's questions were stupid. She tried to intimidate Robin and kept shouting 'No!' to many of her questions. You would have been proud of Robin who stood her ground and persisted with question after question. One time, Selma tried to storm out of the witness box, but the judge told her to stay put. What a fiasco! Well, that's that! The end of the trial has arrived. I think it's a slam dunk for us."

CHAPTER 49

The lady in black got up to follow the other jurors as they went to the deliberation room. She felt Selma's eyes on her. After a quick glance at the judge, she turned and nodded at the defendant. Selma gave her a slight smile in return.

After introductions, the assigned foreman juror, Tony, asked the others what their impressions were of the trial and if they would vote 'not guilty' or 'guilty' according to the evidence. The lady in black quickly answered ahead of the others, "Of course she is not guilty! Did you hear any solid evidence? I sure didn't. How can anyone trust the words of children that age!"

That opened up the discussion. The foreman heard eight of them declare 'guilty'; three were uncertain and the lone dissenter was that strange looking woman dressed in black from top to bottom. Tony wondered if they could ever reach a consensus with her dogmatic statement standing in the way.

The hours dragged by, broken only by coffee breaks and later a meal. Finally the foreman sent a note to the judge that they needed more time. The jury manager came into the room and told them they were to be sequestered overnight. They had until eight p.m. to continue the deliberating, then, they would be bussed to a hotel.

"Rats! "The lady in black muttered to herself. "Wonder if I can get some privacy so I can use the phone in my room!"

Two days after the Nelsons arrived back home, Teri was surprised to hear from Doug.

"Hi, Teri! I'm sure that you know that the jury is deliberating as we speak. I just wanted you to know, that although the defense tried to make a strong case against all you parents, they failed to clear Selma. Robin was tremendously convincing in her two hour wrap up. She focused on the reliability of young childrens' disclosures and how well the kids did in this trial. I'm so happy for you that Robin is your lawyer! What a great job she did!

Did you hear about the judge's final summations? Wow! He took over two hours and described all the different aspects of the case. He certainly leaned towards the prosecution, you will be glad to hear. He praised the courage of the children and emphatically stated that their testimonies rang with truth and should in no way be discounted. He pointed out inconsistencies with the defendant and her witnesses. Selma's face was a picture. What an actress!

Please don't jump for joy yet, Teri! The jury is a strange kettle of fish. You just never know what their verdict will be. They have already been out for twenty-four hours."

Teri paused before she answered. "Thanks Doug! I can't help but be encouraged, but I'm trying to be prepared for the shock if we failed. It would be catastrophic for the children! I appreciate your attending so much of our trial. I know you are a busy man. Do you have any idea how long they will be out?"

"No, I have no idea. Commonly, they take from one day to about three, but those guys have a lot to cover."

Teri told him that Paul had suggested that she travel down to attend court and hear the verdict. After she hung up, she tried to curb her excitement as she rushed over to tell the others. She tempered her news carefully, so that their children would not assume that this meant victory. "We have to just wait and see. Remember that if some of the jury disagree about the outcome, it will make their deliberations longer."

"What's deliberation?" Hannah asked.

Teri looked to her husband, "Do you want to explain? You're better at definitions than me."

Paul laughed,"I'll remember you said that! Hannah, 'deliberation' means a careful discussion, in this case by a jury, of the facts of a case. They look at all that was said during the trial and decide if they are for or against a conviction of guilty for Selma. If there are one or two jurors who disagree with the rest, than they have to deliberate longer until they all agree. It's a good question for the prosecution secretary. Next time we talk to her, I'll ask. Does that help you understand?"

Hannah quickly replied, "Yes, I get it. So, I guess we just have to keep on waiting. " She sighed, "I wish this was all over! I sure can't see why they even have to discuss whether Selma is guilty or not. Why wouldn't they just believe the kids?"

Peter jumped in, "It would be because they think we made it up, Hannah. I think they might not believe what we said anyway."

"Why do you think that, Peter?" Teri asked with concern. She realized that he was not confident that his testimony counted. "I know you got upset on the witness stand, but Robin said that you did a good job."

"Mom, I had to lie about some of my memories, cause I couldn't remember what I said at Brandon's trial." Peter walked away miserably.

Paul exchanged a worried look at Teri. "I think I'd better talk to him. What if he thinks it would be his fault if she's found not guilty?"

He followed Peter to his room. Teri got some cookies for the younger two, then followed her husband. Paul was talking in a quiet voice to Peter, who had turned his face to the wall. "Son, I was there when you testified. You did a great job with the things you remembered. I don't blame you at all for getting frustrated at the defense lawyer as she kept asking questions about where you were at this or that time. There were too many, so called, 'parties' for you to differentiate between them all."

Suddenly Peter turned around and yelled at them. "You don't understand!"

To his parents complete shock, he broke into heartbroken sobs. "Jay, the other lawyer, got mad at me and told me if I didn't remember everything I said at Brandon's trial, he would expose me as a liar. He made me memorize the transcript. I had to lie!"

Teri had never seen him cry like this. His face turned beet red as he tried to stop the tears, but it seemed the more he tried, the louder his weeping became. Teri threw herself beside him and pulled his shaking body close. She had no words to say. She thought that that was one of the worst things anyone could say to her son, who was the most honest child she had ever met. Paul was holding both of them in his arms. "Peter, our precious son, the jury decision has nothing to do with what you said in court. From what I heard, you sounded fine. I am so sorry that Jay bullied you like this. No lawyer should ever act this way! He's the one who did wrong."

Teri cut in, "Oh Peter, I am just so very sorry that you've had to go through all this. Please remember that you are a victim of this monster woman! Your dad and I are very proud of the way you've handled this court business. You are the one who tried to protect others. You have done nothing wrong! If we had known what this lawyer said, we would have confronted him. He was trying to shame you into remembering things that you had already blocked from your memory. We love you so much!"

Finally, Peter settled down and Teri was able to go out and check on the others. Hannah and Jacob were both sitting at the kitchen table without a word. They looked almost as upset as their older brother.

"Poor Peter!" Hannah said sadly, "He had to go to court and I didn't this time." She looked down in embarrassment. "I lied, too. I lied to Robin when she asked me questions about one 'party' when Jamie was there." She looked up with tears sliding down her cheeks. "I said that I couldn't remember, but I did, Mom. That was when she decided that I would not testify. I know that was wrong, but I was terrified of speaking in front of Selma."

Once again, Teri felt sick at what her children had been through. She knew in her heart that she had wanted the oldest two to testify, all because she desperately wanted Selma to be found guilty in court! But at what cost?

Paul and Teri gathered the three children together later that evening to comfort them and pray as a family about this emotional crisis. Finally, the kids were tucked in and asleep.

As her husband snored quietly beside her, Teri lay in the dark, thinking about her children. Was she to blame for Peter and Hannah's court stress? Tears trickled down her cheeks as she considered this. What if she had not obsessed about seeing justice? Should she have allowed their two children to testify at all in the courts? But then, the other child witnesses would have had to carry the brunt of the trial. Would she and Paul have withdrawn Peter from the case, if they had known that this lawyer had threatened him? She tried to pray, but both that and sleep eluded her. Would everything resolve if Selma was found guilty? What if she was acquitted? Robin had told them that if she was declared 'guilty', the defense would probably appeal. If she was found 'not guilty', how could they all survive? Her mind was swirling. Yes, she knew in her heart that God, faithful and true, would see them through, despite the court result. This thought broke through her clouded thinking and she started to pray to her Heavenly Father. *Oh Lord, I'm so confused! Help me to rest in You as we wait for the verdict! Help me to see Your Sovereign will in the jury's decision. You know all things. You know the results already and what lies ahead for us. I still have to ask that You would vindicate our children. Please bring justice! Oh, how we need You now!* She kept praying until the next thing she knew was the morning sunshine warming her face.

CHAPTER 50

The jury had been out for two days now. The families were getting restless and anxious as they waited for a decision. Teri and Paul were working hard to try and distract the kids by planning something fun each day. Despite this, Peter and Hannah continued to be stressed and unhappy. Jacob picked up on the tension and reverted back to his old behavior.

Paul had taken Peter and Hannah shopping in a nearby town. *Peace at last!* Teri thought to herself after she had interested Jacob in the sandbox in the backyard. Of course she had to sit outside with him to ease his fear of being alone. She tried to relax, but her mind kept rushing back to the jury. She was flying down to Hudson the next day to await the verdict. Why were they taking so long? Hadn't the prosecution persuaded them of Selma's guilt? By all accounts, the presiding judge had spoken in their favour. Teri remembered clearly that one juror who favoured Selma. Her body language spoke volumes as she had glowered at the prosecution witnesses and carefully watched Selma's antics. Every day this woman dressed all in black. Was she involved in the occult? Teri sighed at her suspicions. *It's probably my overactive imagination! Could this one juror sway all the others? Maybe I'm right; maybe I'm wrong. Guess I'll never find out! This is such a spiritual battle! I'm so grateful to God that so many are praying for us.*

'Please help me, Lord, to rest in Your Sovereign will. You know all things. You know the result and the consequences of this verdict. I desperately need your peace! So do our friends in this war'.

※

Ms. Cotton looked around her hotel room. Finally, she was alone. Her roommate had gone next door to visit another juror. She turned up the

volume on the TV and reached for the room phone. With her back to the door, she dialed a secret number.

"Hello! Is Selma there? Yes, I need to speak with her now!" she commanded. As she waited, she checked her room again. "Yes! It's me!" She said impatiently, "It's OK! The room's empty. I only have a few minutes."

The hotel room door opened and Ms. Cotton's roommate entered quietly. She had thought that Ms. Cotton would be sleeping. Instead, her room-mate was talking on the phone! Shocked, she knew this was strictly forbidden for sequestered jurors.

As soon as she overheard that her roommate was talking to the defendant, she slipped out and ran to the jury foreman's room. Finally, Tony opened his door, looking half asleep. Urgently, she told him to quickly come with her. Brushing the sleep from his eyes, he followed her down the hall.

She whispered to him, as she quietly opened her own door. "Come in with me! I think Ms. Cotton is doing something illegal."

They slipped inside and stood watching as Ms. Cotton whispered into the phone. "Look! I'm doing my best to persuade the others to find you 'not guilty', Selma. It's a lot harder than you think. Trust me! I'll try to get back to you, but I may not have this chance again. Just get the group to call upon our 'Great One' for help. OK! Thanks !"

She turned and saw the two in the doorway listening. The phone dropped from her hand.

"You were talking with the defendant, Ms. Cotton! " Tony accused."We both heard you, so don't try and defend yourself. I will need to report this to the judge. One thing I know already! You are finished as a jury member in this case."

Ms. Cotton shook in anger. "How dare you come into my room! What you heard was none of your business!"

Even as she shouted these words, she knew she was doomed. Undismayed, the foreman said firmly, "Stay where you are! I'll be right back!"

He hurried back to his suite and dialed the number the judge had given him.

The sleepy judge didn't take long to wake up. "Thank you, Mr. Foreman! Please bring this juror to my quarters at 8:30am. She may be charged with obstruction of justice. Yes! Goodnight!"

Later, Teri heard Paul and the children drive in. Jacob leaped up and ran to meet them.

"Have you heard anything?"Paul asked right away. He looked as tense as she felt.

"No, not a word!" she replied. "I think this is very long for a jury to still be deliberating. I wonder if we are facing a locked jury?"

"Anything could be happening! But you're right, it's taking so long that I wonder the same thing. However, we are not to worry or be anxious. God is on His Throne and we need to trust Him." Paul's faith was stronger than hers right now.

With a trembling heart, Teri swept the sand off her lap and went to make supper..

Before Teri left for the airport the next morning, the phone rang. Paul answered. "Yes this is Paul. (pause) Could you please explain this to me? What happens now? (pause) Wow! Is this unusual?"

The whole family watched his every move and expression. There was a long silence.

Finally Paul replied, "This is amazing! Teri is flying down in a few hours. I wonder how long it will take now for them to reach a verdict? (pause) Yes, I guess they need to adjust to this big change. Ok! Thank you so much for letting us know. Teri will be in touch when she arrives in Hudson."

He hung up, then turned to look at his family. Teri was afraid to move. "What?" she almost yelled.

"Come on, everyone. Let's sit in the living room and I'll tell you what the prosecution secretary just said."

They solemnly followed Paul and sat in silence, waiting. Paul's face was inscrutable as he sat opposite his family. "Something amazing has happened! What an answer to prayer! A jury member was removed after being caught on the phone talking to Selma. Guess who it was?"

Teri burst out, "No! Was it the woman wearing black?"

"You guessed it! This may change everything! They are going ahead with eleven jurors to try and reach a verdict. So glad there wasn't a decision to call it all a mistrial!"

"So, did the secretary say that this will prolong the deliberations? Should I go down to Hudson today as planned? "

Paul quickly answered, "The secretary encouraged you to come down today. She said they had no way of knowing how much longer this will take, but thought it could be anytime."

Teri turned to the kids, "Does this help you see that God is in control? This woman was, perhaps, the one juror who was defending Selma. Now she's gone. The Lord allowed her to be caught in the act. This may greatly change our whole case. We still don't want to get our hopes up too much, though. All the rest of the jury has to be unanimous in their decision."

Hannah interrupted, "So, she was dressed all in black. That's scary! God took her away cause she was a friend of Selma."

"I watched her, too." Peter declared. "I once saw her wink at Selma. She was bad."

Paul continued, "Yes, there are things going on in the unseen world that we can't even imagine. Thank you Lord for your intervention! What a prayer answering God!"

Teri silently asked God's forgiveness for her doubt and anxiety. This turn of events revealed once again, that His ways were higher than hers. She felt a load lifted from her heart. Smiling, she said, "To celebrate, let's make some popcorn and play that new game I bought. I still have a couple of hours before I need to leave."

Later, Teri went to her bedroom to pack a few things. Jacob sat on the bed watching, "I-I-I do-do-don't want you to go, Mommy! Wh-wh-what if something happens to you?"

He started to cry. Teri felt like a betrayer. "I'm sorry, little man! Your job is to pray that the jury give us their verdict really soon. As soon as I hear the news, I will come right home. OK?"

CHAPTER 51

After an uneventful flight, Teri unpacked her small suitcase in Diana's hotel room. Katie had returned to Echo Bay a few days earlier. Diana lay on her bed watching Teri. "Boy, I'm glad you're here! Hard enough being away from my family! Now we can watch our trial ending together. I'm completely blown away by what has just happened! Imagine finding that juror in the very act of phoning Selma! Praise God she's gone! I always had a very bad feeling about her. This could really affect the outcome. I bet she was involved with the occult in some way. That may be one reason that Gladys selected her."

"I totally agree, Diana. We need to continue to pray about the eleven remaining jurors. I let our pray team know already. You can imagine how excited they felt, seeing an answer to their prayers for us. However, we mustn't get our hopes up too high. I realize that the lack of hard core evidence is against us. Selma sure did a good job of hiding all the photos and pornography that the kids told us about! Hopefully, the children's testimonies will be enough. I think Tabitha, you and I did a good job backing up the dates of the 'parties'."

Diana sighed, "Well, I sure hope that we don't have to wait much longer!"

They spent the next day hanging around the court house. They saw Robin once, but she was too busy to talk with them. In passing, she welcomed Teri and said that she was glad that they were both there. They had lunch with Doug, and quizzed him on what would happen after the verdict. He assured them that the child counseling would go on for some time, even if the families all moved away.

That night, after they went out for supper, they visited a game store and laughed hysterically as they played 'Whack-a- Mole'. As she hammered at the pop-up moles, Diana giggled and exclaimed, "I'm pretending they are Selma." The comic relief was refreshing.

The very next morning, the phone rang in the hotel room. Diana answered, listened for a moment and hung up. "The jury has reached a verdict!" she shouted.

They rushed over to the court building and into the room, just as the lawyers settled into their seats. The eleven jurors sat in their rows. Five minutes later they heard, "All rise!"

The judge took his seat and banged the gavel for silence. He turned to the jury and asked, "Have you reached a verdict?"

Tony, the jury foreman stood up. "Yes, we have, Your Honour!"

Judge asked, "What say you?"

Teri trembled like a tree in the wind. Her heart was in her throat. Diana grabbed her hand. They glanced at Selma, who's expression was inscrutable.

Tony answered in a loud voice, "On the six counts of sexual assault, we find the accused guilty, your Honour."

Teri and Diana screamed in unison and leaped to their feet. Selma turned around and glared at them, then slouched in her seat.

The judge slammed his gavel down, "Order in the court!"

Teri vaguely heard him thank the jury for their hard work. "Sentencing will be in two weeks. The defendant will remain in custody."

Teri wept openly as she hugged Diana. She longed for Paul to be there with her. They watched Selma as she was handcuffed. She jerked her hands away and started to curse. Roughly, the guards pulled her arms forward and clipped the cuffs shut. Teri had a hard time feeling any sympathy for her as she remembered all that she had heard from the mouths of her little children. She only felt enormous relief!

Finally, the two went out into the outside hall. Robin met them there. Teri resisted the urge to wrap her in a huge hug. She smiled, "Let's go down to my office!"

As the three entered the office room, the secretary leaped to her feet. "Congratulations, Robin! All our hard work rewarded!"

The two hugged. Then Robin turned to Teri and Diana. With joy barely suppressed, and said, "Let's sit down! We have a few things to discuss.

I realize how much you want to let your families know, so this will only take a few minutes. As I've warned you before, Gladys and crew have already threatened to appeal this decision. They will need to find something amiss that happened during court. We have been very careful to avoid anything that could cause a successful appeal. The defense will need to take any evidence to the Appeal Board before several judges. If they agree to this appeal, it will go to a higher court before a panel of judges. The good news is that witnesses do not need to reappear at this hearing. Also, we need to discuss if the families want to pursue some of the other accused in this case. If you decide to do this, then you will need to go to trial again."

Diana interrupted, "I think I can speak for my family. We do not want to go through any more trials. It would be way too hard for our children."

"Yes, I definitely agree!" Teri continued. "I am absolutely sure Peter will not be able to testify again. He has already blocked out much of what has happened."

Robin replied, "I thought you would feel this way. Personally, I agree with this. You need to think of your children and move on. There are just so many accused. These court cases could go on for a very long time."

"We need to talk to our husbands, but I believe we all feel this way." Teri added. "So, at this point, we can tell all our children that court is over. We will only have to wait about this appeal possibility. I think I can speak for Diana, too, that we are so thrilled with this result. Isn't it amazing how that one juror was removed! This could have made all the difference with the jury verdict."

Robin agreed. "Yes! Instead of helping the defendant, this juror revealed that Selma was, actually, jury tampering."

Teri looked at Diana with a knowing smile, than continued, "We all want to thank you, in a huge way, for the supremely capable and excellent job you have done with our two court appearances. We are so grateful that you took on this extremely difficult case."

Diana exclaimed, "There is just no way to adequately express our gratitude. All I can say is thank you from the bottom of our hearts!"

"Is it possible to phone our two families from your phones?" Teri asked.

"Yes! You are very welcome to do so. In fact, we have several phones that you can use to contact your homes."

Eagerly, Diana and Teri each dialed their numbers.

Paul paced back and forth in the living room. He hadn't dared go out until he had heard the verdict. *Why hasn't Teri called yet! Maybe something has gone wrong! Maybe she is too upset to phone! Please Lord, help her to communicate soon. I can't wait much longer!*

Peter, Hannah and Jacob were playing in Peter's room. It was a silent game. Finally, Peter could take it no longer. He stood up to go talk to his dad.

Suddenly, the phone rang shrilly in the kitchen. All four rushed to answer it. Hannah felt sick with dread mixed with hope.

Dad grabbed the phone and said, "Hello!" before he got it to his ear. "It's your mom." He said to the waiting three.

"What, they found her guilty!"

The room erupted into screams of tremendous relief. "I can hardly believe it! God has given us justice!" he shouted.

Then he listened quietly as Teri described what had happened. The kids were bouncing around the kitchen like little rabbits.

"Yes, I will pass this on to everyone, after I explain all this to the kids. I can't help thinking of God's promise in, I think, Psalm 37, 'He will bring forth your righteousness as the light. and your justice as the noonday.' Praise His Name! Are you booking your flight for tomorrow? We can't wait to see you! Has Diana phoned Sam yet? Okay, good! So just phone back to confirm your flight. Bye! Love ya!"

After a big celebration in the kitchen, Paul suggested that the three go over and play with the Haywood's kids. "Then you can all have fun together. You are the bravest children I know! Now we can get on with our lives!"

Peter nearly yelled as he said, "No more court! Selma got what she deserved alright! Maybe I didn't do so bad as I thought I had! Yes!!! I'm going to spend the rest of my life forgetting about it."

Hannah added happily, "Now we can all be normal kids again!"

Paul didn't think it was time to burst their bubbles of joy. He knew that difficult days lay ahead. He wondered how well his children would recover. He knew it would take many years and many struggles until they were all able to rise above this horrendous abuse.

CHAPTER 52

A week later, the family met with their mission director, Drew. He and his wife had flown up from Hudson. As they all walked along a nearby beach, he warmly congratulated them and asked many questions about their time in court. Teri was glad that Paul did most of the talking. She just didn't feel up to talking about it anymore. Drew's wife, Fiona, had taken all three children into the kitchen to make cookies while their parents visited with her husband.

Teri leaned against Paul as they walked. With a sigh, Drew said, "Our Board met again to discuss your future. We all firmly believes that it is time for you to move to a different ministry. We had a meeting, before I flew up here, to again go over the options for you. Together we decided on one particular place for you to consider."

He then went on to describe an abandoned Bible camp site hundreds of miles south of Echo Bay. "I know you all need a vacation. Before that, however, I would suggest that you drive to this camp and check it out as soon as possible. Fly down to Hudson as soon as you can. We will have a rental car ready for you to use. Remember, as you explore this camp, that you would be starting from nothing! We have researched the area and found out that there are many children who have not experienced hearing about the gospel at all. Most of the local churches don't even have Sunday School!

You will be happy to know that it's located at a beautiful site on the edge of a lake. The property already has a nice little log house on it, so you could move right in. A great place to heal and raise your children! The board will pay for this trip, which includes a one night stay at a motel." He stopped and looked intently at the Nelsons. "We don't want you to decide yet. Please go, as soon as possible, and have a look to see if this is where the Lord wants you to move! Pray about this in the next few days and let us know how God is leading you."

A general feeling of excitement filled their hearts as they prepared for this new adventure. Teri, although exhausted, felt at peace about moving from their beloved Echo Bay. Yes, there was a lot of healing that needed to take place. The children were to have on-going counseling where ever they lived. Teri couldn't help feeling that the Lord was leading them to just the right location for this to happen.

CHAPTER 53

Five Years Later

Teri waved goodbye as seventeen year old Peter drove out the drive way. He was going on another solo trip into the mountains. He had found hiking to be his niche in this mountainous community. His dad had taught him well and often went with him. Teri stood in the dust and marvelled at the changes in her son. He was a pleasant, responsible young man. Teri always felt trepidations when he left on these outings. He would be away for five days this time. She rested in his reliability, as she knew he would be back right on time, as usual.

Hannah and Jacob ran up to her. "Awww! Did we miss saying goodbye to Peter?" Hannah's curls were tangled and messy from jumping on the trampoline." Mom, can we go riding today?"

Paul and Teri, realizing their daughter's passion for horses, had bought a horse that suited her ability. Mom had a pony that she could borrow to go on trail rides with Hannah. She marvelled in how 'normal' her daughter had become. A teen of joy and contentment. She openly shared about what she had been through and gave God the glory. She had been the first one to express that she had forgiven Selma, "Because I don't want to spend the rest of my life haunted by this woman and what she has done to me."

Jacob's speech had improved with the help of a speech pathologist. His terror at night had finally been relieved by his faithful dog, Gabriel, who slept beside his bed all night. To his parent's delight, he didn't panic when his parents shut their bedroom door. Teri loved his affectionate nature and desire to please his parents. What a different child from Echo Bay days!

Paul and Teri had never been busier as they directed Lake Side Bible Camp. They loved the work the Lord had given them. The camp facility had been improved and the number of kids attending continued to grow.

To Teri's great joy, her mother had read the Gospel of John and, as a result, had decided to follow Jesus. What a different person she had become! She had shared with her daughter that her decision was partly because she saw how God had helped her family through the unspeakable tragedy that had happened in Echo Bay.

A few years back, Paul and Teri were distressed to hear from Jean, still living in Echo Bay. On the phone she described the continuing turmoil in the community. "The town is in complete chaos, Teri. So many children here are still traumatized by what Selma and her group did! There is an epidemic of attempted suicides, sexual acting out, increased criminal activity and kids running away. The community has called in an 'Emergency Response Team', cause the situation here is out of control! Rob and I are so glad you are out of this. He has just received a new job near Hudson. We are moving in a couple of days. Thank goodness!

This will be our last call to you for awhile, but please keep in touch!"

Paul exclaimed after they hung up, "That evil woman and her cohorts have done such great harm to so many. Too bad she was only sentenced to five years in jail! I heard that she has already being released from prison with few restrictions. She's a great manipulator! No doubt she has come across as a poor victim to the authorities! However, we know that Our Sovereign Lord is in command, even of her."

Teri responded, "Yes! Praise God! We will never completely get over what has happened to our children, but God has led us out into green pastures, hasn't He! He has seen us through!"

Paul reached for her and they embraced in the joy of God's deliverance.

EPILOGUE

Hannah Nelson. (age: 16- years-old).
Suffering

There is no doubt that Christians encounter suffering. Following Christ does not mean they are exempt from the pain of this world. When Christ states, "Whoever desires to come after Me, let him deny himself and take up his cross and follow Me." (Mark 8: 31). He was not telling His disciples to literally carry crosses. He was making the point that following Him was not easy, but full of blood, sweat and tears. The Christian faith was never promised to be easy.

I know one girl who loved Christ from age three and she went through great sufferings, even though she was Christ's. She never wanted to suffer, but when you follow Christ you should expect trials. As Oswald Chambers said in his book,' Cry the Beloved Country', "No normal healthy saint ever chooses suffering, he simply chooses God's will, just as Jesus did, whether it means suffering or not."

And as Jesus Himself said in the book of Acts, referring to Paul, "I will show him how many things he must suffer for my Name's sake."

This girl, at a very young age, faced great tribulation. She was sexually abused by haters of Christ, who had infiltrated the church where her dad was the pastor. Because of threats too horrendous for a small girl to fathom, she couldn't tell her parents. So all she had to depend on was Christ's promise, "I will never leave you or forsake you." (Hebrews 13:5). This is a promise that Christ gives to all His followers.

While Jesus allows His followers to suffer, He not only goes through the trials with them, He gives great joy at the same time. Paul states, "I am exceedingly joyful in all my tribulations."

This girl, in the midst of some of the greatest heartaches, was able to testify that Christ gave her strength, comfort and even joy when she had to face lawyers and policemen to answer their blunt and painful questions. As Oswald Chambers stated, "We are super victors with a joy that comes from experiencing the very things which look like they will overwhelm us." As she walked forward to testify in front of many people, including her abuser, she brought to life Psalms 55:22 which says, "Cast your burden upon the Lord and He will sustain you. He shall never permit the righteous to be shaken."

In the midst of her suffering, Christ was there. As it is written, "When you pass through the waters, I will be with you.....For I am the Lord your God. Fear not, for I am with you." (Isaiah 43:2,5).

The things we face in life are powerless to separate us from the love of God and His presence with us. O. Chambers wrote, "We never realize at the time what God is putting us through- we go through it, more or less, without understanding. Then suddenly we come to a place of enlightenment, and realize- God has strengthened us and we didn't even know it."

Jesus does not let us suffer for no reason, but to equip us with skills and knowledge to serve Him and others. The girl, because of her suffering, has been given opportunities by God to help others through similar sufferings. Looking back, she sees God's Hand on her life, even through these trials, and realizes God does work everything together for good. I can even say that she is thankful for the trials with all honesty, because that girl is me.

In conclusion, there is no doubt that Christians experience suffering just like the rest of the world. As followers of Christ, we are not exempt. Christ Himself suffered greatly. He promises His people that He that He will go through the trials with them. He promises strength, comfort and joy in the midst of pain. This girl found all of this to be true. Others have been helped and encouraged by what this girl shared about what she had experienced.

"In this you greatly rejoice, though now for a little while, if need be, you have been grieved by various trials, that the genuineness of your faith, being more precious than gold that perishes, though it is tested by fire, may be found to praise, honor and glory at the revelation of Jesus Christ-" 1 Peter 1: 6-8.

CPSIA information can be obtained
at www.ICGtesting.com
Printed in the USA
LVHW031923290319
612383LV00001B/4/P